lure

THE ALLURE CHRONICLES

ALYSSA ROSE IVY

Cover Design: MaeIDesign and Photography
Formatting: Polgarus Studio

OTHER BOOKS BY ALYSSA ROSE IVY

AUTHOR'S NOTE

Dear Readers:

If you've already read the prequel novella to Owen and Daisy's story, *Seduction's Kiss*, you can skip ahead to chapter one of *Lure*. If not, please enjoy reading their story straight through starting with *Seduction's Kiss*.

Seduction's Kiss

The Allure Chronicles

ALYSSA ROSE IVY

PREFACE

You're probably not going to believe a word I say. If you're like everyone else I've told, you're going to read this and tell me to get help. That's fine, because the only thing I care about is finding my winged hero. So whether you believe me or not, if you see him, tell him I'm searching for him, and I have no plans to give up. Because when a man can kiss like that—can make you feel alive in every grain of your being—there's no comparison. The only clue I have to find him is his first name. Owen.

CHAPTER ONE

"Please, Daisy. It's going to be fun." That one line out of Reyna's mouth was the beginning of the end for me.

"I don't know. I was hoping to just have a quiet Halloween this year. Driving all the way to New Orleans seems a bit extreme." I set aside my sociology textbook. There was no way I was getting reading done until Reyna said her piece.

"There's nothing like New Orleans on Halloween. This is going to be epic." She took a seat next to me on my bed and grasped both of my hands in hers. She was getting ready to plead.

"But why the sudden decision to go? Is it about a guy?" Reyna was usually motivated by a member of the opposite sex.

"No, not exactly. I just want to do something fun for a change."

Not exactly? That meant yes. "Ok, who is he?"

"Just this guy I knew back in high school. We've started talking again, and he invited me and any friends to come crash at his place for Halloween." She suddenly turned serious. "I'm so sick of the scene here. I need a break, but I don't want to go alone. Please, pretty please."

I sighed, realizing that saying no would just lead to a pouty roommate for the next few days. "You promise you're not just going to ditch me?"

"Of course not! It will be awesome. He's got so many hot friends. It's crazy."

I tuned Reyna out as she went on and on about Tulane boys. Admittedly, my dating life at East Madison wasn't great, but I knew a random hook up with a guy I didn't know wasn't going to help matters either. "There's just one problem. Isn't New Orleans a full day's drive from here?" I wasn't an expert on driving distances, but Atlanta and New Orleans aren't exactly next door.

"It's doable. About seven hours. I'll do all the driving. All you need to do is keep me company."

"You really want to do this?" Despite her obsession with guys, Reyna was actually a really good roommate. We'd both joined the same sorority, Delta Mu, the year before and hit it off immediately.

"Yes." She turned her doe eyes on me.

I wasn't exactly jumping at the idea of the trip, but Reyna's one of those people who always manages to find a good time, and sometimes I just liked to go along for the ride. "Okay."

"Yes!!!" She jumped up and ran around the room. "I can't wait to tell Chad!"

"Great." I leaned back against my pillows. "I guess I really need to find a costume then."

"Just sex up that black cat costume you wore last night." Reyna rifled through her closet.

"Sex it up?" I'd donned cat ears for our Halloween kid's philanthropy event, but I had no plans to wear them again, and sex them up? Did she forget who she was talking to?

"Yeah. Tight shirt and short black skirt. It's easy enough." She tossed one of her skirts at me. "Try this."

"You're way shorter than me. This skirt is going to be up to my ass."

Reyna grinned. "That's called sexing it up. Wait until you see my firefighter costume. It's hot."

"Hotter than me wearing this?" I held up the black fabric.

"It's a short skirt, but also just a jacket over a red bra. It's a little over the top, but Chad said that's what Halloween is like there. I'm embracing my inner skank."

"Ugh." I put a pillow over my head. "Please don't make me go."

"You don't have to wear that skirt. Wear one of your own, but please try to look decently sexy. We don't want to stand out like sore thumbs."

"Then ask someone else to go."

"Nope. It's only going to be fun if you go."

"In other words, I'm the only one you can dupe into going."

"Come on. Who else would be willing to miss the Iota party? I know you don't care about that."

I didn't care because none of those guys gave me the time of day. The fact that every woman in my family had been Delta Mu was probably the only reason I'd gotten a bid from my sorority in the first place. I didn't regret my decision to join, but living with a bunch of tens when you're a seven, on a good day with the right makeup and hair products, can get old. "Fine, I'll come up with a sexy enough costume."

"Perfect. We'll need to get on the road early Friday."

"But I have three classes."

"And perfect attendance. I'm sure you can miss one of each. This is going to be epic!" She hugged me around the neck.

I decided not to point out that she'd called the trip epic twice. "I'm sure it will be."

"I'm going to text Chad and let him know."

"Great." I picked up my textbook and tried to get back into my reading. Not that social phenomena particularly interested me.

"He says awesome. We're going out on Bourbon Street for Halloween and everything."

"Cool." I plugged a set of headphones into my phone and turned on some music. Reyna would never stop talking if I didn't, and this method usually worked better than telling her to shut up.

I made it through all of three paragraphs before she pulled one of my ear buds out. "You're the best. Just wanted to tell you that."

"Yeah, Yeah." I smiled.

"I need caffeine. Want to go over to the Java Circle to read? I heard they've got that white hot chocolate stuff you love."

"Sure." Reyna knew the way to my heart. Hot chocolate. I had a mild addiction.

"Great. We can strategize costumes on the way over."

I laughed. "I'll go with the cat idea if I don't find anything else."

"There's no reason not to. It's classic."

"All right, I'll stick with it. It's not like I have a lot of time."

"Nope. We leave in two days."

"Exciting."

She pushed my arm playfully. "Please try to get hyped up, for my sake."

"Of course. If nothing else I'll get hyped about the food. I've heard it's amazing."

"See." She linked her arm in mine as we headed toward the stairs. "There's always a bright side."

CHAPTER TWO

Seven hours is a long drive. Add on an extra two hours thanks to traffic, and it's pretty much endless. I wasn't the one driving, but sitting in the passenger seat with Reyna driving wasn't much better. She didn't 'believe' in GPS. Instead she tossed a tattered old map on my lap. "I know where we're going, but we have that just in case."

Although at first I missed the familiar computer generated voice reading directions, it didn't take long to get used to using a paper map again. It brought me back to my childhood. My dad's one of the types that is all about life skills. Evidently reading maps was still a life skill in his book, because he made my brother and I master the art before the end of elementary school. I planned to call him later and thank him.

A few hours into the drive I decided to ask some more questions about Chad. Reyna had been surprisingly reticent on the subject. For a girl who usually gave details, way too many details, her silence made me a little suspicious. "Are you ready to tell me about him?"

"He's just a guy I knew."

"Knew how?" I turned down the radio.

"He's the one who got away," she said in barely a whisper.

"What?" I said in anything but a whisper. Hooking up with an ex-boyfriend was always a bad idea. I knew from experience. "We're going to New Orleans so you can hook up with an ex?"

"Calm down." She looked right at the road. It wasn't for safety reasons. She was avoiding my gaze.

"So how do I fit in? What am I going to do while you guys *reconnect*?" I resisted the urge to use air quotes.

"I don't know what's going to happen. I just couldn't do it alone. I needed my best friend with me."

Best friend? Did she really see me that way? "Since we're hours from Atlanta I'm coming, but I wish you'd been honest with me from the beginning."

I was such a pushover. I could practically hear my brother lecturing me. He said I couldn't spend my whole life as a doormat. He was right, but that didn't mean I knew how to change it.

"His roommate's single and excited to meet you."

I groaned. "I am not hooking up with the roommate."

"I never said you had to. I was just letting you know. He's really cute."

"Wonderful." Reyna might as well have been getting a degree in matchmaker for all the effort she made trying to set other people up on dates. It wasn't something she was particularly good at. To be honest, I couldn't think of a single success story.

She changed lanes and gunned it to pass a truck. I held onto the 'oh my god bar' for dear life. She reduced speed once she was settled back in the right lane. "I really owe you for this. I promise I'll make it up to you."

"Just don't completely ditch me. That's all I'm asking."

"I won't."

"Didn't anyone ever tell you not to make promises you can't keep?"

She laughed. "Trust me on this one. I don't even know if anything is going to happen. He invited me as a friend, remember?"

"You really believe that?" I didn't. A guy wouldn't invite an ex to stay with him unless he planned on rekindling the old flame—or getting her in bed—or most likely, both.

"I do. We flirt and stuff, but it hasn't passed that."

"If you say so." I wasn't in the mood to argue, but I steeled myself for a long few days. Hopefully I'd be able to navigate New Orleans on my own.

***

I checked the address twice after Reyna parked along the curb. When she said we'd be staying in an off-campus apartment I assumed it was going to be a complex or something. Instead we were parked in front of an old house that looked like it should have been condemned. Ok, that might be a slight exaggeration, but it didn't exactly have curb appeal.

"You coming?" Reyna asked leaning in through her open door. Miraculously she didn't look like she'd been sitting in a car for seven hours. Now me on the other hand, that was an altogether different story. I'd barely slept the night before, and even if I wore makeup it wouldn't have covered up the bags under my eyes.

"Yeah, I'm coming." I reluctantly unbuckled and got out. I wasn't looking forward to what I knew would be an awkward introduction.

Reyna pulled out my duffel in what she probably viewed as a peace offering. I put it over my shoulder and followed her over to the questionable looking set of stairs. I tentatively touched the bottom step before taking a deep breath and following her up to the porch.

She knocked on the door, and I was surprised it didn't fall off the hinges.

A guy with brown hair opened the door and pulled Reyna into his arms. "Hey, Baby!"

My stomach dropped. Baby? They were on pet name terms?

"Hey, Chad!" Reyna kissed him on the lips playfully. "We made it."

He rubbed her back in a very familiar way. "I'm glad you decided to make the trip. I promise to make it worth your while."

I just stood there in the doorway holding my bag. I wished I had the nerve to clear my throat, but I didn't want Chad to hate me already.

I settled on a light sigh that came out sounding like more of a grunt.

"Oh, sorry." Reyna stumbled back from him. "Chad, this is Daisy, my amazing sorority sister and roommate."

"Hey, Daisy. Thanks for going along for the ride with my girl, Reyna."

Yeah, I was on my own for the weekend. "Of course. Anything for Reyna." Door Mat. Door Mat. I repeated to myself.

Chad and Reyna exchanged a look, and I knew it had something to do with me. I assumed it couldn't be good so I showed myself into the cramped apartment.

I eyed one worn out leather couch. I assumed I'd be sleeping there. I walked over to drop off my stuff and noticed a few suspicious stains. Gross. Completely and utterly gross. I was so glad I'd brought a sleeping bag with me. At least I wouldn't have to sleep right on the thing.

"Hey."

I turned and nearly collided with a guy with spiky black hair. "Hi."

"I'm Shaun."

I looked around Shaun to see Reyna flirting with Chad. Might as well make friends with the roommate. At least Reyna had been right about one thing, he was cute. "Hi Shaun, I'm Daisy."

"Really? Like from *The Great Gatsby*?"

"Uh, yeah." Wow, a guy my age who knew something about literature.

"Cool. Listen, just to put it out there, you can sleep in my bed if you want. I wouldn't want to subject you to the couch."

I shook my head. "Oh, that's okay." First he appreciates literature and now he's a gentleman? Double points.

"Come on, I saw you eyeing it's, uh, worn in condition." He smiled, immediately putting me at ease.

"I was just glad I brought a sleeping bag." I felt like a weight had been taken off me. Things might not be quite as awkward as I anticipated.

Shaun laughed. "Really, I'd only offer my bed if I wanted to. Save the sleeping bag. Besides, I wouldn't want to leave you out here with our other roommate around."

"Other roommate?"

"Yeah. Duncan. He's a weird one."

"Oh." Reyna hadn't mentioned a third roommate in the apartment. Interesting omission. In order to avoid any unnecessary drama I decided not to ask more about Duncan. If he was really that weird hopefully I wouldn't even meet him.

"Here, I'll help you with your stuff." Shaun grabbed my duffel before I could stop him.

"Really—"

"I'm telling you it's not a problem," He interrupted.

Reyna caught my eye and winked. I shook my head in return. If she thought she was playing matchmaker she had another thing coming. Nice or not, I wasn't interested in hooking up with some random guy. If that's all I wanted I might as well have just continued trying my luck with the dating pool at East Madison.

"Reyna? You coming?" Chad called from the doorway of his room. Wow, he was moving fast. I hoped Reyna knew what she was doing. Hopefully they were on the same page.

"Looks like you have someone to keep you company." Reyna grinned. "I'm going to take a quick nap with Chad."

"Oh, a nap?" I rolled my eyes. "Enjoy that."

With a sigh I walked into Shaun's room. The room was sparsely furnished with just a bed and a desk in the corner. His walls were bare which surprised me. I guess most guys I knew at school had posters and stuff up. His looked like he'd just moved in. A window AC unit sat precariously on the sill appearing like it could fall at any moment.

"I just changed my sheets today." He gestured to his bed.

"Really?"

"Yeah. I always do laundry on Fridays."

"And you change your sheets?"

He laughed. "You don't wash yours?"

"I do, but most of my guy friends don't with any regularity."

"Oh, that's kind of gross."

I laughed. "Are you as much of a neat freak as me?"

"I prefer to think of myself as orderly."

"Orderly. That works too."

I took a seat on the edge of his bed. My guess was that Reyna's 'nap' was going to last awhile.

CHAPTER THREE

"The Boot isn't anything special, but it's where we always start." Chad was all smiles as we walked toward the unofficial campus bar of Tulane.

"Cool, we're up for anything." Reyna appeared equally happy, ever so often stealing glances of her hand held by his. If I didn't know any better I'd say this guy really meant something to her.

"Great." It was already Friday night. All I had to do was make it until Sunday morning and we'd be on our way back to campus.

"What's the scene like at EMC?" Shaun asked.

"It's a big Greek scene." Which was why joining a sorority was a no-brainer. Social life pretty much revolved around it. "There's obviously tons to do in Atlanta, but we're just outside the city."

"So you're in a sorority?"

"Yeah. Delta Mu."

"Nice."

"I'm guessing you're not Greek?"

"No, it's not really my scene."

"Cool." I didn't care whether he was or not, but there went a potential conversation. "So this is an eighteen and up place?" I didn't particularly feel like broaching the whole fake ID subject.

"Yeah. You're good."

"Ok, great." Our conversation was getting stilted so I really hoped we got there soon.

We turned a corner and suddenly we were surrounded by crowds of college students. Evidently this was where everyone hung out on Friday night. The door to the bar was wide open, but a large guy who couldn't have been more than twenty-two or so sat at the door. I showed him my license and he grunted something. I assumed that meant I was fine so I trailed the others inside.

The bar was smoky and crowded as I followed the others. One long bar spanned the back of the space, and loud music blared from speakers somewhere.

"I'll get us a pitcher." Chad dropped Reyna's hand, and we searched around for a place to sit.

"Shaun, hey." A guy called him over. Reyna and I followed him.

"Hey, man. Mind if we join you?"

The guy looked Reyna and I over. "No feel free."

Sometimes being a girl did come in handy. I took a seat next to Shaun, knowing Reyna would want the two seats on the other side of the table so she could sit with Chad.

I made some more awkward conversation. That seemed to be the theme of the evening. When Chad arrived with the pitcher of beer I gulped down my cup in record time. I needed something to take the edge off. After about an hour we left the Boot and piled into Chad's car to drive over to a place called the Bull Dog. This one had a different crowd. It seemed a little bit older, but definitely still college.

As I stood sipping my Abita beer, it was a local beer I was told I had to try, I largely tuned out the conversation of the group we were with. They'd stopped even pretending to include me, and it wasn't worth the effort to push myself in. Instead I people watched.

That's when I saw him. Tall, broad, and blond, he stood out in the sea of students. Even flanked by two equally tall and attractive guys, he commanded all of my attention.

He was too far away to see the color of his eyes, but whatever they were they probably fit perfectly with his chiseled features. The guy could have been a model. As hard as I tried, I couldn't pull my eyes away from him.

"What are you staring at?" Reyna asked. She'd separated herself from Chad for the moment.

"Nothing."

She followed my line of vision. "Oh. Which one?"

"Blond."

"Of course." She laughed.

"Hey, I've dated guys with dark hair."

"Yes, but when given the choice you want a blond." She brought her beer to her lips.

"So? We all have our preferences." Reyna always went for the brooding types, although Chad didn't fit that description.

"Go talk to him." She nodded toward him.

"Yeah… right."

"Why not? If he isn't interested you never have to see him again."

She had a point. That was the upside of being hundreds of miles from home.

"Come on. Live a little. He's gorgeous. You can't give up this kind of chance." She placed her empty beer bottle down on the table.

"Only you can make talking to a guy sound like a monumental life event."

"Not a monumental event, but a fun one. Go ahead."

"Fine." Normally I would have just stood there staring at the guy, but she was right. What's the worst thing that could happen? I wouldn't have to worry about running into him again or anything.

I finished my beer and set it down before forcing myself to walk toward the three inhumanly attractive guys.

I stopped right next to him. "Hi."

He didn't say anything.

I tried again. "Hi there."

He gave me a funny look. "Hi? Can I help you?"

"Can I help you?" His friend with the black hair elbowed him. "Ignore his manners, he's rusty."

"Oh." Humiliation had taken on new meaning.

"Shut up." He glared at his friend before turning back to me. "Is there something I can do for you? Do we have a class together or something?"

I wanted to run, but I forced myself to hold my place. "No. I was just saying hello."

"Ok, hello." He just stared at me, and I was ready to be swallowed into the floor.

His friend with brown hair shook his head before turning to me. "Sorry about him."

I couldn't take a second more. I spun around and headed back to Reyna.

"How'd it go?" she asked. She'd already returned to Chad's side so I didn't want to talk about it.

"I'm not feeling great. Any chance you guys want to go home?"

Chad put his hand around Reyna's waist. "We can definitely head back."

I probably earned points from the guy, my request meant he'd get laid sooner. "Thanks."

"Should we wait for Shaun and the others?" Reyna asked. Shaun disappeared within twenty minutes of us arriving at the second bar. He'd run into some of his other friends.

"Nah, he'll probably stay out late, and I'm sure he can find another ride." Chad started heading toward the entrance.

I stared at the floor as we passed by those guys again, but I allowed myself one glance as we reached the stairs.

They were still in the same place completely oblivious to my exit. Wow, talk about a strike out.

Reyna noticed the direction of my glance and she leaned in to whisper, "Don't worry about it. We all have those nights."

I smiled to make her drop the subject, but I was pretty sure Reyna had never been shot down by a guy like that before. At least I was able to leave.

We made the quick drive back to their house, and I kept a smile plastered on my face when I said goodnight to both of them.

I could already hear Reyna's giggles as I got ready for bed in the bathroom. I was ready to go to sleep and forget the embarrassment. Most people would have just moved on from it, but I was analyzing every detail. Was I really that unappealing? He hadn't even smiled.

Oh well, at least I wasn't sleeping on the couch. I pulled down Shaun's blanket and checked the sheets. They looked fresh and clean.

Satisfied I wasn't sleeping in anything gross, I turned off Shaun's desk lamp and slid into his bed. The mattress was surprisingly comfortable. He must have had one of those ultra-padded mattress covers. I made a mental note to pick one up for myself. Thinking about shopping for bedding accessories was better than thinking about the earlier rejection.

Going to sleep in a strange bed is always a weird feeling, but add in the fact that I knew the bed belonged to a guy I'd just met, and it was even weirder. I wondered why he was so willing to give it up since, as a neat freak like me, he couldn't be thrilled at the thought of sleeping on the couch. Maybe he had somewhere else to crash.

Eventually after my mind had run a few dozen laps around the evening's events, I finally drifted off to sleep.

***

Someone's hand was on my breast. Not just on my breast, but cupping it. My eyes flew open. Where was I? As I felt something hard poking my back I remembered. I screamed and jumped out of bed. "What the hell?"

"Hey, Daisy. Didn't want to wait up for me?" Shaun's voice was level like we were talking casually, but he'd said my name which meant he'd known it was me. That ruled out any possibility of him being drunk and forgetting who I was.

I stumbled around looking for the light. I didn't bother with the lamp. Instead I went for the overhead light.

"Fuck." Shaun cursed as the light blinded us both.

"What were you doing?"

"I was enjoying the beautiful girl in my bed, what did you think I was doing?"

"You told me I could sleep here." I wrapped my arms around my chest. Even though my t-shirt provided good coverage, I wasn't wearing a bra.

"Yes, I did." He grinned.

"And that offer implied you weren't sleeping here."

"No, it didn't. I'd never agree to sleep on that couch." His face wrinkled up in disgust.

"I thought of that. I assumed you had somewhere else to sleep."

"Somewhere else?" Understanding crossed his face. "Oh, no. I wasn't planning on crashing anywhere else."

"You somehow got the impression that I wanted to sleep in the same bed as you?"

"You want exactly what I do." He arched an eyebrow.

"No, I don't. That's why I jumped out of bed."

"You were surprised—that was the point. Now why don't you come back to bed so we can get things started." He pulled away the blanket and sheet revealing what I already knew. He was completely naked. And completely aroused.

"Oh god." I grabbed my stuff as I headed for the door. My clothes from the day slipped off the top of the duffel, so I bent to pick them up where they landed right next to his bed. As I reached for my shirt I came face to face with a picture of a half-naked woman, and from the looks of the rolled-up posters beside it, there were more like it. Of course. This perv had planned this all along. What a creep. I stood up, and did one quick look around for the rest of my stuff. I wouldn't be stepping foot into his room again. I'd rather sleep on the floor or outside.

I turned the doorknob, and it took an extra turn. "You locked the door?" I said mostly to myself as I opened the door.

"I figured you wouldn't want anyone walking in on us." Shaun's voice came from right behind me.

I didn't turn around. What if he was still naked? "I'm sleeping on the couch. Stay far away from me."

"You don't have to be this way. No one's going to judge you."

"Uh, this isn't about being judged." Why was I even arguing with this weirdo?

"If you change your mind, the offer's still open."

"No." If I hadn't been exhausted and humiliated, I probably would have done more. It wasn't until I was curled up inside my sleeping bag that I started to beat myself up about how I wished I was the kind of girl who would have slapped him. I just wasn't, at least not when I was sleeping in some crappy apartment in a city I'd never been to before. The trip was definitely epic—epically awful.

I remained staring at the wall until I heard Shaun's door close.

"Want me to hurt him for you?"

"What?" I whirled around quickly, but since I was in the sleeping bag that meant I ended up half on the floor. I say half, because a guy gently helped me back onto the couch.

"Who are you?" The room was dark enough that I couldn't really see his face. Could things get any worse? First the most attractive guy I'd ever seen rejected me, then a weirdo groped me, and now this?

"I'm Duncan. I live here. I'm guessing you're here with the girl who's in Chad's room?"

"Uh, yeah." All right, hopefully this roommate wasn't as pervy. Shaun had called him weird, but I no longer trusted his judgment.

"You didn't answer my question." He just stood there. I tried to get a better look at him, but in the nearly absent light I couldn't make out all of his features.

"What question?"

"Want me to kill him?"

The question had to be a joke, but he said it completely serious. He'd stepped closer to the window so I got a quick look at his face. He wasn't bad looking—he had nothing on the Blond though. Not that his attractiveness mattered. "I think he can live to see another day, but if he goes near me again I might change my mind."

"Ok, suit yourself." Duncan turned and walked away. I heard a door open and close, and repositioned myself in an attempt to actually get some sleep.

To keep my mind off the horrible night, I started going through the list of work I'd have to do when I got back to campus. Somehow my tedious assignments were relaxing to contemplate. Despite the craziness of the night, I eventually fell asleep.

The next time I woke up, no one was copping a feel, but Shaun was sitting in a chair staring at me, and he was only wearing a pair of briefs.

I groaned. "What part of stay away from me don't you understand?" I pulled the sleeping bag tighter around me.

"I'm just sitting in my living room."

"Staring at me."

"It's not like I'm jacking off in front of you." There was something in the way he said it that made me think he'd done that in his room not too long before. So much for the polite gentleman. Between the near nudie pictures, the groping, and now the jerking off comment, I was pretty sure his entire personality the day before had been an act.

"Lovely image." I unzipped my sleeping bag.

He smiled. "Yeah? You like it?"

"Oh my god. No. I was being sarcastic." I picked up my duffel "Now if you'll excuse me I'm taking a shower." The thought of using a shower in that apartment scared me, but I desperately needed to wash away the remnants of the horrible night. I hoped there was a good lock on the bathroom door.

"Want some company?" He called after me.

I spun around. "Are you serious?"

He smiled sheepishly. "You can't blame a guy for trying."

"Yes, I can." I headed toward the bathroom. I needed to get changed and out of that apartment as soon as possible. I had a feeling that Reyna wasn't getting up for a while, but that didn't mean I had to wait around.

"Man, you like this hard to get stuff."

"It's not playing hard to get, it's telling you to get lost." I didn't bother turning around. I didn't want to encourage him at all.

Thankfully the lock was a strong one, and the water was hot. I gave myself a few minutes to enjoy the spray before drying off and getting dressed. I brushed out my wet hair and tied it back into a low pony tail. That would have to do.

I braced myself for facing Shaun again when I opened the door to the bathroom, but he was nowhere to be seen. I let out a sigh of relief. I grabbed my purse and camera and stowed the rest of my stuff behind a chair. I glanced at the microwave clock in the kitchen on my way out. Eight thirty. Hopefully I'd find something to do that early on a Saturday morning.

I had no real idea of where I was going, but I assumed my best bet was the streetcar the guys had pointed out the night before. If I got on heading downtown, at least I could explore the city and get something out of the trip.

The neighborhood had a different feel in the morning. There was a quiet calmness that made me nearly forget my insane experience with Shaun. I walked the few blocks to St. Charles and waited on the median. I wasn't sure how often the cars ran, but at least I'd left Mr. Crazy behind.

CHAPTER FOUR

After a few frantic moments of searching, I found the exact change the driver said I needed to ride the streetcar. I slid the cash and change into the machine, and the driver closed the door behind me. Without any warning the car started moving, and the jerking motion nearly had me flying through the air. Luckily I was able to grab hold of a pole, and then I held onto the first few rows of seats before falling into an empty one. The car was mostly empty, and I was glad no one seemed to notice my latest awkward moment.

As the car moved downtown, I opened the travel app on my phone. Reyna might not believe in GPS, but I did. I also believed in any app that could make my life easier. I searched for cafes, and quickly recognized the name of one. Café Du Monde. Evidently they were known for these donut like things called beignets and chicory coffee. Both sounded pretty good at the moment.

The outdoor café, covered by a huge green and white stripped awning, was busy, but I had no trouble finding a place to sit. I'd barely sat down when a waiter walked over.

I'd already decided on my order thanks to my app. "One order of beignets and a coffee."

The server smiled and walked off. I was positive I wasn't the only one ordering that same thing.

While I waited, I opened the app and tried to keep planning my morning. It looked like most of the shops and galleries in the French Quarter wouldn't open for a while, but it could still be fun to walk around.

My breakfast arrived, and I bit into the hot and sweet beignet. On the first bite I got powdered sugar all over my black t-shirt. Perfect. Oh well, I'd dust it off. The beignet was delicious, and the chickory coffee gave me the pick me up I needed. Hot chocolate was my comfort drink, but after the night I'd had and the lack of sleep, I needed something stronger.

I glanced at my phone. Nine thirty. Less than twenty-four more hours left. We were planning to leave at eight the next morning so we'd be back in time for a mandatory sorority meeting.

After finishing my breakfast, I paid and wandered around Jackson Square for a while to admire the artwork hanging from the wrought iron fence. I took some pictures of the large Cathedral and listened to a solo violinist performing a jazzy tune before heading over to Royal Street.

I stepped into a few galleries, but the owners all looked at me skeptically. I wasn't sure if it was the remaining powder I couldn't seem to get off my t-shirt, or my age, but none of them thought I could afford their work. I couldn't, but that didn't mean I couldn't look.

The one exception was the owner of a photo gallery I stopped in.

"Nice camera." He gestured to the Nikon around my neck.

"Oh, thanks. It was a graduation gift from my parents."

He set aside some sort of book he'd been reading. "Graduation from?"

"High school. A few years ago."

"Great gift. What do you use it for mostly?"

"Oh, pretty much everything. I've been into photography for a while." My parents had bought me my first camera when I was seven, and I'd never stopped clicking away.

He laughed. "Same here."

I really looked at the guy. He was probably in his thirties. Owning a gallery in downtown New Orleans in my thirties didn't sound so bad.

I gazed around at his street scenes and portraits. "Your work is beautiful."

"Thank you. I try to capture the essence of the city."

"This is my first time here. I'm impressed."

"Really? You're first time in New Orleans? What do you think of the Crescent City so far?"

I thought over my experience. "I'm enjoying my morning."

He laughed. "Not so much the rest of the visit?"

"I had a bad night." Ok, that was too much information, but who cared. I wasn't going to see this shop owner again.

"Ah. I think I catch your drift."

I shrugged.

"You should check out the Midnight Cauldron."

"The Midnight Cauldron?"

"It's a Voodoo shop, but with a different feel from the rest. I think you'll find Kalisa, the owner, entertaining."

"Voodoo? Like witchcraft?"

"Yes and no. You should check it out. She's just off Bourbon, but don't let the address fool you. Tell her Harold sent you."

"Okay." I took another look at his work not sure what he meant by letting the address fool me. "Thanks."

"No problem." He handed me his card. "Don't be a stranger."

"Ok." I pocketed the card and headed out.

The Midnight Cauldron didn't look like much on the outside, but I decided to take Harold's advice and check it out.

Unlike most of the shops nearby, the door was closed, but I pushed it open. A chime jingled as I walked inside. The smell of incense hit me as I gazed around the crowded shop. A counter spanned nearly the whole store. I walked up to it and looked into the case.

Rabbit feet? Frogs legs? Yeah, not the kind of stuff I needed.

"Can I help you?"

I jumped back startled by the sudden appearance of a woman that I assumed was the shop owner. Her long dreadlocks and mouth full of metal capped teeth weren't what caught my attention first. Instead it was the ample cleavage that she had on display. The woman gave a new definition to well-endowed. "Hi. I was just looking around. Harold at the gallery down the street suggested I stop in."

Her lips spread into a wide smile. "Harold's lovely, isn't he?"

"I just met him for a few minutes, but he seemed nice." I looked around at the candles lining the store. They were in every color imaginable and created an eerie glow despite the small amount of sunlight filtering in through a crack in a window.

"I see." Her eyes narrowed like she was sizing me up. "Is there anything in particular you're looking for?"

"Not really. I'm just exploring."

"Exploring? Where are you from?"

"Right now I'm living in Atlanta, but I'm from Charlotte." I'm not sure why I was so forthcoming with details, but I didn't see any harm in it.

"Are you here with a boyfriend? Lover?"

I laughed dryly. "No."

"Meaning you don't have either?"

"Exactly. I'm with a friend." No reason to explain more.

"Your friend has a man?"

"Yes."

"And you're happy for her, but secretly you're jealous." She stuck out her tongue slightly as she smiled.

"I'm not jealous." I crossed my arms over my chest.

"No? You don't yearn to be desired, wanted?"

Of course I did, who didn't? "Sure, but I'm not jealous of her."

"Fair enough, but you want a man. I can tell."

"Sure, who doesn't?" I shrugged. The conversation was turning awkward. I needed to find something to buy so I could make a polite exit.

"I have the perfect thing for you." She turned and started rifling through a number of little vials. "Yes, this should do the trick."

"What?"

"Come on back with me."

"Now?" I asked nervously. Wasn't this a voodoo shop? What were the vials for? I didn't know voodoo involved potions. I decided to voice my concern. "I didn't know voodoo involved this stuff." I gestured to the vials and bottles.

"I practice many different types of magic." She moved around to my side of the counter before walking over to the door to turn around the open sign to closed. She locked the door. I assumed that was all part of trying to create an authentic experience. Kalisa took things seriously for the owner of a tourist trap.

What had I gotten myself into? "You know, I really think I'm fine."

"No honey, you are not fine." She took my arm and led me back around the counter. Every part of me screamed to run, but one small part begged me to stay and see what she had in mind. How many chances like this would I have? Besides, I was in New Orleans. I might as well experience all it had to offer. When in Rome, do what the Romans do, right? I smiled to myself thinking about what Reyna would think of what I was doing. She hadn't called which meant she was still sleeping—it must have been some night.

She gathered a bunch of bottles and herbs and stuff as we walked into the back room. The worn floor boards beneath us creaked as we ducked under the sloping ceilings.

She started putting a few vials into a pot cooking on an old stove. I watched curiously until a large flash of fire had me stepping away. You couldn't deny that Kalisa had the theatrics down.

A strong breeze blew out a few of the candles Kalisa had set up. I shivered. I glanced around. There were no windows. Strange.

"Do you want to drink this or use it as a paste?"

"Uh, the paste." The atmosphere was great and all, but I wasn't drinking anything.

She laughed. "I was only kidding. I'd get shut down if I gave you anything you actually drank. Regulations and all."

I laughed uneasily. "I bet."

Without warning she pressed her thumb across my forehead. "I call this Seduction's Kiss." She ran her finger back and forth over my skin. The mixture was warm—nearly hot.

"Be very careful, child. Seduction's Kiss can be extremely dangerous."

And she was telling me this after putting it on my skin? If I'd actually believed anything she was doing was real I'd have run the other way. This was just a silly 'rip off the desperate tourist' routine I was positive I'd pay an arm and a leg for.

I rested a hand on my forehead as I ducked to leave the back area. I could feel the beginnings of a headache. "What do I owe you?"

"Nothing, child. It's on me."

"Are you sure?" I glanced around the shop again settling on a rabbit foot. I could use the good luck. She let me pay for that.

"Thanks, that was interesting."

She used a moist cloth to wipe of the remainder of the paste. "Remember what I said about Seduction's Kiss being strong. Beware of the night."

"Okay…" I stumbled out of the store with a full on headache, but I knew it was probably from the incense. I knew whatever she'd performed wasn't real, but she sure put on a convincing show. I'd have to recommend this store to people looking for an authentic experience. I'd add in my anecdote to the app when I got on Wifi again.

I checked my phone on my way to the streetcar. Two calls from Reyna. At least she was finally awake.

I called her back, and she answered on the first ring. "Where are you?"

"I needed to get out of there."

"What happened? Shaun said you were all weird today."

I laughed dryly. "The guy groped me last night. He told me I could stay in his room—I assumed that meant alone."

She gasped. "No way."

"Yes. He's a creep. This morning I woke up to him staring at me."

"I'm so sorry, Daisy." I heard the ruffling of something. Was she back in bed? I assumed if she'd talked to Shaun she was already up. "I promise I'll make this up to you."

"It's okay." I expertly slipped my money into the streetcar this time. I was learning. "I'm just going to avoid him until we leave tomorrow."

"That's going to be hard."

"Why?" my stomach dropped.

She didn't answer.

"Why would that be hard, Reyna?"

"We have reservations for dinner already, and then we're going out downtown."

"Who's we?" I knew I wouldn't like the answer.

"The four of us."

"No way. I'll just stay in their apartment and watch TV or something. If he's out of there I'm fine."

"I heard their other roommate is really weird. I wouldn't leave you alone there."

"He was nice to me last night." Admittedly he did weird me out, but he didn't scare me as much as Shaun. At least Duncan seemed to know how to keep his hands to himself.

"Still, you have to come. Otherwise it's just going to be the three of us."

"Can't Chad just tell Shaun not to come? Then you two could have time alone."

"Why? So he can stay back and annoy you? At least if you come with us we'll be in public, and I'll protect you."

"Protect me?" I lowered my voice when I noticed the woman next to me staring.

"Yes. What have you been up to all morning?"

"Not too much. Taking pictures, getting breakfast, and hanging out at a voodoo shop."

"A voodoo shop?" Reyna didn't hide her surprise from her voice. "You're brave."

I laughed. "Just trying to enjoy what I can." I noticed the woman staring again. "Ok, I have to go. Are you at the apartment?"

"Yes. I'll see you when you get back."

CHAPTER FIVE

I don't know what made me agree to dinner. Sure, Reyna would have been annoyed, and it would have made my living situation awkward, but Shaun was a creep. Surely that won out. But I did say yes. I felt a strange surge of confidence that made everything seem easier. Maybe Kalisa had actually done something with that ritual. Only instead of Seduction's Kiss she should have called it Confidence's Kiss.

Whatever the reason, I found myself sitting next to Shaun at an Italian restaurant less than twenty-four hours after creep-fest had started.

"I can't wait to see your costume." Shaun took a big bite of his pasta. "I know you're going to look so hot."

"Oh, I'll look hot." I'd decided to take a different approach with Shaun. He wasn't getting the time of day from me, but that didn't mean I couldn't mess with him a little.

He swallowed hard, and I struggled not to laugh.

"How was your morning exploring, Daisy?" Chad asked.

I paused to take a sip of water. "It was mostly uneventful."

"Uneventful?" Reyna laughed. "You found a Voodoo shop."

"Like I said, *mostly* uneventful."

"Was it down on Bourbon? Because those places are all tourist traps." Shaun sounded proud of himself, like he was saving me from having the wool pulled over my eyes.

"Yeah. I know." Something felt off agreeing with him though. Kalisa may have played with me, but I didn't like saying the Midnight Cauldron was a tourist trap. If nothing else the ambience had its own value and place.

Shaun set down his fork. "You should have asked me to come with you. You didn't have to do that alone."

I laughed dryly. "Yeah, asking you wasn't in the cards."

Chad suddenly grinned. "What? One night with him was enough?"

Wait. Did Chad actually think something had happened? Hadn't Reyna set him straight?

Before I could mull it over for too long, I felt a hand settle on my leg. I was already wearing the black skirt that was part of my cat costume. I'd packed one far less short than the one Reyna had suggested I wear.

"What can I say? I wore her out." He slid his hand up higher.

I smacked his hand away. "If by wearing me out you mean sending me out of his room running and screaming, then sure."

Chad laughed. "Ouch, man."

"To set the record straight absolutely nothing happened last night except this jerk trying to take advantage of me." Take that. I was on fire. If I'd felt this way the night before Shaun would have had a hand print across his face and a sore groin from me kicking him.

Reyna shot me a funny look, but I didn't care. Chad should know that his roommate was a total pervert. I hoped he didn't already know it. If so, he'd knowingly sent me to the lions and was not someone Reyna should be giving the time of day. You can tell a lot about a guy by the way he treats your friends.

"How drunk were you, Daisy?" Shaun smirked. "I think you're remembering things wrong."

Seriously? He was going to play that game?

"Remembering things wrong?" I tossed my napkin on the table. "No, I'm remembering things perfectly. If we had such a great night, why did you have to self-service this morning?"

The couple at the next table turned to look at us. I didn't care. I wasn't holding it in.

Shaun's response was to put his hand back on my leg.

I pushed my chair back.

"Shaun, please stop creeping out Daisy." Reyna glared at him.

I headed to the entrance without worrying about who would cover my tab. Considering the circumstances, I figured I deserved a free bowl of pasta.

Reyna ran after me. "Daisy!"

I stopped walking and turned around.

She pulled me into a hug. "I'm sorry. I'm being an awful friend."

I didn't disagree with her there. If the tables had been turned I'd be finding a hotel room or driving us home.

"It's just that I want things to work with Chad. I've never met anyone who makes me feel this way."

I believed her. The emotion in her words and face seemed real, but it was the way she glowed that made it impossible to deny. "I get that, but I still don't need this."

"I know. I know. I'll leave tonight if you want." She meant it. Reyna was a horrible actress. That reality alone was enough to keep me there.

"I think I can handle waiting until tomorrow. Just get Shaun to go out with you guys and without me."

We reached the apartment, and Reyna unlocked the door. Chad must have given her the key. "Why can't we do the reverse? You come, and he does something else?"

"Because I'm still going to be the third wheel. I get you're into Chad, and that's fine, but I'd rather do homework than tag along with you guys."

"Daisy? Do you hate me?" She gave me her puppy dog eyes again.

I sighed. She shouldn't have been the one making me feel guilty, but it wasn't worth a fight. "Hate, no. I just wish I'd stayed back at school. I can't go back and change that though. At least I had fun this morning."

"And you can have fun tonight."

Shaun and Chad walked inside the apartment, and I saw Reyna and Chad exchange a look.

"Don't worry. I won't sit at home tonight." I grabbed my cat costume from my bag and walked down the hall to the bathroom.

"What the hell, man?" Through the door I heard Chad. "Please don't screw this up for me."

"I'm not doing anything."

I rolled my eyes at Shaun's denial.

"You groped the girl, and from her reaction at the restaurant you were going there again."

"She's into me." Shaun was delusional. Completely and utterly delusional.

"No, she's not. My girlfriend's friends aren't yours for the taking. If she wanted to mess around then great, but she's made her feelings abundantly clear."

Girlfriend? That was fast.

"I'll back off."

"Stay away from her. They leave tomorrow. Think you can keep it in your pants for a few more hours?"

"Does Reyna have any other friends she can introduce me to?"

I was about ready to burst through the door and let him have it for that comment, but evidently Reyna was listening in too.

"Not a chance, and you owe Daisy about a million apologies. You were rude and gross to my best friend, and that's not okay."

I heard the telltale sound of a slap. Wow. Reyna's path to forgiveness had just been shortened considerably. I put on my cat ears and drew on my whisker s before walking out of the bathroom.

"I'm sorry," Shaun said as unconvincingly as possible as he still touched his cheek.

"Great." I started toward my bag so I could drop off my clothes, but Duncan walked out of his room at the exact moment, and we collided.

He put his hands on both of my arms to sturdy me. "Hi."

"Hi."

He still didn't let go. "Nice costume." His eyes had a faint ring of greenish-yellow color in them that seemed out of place in his brown eyes. I wondered if he was wearing contacts.

"Oh. Thanks." I looked at his all black ensemble consisting of a dress shirt and slacks. I guess that was as far as he went to dress up on Halloween. Given a choice, I would have skipped my costume all together.

"Do you have plans tonight?"

"None I particularly want to be part of." There wasn't a chance I was spending any more time with Shaun.

"She has plans." Chad walked over. "We're all going out."

"Come out with me instead." Duncan looked at me seriously. "I'm going downtown to meet some friends."

"Daisy's not hanging out with you." Shaun pulled on my arm. Duncan didn't let go.

Duncan narrowed his eyes. "Why would you have any say on what she does?"

"She's coming out with us." Reyna said from somewhere behind me.

"Aren't you guys going downtown too?" I turned to look at Chad.

Chad nodded. "Yes, and I promise you'll have a better time with us."

I turned, offsetting one of Duncan's hands. "Why don't we all hang out together? Then you can meet up with your friends, Duncan." That seemed like a nice compromise.

"No way." Chad, Shaun, and Duncan all said it at the same time. Why were they being so strange?

"How about we just do a girl's night then, Reyna?" I joked.

She gave me a panicked look which told me everything. She would have agreed to it if she thought I really wanted to. That's all I needed to see.

I smiled lightly. "I really want to hang out with Reyna tonight, Duncan. But I appreciate the offer."

"I have a better idea. Are you ready to go, now?" Duncan asked.

"Yeah, why?"

"Why don't we go hang out with my friends first? We can meet up with these guys later." He gestured to Reyna and Chad.

I thought about it. The idea seemed reasonable enough. If I was having tons of fun with Duncan's friends I could just stay with them. If not, I had an out. "Sounds good." I grabbed my purse and double checked I had everything inside that I needed.

Duncan waited for me at the front door. I hugged Reyna to put her at ease. "Call me when you get down there."

"I will… be safe." She held on longer than necessary.

"I will be." I followed Duncan outside.

From inside I heard Reyna. "Is she safe?"

Chad reassured her. "Yes. At least I think so."

I shivered. Did Chad dislike his roommate that much?

"Don't worry about him." Duncan patted my arm.

I waited for more of an explanation of why I shouldn't have worried about Chad's hesitation, but none came.

"How are we getting downtown?" I didn't want to make a scene, but I also didn't plan on getting into a car with a guy I barely knew.

"The streetcar. Finding parking on Halloween would be impossible."

"Oh, the streetcar sounds great." Public transportation sounded perfect.

"You were afraid to get in my car." He gave me a small smile as we walked.

"Maybe a little." For good reason. From what Shaun had demonstrated, you couldn't be too careful. I figured I'd be safe enough in public though. At least I hoped I was. "Why did you invite me tonight?"

He looked at me like I was crazy. "Because I wanted you with me, and I thought you'd prefer to spend time with me than Shaun."

"You've got that much right."

He stopped walking. "My offer from last night is still on the table."

"Your offer? Wait, about killing him?" I contemplated an excuse of why I couldn't go.

He smiled, and I relaxed. Had I really thought it was anything but a joke? "He's okay. I'm leaving in the morning anyway."

"Oh. Leaving to where?" He stopped on the median to wait.

"To school. This was only a weekend visit."

"You want to go back?" He put an arm around me as a group of guys without costumes walked over.

I assumed it was a protective gesture and didn't shrug it off. "Yes. I've been ready since I got here."

"Because of Shaun?"

"Because of everything. I knew Reyna was into Chad, but I should have predicted just how into him she was."

"You're single." It was a statement and not a question.

"Yes. Very much so." What was with everyone asking me that? Kalisa was obsessed with it.

"Are you a virgin?"

If I'd been drinking, I'd have choked. Instead I coughed. "What?"

"A virgin. Have you had sex before?" He watched me carefully.

"How is that any of your business?"

"It's not, I'm just curious." He buried his hand in his pocket.

"I'm not a virgin." Considering the less than stellar experiences I'd had though, I'd have been better off being one.

"Good."

"Good? Why is that good?" Shaun and Chad were right. This guy was really weird.

"Because I'd feel guilty having the thoughts I'm having right now about someone untouched."

"Uh." Seriously? He had to get creepy too?

"Maybe I should just call Reyna."

"No." he removed his arm from around me, but stayed close. "I want you to stay."

"Evidently."

He smiled. "I promise you'll enjoy yourself."

"No weird, creepy business then?" I knew his word didn't really mean anything, but maybe it would help me emphasize I wasn't in the mood to be toyed with.

"No. Just a fun night out."

I needed to keep the conversation going. "What year are you?"

"Oh, I'm not in school right now. I was at Baylor for a while, but I'm taking a break."

Not in school? There went the comfort from knowing he went to college with people I knew. Not that that fact would have changed anything. "How'd you end up living with Chad and Shaun then?"

"They put up an ad looking for a third roommate, and I responded. The place isn't great, but I wasn't allowed to stay where I was living before."

"Were you living with your family?"

"Something like that." He looked down the road. "It's coming."

Although the streetcar was mostly empty when it pulled to a stop, it was nearly full by the time Duncan paid our fare, and we walked on. He gestured for me to sit in a seat next to a girl. "I'll stand."

I wasn't sure if he was doing it because he wanted other people to find seats or because for some reason he enjoyed standing, but either way I appreciated having a seat. I still wasn't used to the jerky stops and starts of New Orleans' most famous form of transportation.

By the time the streetcar reached Canal Street, it was filled to capacity. I couldn't see Duncan when I got off the car from the back. I hadn't even realized you could do that. He was waiting for me on the sidewalk.

"Where to?" I asked. It looked like there was a party pretty much everywhere.

"This way." He took my hand in his, but I didn't fight it. Otherwise we probably would have been separated by the endless crowds. I was really glad I'd visited the quarter in the morning so I at least had an idea of what it was like without thousands of people filling every nook and cranny. "I want to take you to one of my favorite bars."

"Ok, cool." I hoped this one was eighteen and up too.

We wove our way through the crowds. I glanced into the rows of bars and clubs teeming with people dressed in various degrees of costumes. Despite my apprehension of hanging out with someone I barely knew, the excitement seemed to be rubbing off on me. I found myself moving along to the music spilling out of one club when we were momentarily stopped.

"Duncan!" A girl with long blond hair yelled and proceeded to wrap her arms around Duncan's neck. She was dressed as a pumpkin, if a pumpkin was just a skimpy piece of orange fabric. "Come dancing with us." She was visibly drunk.

"Oh, hi." He gave me an apologetic look.

I shrugged. It wasn't like we were on a date.

"Why aren't you dressed up? It's Halloween. You're supposed to be dressed up."

He shoved a hand into his back pocket. "How do you know that I'm not dressed up?"

"Laurie!" The girl yelled. "It's Duncan, the stripper who did Debbie's party last week."

Wait. What? Did he strip? Wow, that was pretty surprising. He wasn't bad looking, but I hadn't met a male stripper before.

Another girl ran over. This one was appropriately attired. She had an awesome lollipop costume on. She also gave Duncan a hug, so I decided to people watch while I waited. That's when I saw him. The gorgeous guy from the bar. All six plus feet of his perfectness. This time he was wearing one of those sleeveless white t-shirts that showed off his muscular arms. But it wasn't his muscles that jumped out the most. It was his beautiful set of black wings. Now that was a costume.

He glanced up just as he passed, and my chest tightened. He looked at me with curiosity for a second before continuing on. Maybe he vaguely remembered my face but didn't know why. I wasn't sure what would be worse, if he remembered the humiliating moment, or if he didn't.

I suddenly felt embarrassed of my cat costume. Were the whiskers too much?

"Daisy?" Duncan called my name and snapped me out of my daze. "Ready?" The girls must have walked off while I was distracted because Duncan was alone watching me. I wondered how obvious my ogling was.

"Yeah, sure."

Duncan towed me along until he turned into a dark and completely unappealing dive. This was his favorite place? I kept my mouth shut. I didn't want to offend him. Maybe this was one of those hidden gems you always hear about. Just to be safe I texted Reyna the name of the place as inconspicuously as possible, Grounddiggers.

"Who are you texting?" Duncan asked as we walked through the entrance.

Evidently I wasn't as inconspicuous as I thought. "Just a friend." I'm not sure why I didn't just tell him who it was. I just felt like it was safer not to.

He nodded at a bouncer, who like Duncan was dressed all in black. The bouncer grunted something unintelligible to Duncan. Duncan must have taken the grunt to mean enter because he pulled me further inside.

CHAPTER SIX

The interior of the bar was no more appealing than the exterior. The faded black paint on the walls looked like it hadn't been touched in years. The worn wood floors made the stairs at Chad's apartment look high quality in comparison.

I tried not to make a face, but with the musty smell in the air, I was having some doubts about whether the place could pass any health code.

A large, dilapidated bar dominated the room. Otherwise there were a few tables all of which had no chairs. Compared to the other bars on Bourbon Street, this one was mostly empty. The dozen or so customers were all dressed exactly alike. Black dress shirts and matching slacks.

Black was a popular color for Halloween, but wearing it head to toe seemed a bit much. Then again I was wearing all black.

"Can I get you a drink?" Duncan asked.

"No thanks." I needed a few minutes first. This was not the type of bar I was used to. The bars we'd been at the other night were similar to the ones near East Madison, but this place was something else entirely. I couldn't ignore the sense of unease spreading through me.

I took a closer look at the customers. They were all male as far as I could tell. Was this a gay bar? If so, it was probably the worst looking one in the world. I had no problem if Duncan was gay, but why bring me here? And hadn't he admitted to having inappropriate thoughts about me? The last thing I needed was some confused gay guy trying to use me to experiment or something. That would have fit with the theme of the weekend though—messed up.

"You brought some company, Duncan." A deep throaty voice asked from behind me. I turned around and came face to face with a tall guy, maybe in his mid-twenties. He was wearing black like everyone else, but his shirt was satin. "Hello, little one."

Little one? What was that about?

"She's in town visiting."

"Oh. She's from out of town." The new guy smiled in that 'I'm picturing you naked' sort of way.

I stepped closer to Duncan. "Do you not like locals?"

He laughed. "I just like meeting new people. I am Jeryl." He held out a hand, and I accepted his awkward handshake. He then brushed his lips against my hand. "Lovely to meet you, little kitty."

Kitty? Oh yeah, the costume. "My name's Daisy. Nice to meet you."

"Daisy? Isn't that perfect?" He rubbed a thumb against my cheek. Was he checking to see if the whiskers were real? I stepped back. He was definitely stepping over the socially acceptable behavior line. That also fit perfectly with the weekend's theme.

"Perfect?"

"Yes." He still held my hand. I wanted to pull it away, but how did I do that without offending him? "You're named after a flower, a symbol of life."

"Oh. Yeah." My name seemed to always get people talking. Sometimes in good ways, and sometimes in bad ways.

"Nice find, Duncan." Jeryl nodded at Duncan.

"Find?" I looked up at Duncan. What in the world was Jeryl talking about?

Duncan put a hand on my shoulder. "Isn't she? I noticed her yesterday, but tonight I couldn't resist her."

"Absolutely perfect," Jeryl repeated himself.

Duncan squeezed my shoulder. "Let me show you around." As weird as he was being, he sure wasn't getting frisky. That was something.

"No." Jeryl put a hand on my other shoulder. "I'll show her around."

The two men stared each other down. Something seriously weird was going on. This exchange caught the attention of several of the other customers who turned to look at us. Or maybe I should say turned to look at me. There went the gay bar question. The looks on their faces left no doubt of what was on their mind. Maybe these guys just didn't get out much.

"I will be showing her around," Jeryl once again repeated himself. This time Duncan nodded. Jeryl didn't seem particularly bigger or stronger than Duncan, so I wasn't sure why he caved to him so easily. I also didn't get why he thought it was okay to hand me off.

"Uh, I'm going to stay with Duncan. You know the whole rule that you stay with the guy you show up with?" I didn't know if it was actually a rule, but it was a pretty good attitude to have.

"Is that some sort of joke?" Jeryl narrowed his eyes.

"Yeah…" His gaze made it hard to think straight. Agreeing seemed like the only option.

"Why don't we both show her around?" Duncan's hand returned to my shoulder, and although I took some comfort knowing he wasn't ditching me, awkward took on new meaning.

My two escorts walked me over to the bar. "Would you like something to drink?" Jeryl asked.

"Uh, no thanks." I may have made some bad mistakes this weekend, but I wasn't going to add getting wasted in a bar full of weird guys to the list.

"Are you sure? We keep a full bar of liquor, wine, and beer."

"Great." Didn't most bars? "But I'm fine."

"Perhaps something nonalcoholic?" Jeryl gestured for me to take a seat on a stool. "A club soda? Juice?"

Theoretically, they could drug any drink. "No, thanks. I actually think I'm going to get going."

"But you just got here, Daisy." The way Jeryl said my name was creepy. I would have taken more quality time with Shaun over the shiver inducing situation I was currently in.

"Yeah, I'm pretty tired, and I'm not feeling great." I turned to Duncan. "Thanks for inviting me." I eyed the closed door like a life boat. I'd have much rather been stuck alone in the crowd outside.

Duncan shook his head "You can't leave yet, Daisy."

"Yes, I can. I remember where the door is." I tried to shrug off Jeryl's hand. Duncan had dropped his.

Jeryl pushed down on my shoulder slightly. "But we haven't even finished the tour."

"Maybe another time." I attempted to step forward.

He turned me so I was looking at him. "Oh, Daisy." He waved a finger in front of my face. "It's impolite to make promises you don't intend to keep. You're from out of town. You're not planning to come back anytime soon."

He could say that again. No matter how many times I visited New Orleans I wouldn't be taking a step into this dive. "Ok, nice meeting you. I'm going to go now." I tried to step away again.

I was immediately pulled back by Jeryl. "I insist you at least let me finish the tour. There's so much more to show you."

"I suggest you let him." Duncan wore an unreadable expression.

"I really need to go." There was no way I was willingly walking any further into that place.

"Not yet." Jeryl wrapped his hand around my wrist. The contact hurt. My whole body shuddered. I was in some serious hot water. What was this creep going to do to me? And why was Duncan just standing there?

"Are you going to join us, Duncan?" Jeryl now seemed to want his friend's company.

Duncan nodded. "Yes."

Jeryl pulled me along as he walked toward the back of the bar. His nails dug into my wrist, and I winced. If Jeryl noticed my discomfort he didn't show it. Somehow I wasn't surprised.

"Here, let me show you the VIP room." He leaned in, and he definitely smelled me that time. "Lovely, lovely Daisy."

"You have a VIP room here?" I didn't bother keeping the surprise out of my voice. I doubted Jeryl would even notice.

"Of course. Doesn't any fine establishment have one nowadays?"

"Fine establishments. Right."

Duncan held up a set of those bead curtains you only expect to see two places—a hippie's van or a strip joint. I wasn't in either, which made their appearance unsettling.

"Go on in and have a look around." Jeryl released my hand and gave me a slight shove forward. I stumbled into complete darkness. My body went into panic mode. I squinted and carefully reached a hand out around me.

"What do you think?" Jeryl asked.

"Uh, I can't see anything." Please let this just be him being weird, I pleaded silently.

"Oh, sorry. I forgot about that."

My eyes stung as a bright light suddenly blinded me. The change from pitch black to bright light was overwhelming.

I blinked a few times before I could fully open my eyes. "Oh."

"It's nice isn't it?" Jeryl asked.

I glanced around at the peeling neon pink paint on the walls and the crushed velvet couches that looked they were straight from the seventies. I guess that explained the beads. The two poles anchored into the floor and ceiling made me more than a little uneasy. They had better not have expected me to be using one of them, but none of that could compare to the giant cage off to the side of the room. Either they had huge dogs, or these people were even freakier than I thought. "Oh."

"I'm glad you like our VIP room. We don't let just anybody see it."

Maybe this was a cult? A cult of escapees from a mental hospital? I searched for a rationale for who Jeryl was and why Duncan gave him any deference.

"Why don't you take a seat?" He gestured to a couch. "And maybe you've reconsidered that drink?"

What the hell was going on? Was this guy for real?

I blurted out the only thing I could think of that would give me an excuse to leave the VIP room. "Where's the restroom?"

"Oh, I'll show you." Jeryl offered.

"Thanks." Luckily I didn't actually need to use the bathroom, because I doubted it was any nicer than the rest of the place.

"It's just this way." Jeryl pushed me toward a set of spiral stairs.

"The bathrooms are upstairs?" Could this situation get any creepier?

"Yes. Is that a problem?"

"Uh, maybe I'll wait." Walking upstairs meant getting further into the decrepit building. That wasn't high on my to-do-list.

"I know women, Daisy. You're not the best at waiting." He shoved me up onto the stairs.

I doubted he knew too many women, at least not normal ones, but it didn't seem like I was going to be able to turn around, so I took tentative steps up the stairs. Finally I reached the floor above. Once again I was in complete darkness.

"It's the third door on the left."

"I can't see any doors."

"Let me show you." Jeryl's hand settled on my arm. He led me into the darkness. "It's this one. The light switch is just inside the door."

"Ok, thanks."

"Want me to hold your bag for you?"

"Oh, no thanks."

"Why not?"

"Because I need it." Like I was letting my bag and phone go?

"You're not menstruating."

Crazy? No, this guy was a lunatic. "Ok, I'm going in there."

"Give me your bag."

"No. I want it." I hurried inside and closed the door. I flicked on the lights, temporarily blinding myself.

"Your phone isn't going to work in there anyway," he mumbled.

He'd evidently figured out what I was going to do. I walked into a stall. It was actually a restroom. A dingy gross one, but at least he hadn't led me to a torture chamber or something. I tried to send Reyna a text, but it wouldn't send. I checked the signal, no bars. No bars in downtown New Orleans? Was that possible? Next I tried the internet. Could I email her? Nothing.

I checked each stall for windows so maybe I could get to the roof, but I came up empty. Okay, plan C. Run for the hills.

I thanked my lucky stars I wasn't wearing heels, flip flops left my feet open to the ickiness of the Grounddigger, but at least I could move in them.

I waited a few more minutes for good measure, before pushing open the door. I expected to see Jeryl standing there, but the hall was empty. I followed the light to make my way downstairs.

"What are they doing in here?" Jeryl barked.

They? Were there other normal people inside now?

"They insisted they knew Duncan and had to come in. They were making a scene." Another man I assumed was the bouncer replied.

I tried to quietly take the stairs so I could get closer. The problem is even in flip flops, walking down shaky, dingy metal stairs quietly was difficult.

"That didn't mean you should have allowed them in. We're busy tonight."

Busy? If a dozen people was busy.

"What should I do with them?" the same man replied.

"You have to bring them back now. Who knows what they saw?"

"Daisy!" a female voice shrieked.

I knew that voice. "Reyna!" I tried to take the stairs faster, and I nearly fell down the last few.

Duncan caught me at the bottom. "You shouldn't have told your friends where you were."

"Why not?" My gut told me I wasn't going to like the answer. The dozen patrons were circling in around my friends.

"No one was going to kill you because we wanted you. The rest of them will be dead by the end of the night."

"What?" I gawked at Duncan. "Is this a joke, like the Shaun thing?"

"I'm not in charge here."

"I'm guessing Jeryl is." I turned to look for the creepy guy. "And what do you mean you want me?"

"You call to all of us, so we're going to keep you. That's why I brought you. It also means I'm invited back into the nest." He smiled.

"Nest? What the hell is this place?"

"Oh, this isn't the nest. It's just our place in the city." Duncan grabbed my arm.

"What?" Dread hit me like a fifty pound weight in my gut. What had I gotten us into?

CHAPTER SEVEN

"Reyna!" I screamed her name. We had to get out of there and fast.

I fought to break away from Duncan only to find that all three of my friends were being held by two men each.

"Daisy." Jeryl broke into a smile. "Lovely to see you again."

"Why are my friends being held against their will?" Of course I realized I was also being held, but I decided not to go there yet.

"We run an exclusive club. We can't have just any riff raff running around."

"You mean the VIP room isn't the only exclusive spot?" I tried my best to sound genuine.

"Entry to our club has certain requirements." He clasped his hands together. "We are willing to waive those requirements for you, dear, but not for them."

"Why? If it's a female thing, why are you holding Reyna?"

"She smells like sex." One of the guys holding Shaun wrinkled up his face. "Human-human sex."

"Uh, yeah I don't have sex with non-humans." Reyna paled. "If you guys are into bestiality I'm sorry, but you're sick."

"Who said anything about bestiality? We enjoy sex with humans." Duncan returned his hand to my shoulder. I recoiled. This was all his fault. Or mine. I was the one who had insisted on going out with him, wasn't I?

"So you're holding us hostage because we smell like sex?" Shaun sneered.

"You don't smell of sex." Jeryl gave him a patronizing smile. "You smell of desperation." The crazy guy got that right.

"Is that so? Then why was Daisy in my bed last night?" I was about to argue when Shaun shot me a look. "If you're looking for a virgin sacrifice or something, Daisy isn't going to cut it."

Was the creep really helping me?

"She's definitely not a virgin," Reyna added.

I'd never been happier to have people talk about my sex life.

"She hasn't had sex in months." Jeryl said it as a statement. He was right, but that didn't mean I was going to agree.

"Shaun's telling the truth. I was in his bed last night."

"And you jumped out screaming." Duncan squeezed my shoulder. "I was there, or did you forget?"

I groaned internally. Oh yeah.

Jeryl kept his gaze on me. "We can discuss this later. We have to move."

"Move?" I looked to Jeryl with my question.

"We can't get caught with the evidence here." He reached for my hand, but I pulled it back.

"Come now, I assure you we're going to get to know each other very well." He licked his lips.

"No, we're not." I looked him straight in the eye. That's when I noticed he had this same weird colored ring in his eyes that Duncan had. I looked at the other men, they had the same thing. Freaky.

"We are. And right now you're going to put your wrists together so I can bind them."

"Excuse me?"

"You heard me."

"Why would I do that?" I stepped back. That turned out to be a mistake as I walked right into Duncan's chest.

"Because you'd rather I didn't kill your friend."

I noticed he said friend in singular. Perceptive. Not that I wanted anything to happen to the guys.

"Please, just let us go. Is it money you want? I don't have much, but I'll give you what I have."

Jeryl laughed. "Money? You think we want money from you?" He stepped closer just as Duncan wrapped his arms around me from behind. "We want something more primal from you." He held his hand over my neck like he was going to choke me "Much more primal."

"Don't touch her!" Shaun yelled.

Jeryl laughed. "Showing concern for the girl who rebuffed you? Humans are so interesting."

"Like you're not human?" Chad asked.

"No. We're not."

In a flash, one of the guys holding Reyna leaned her head back and rested his long sharp teeth on her neck. Fangs. The guy had fangs.

Jeryl laughed at my obvious fear. "Hold your hands out behind your back, or he bites."

"What the fuck are you?" Chad struggled against his captors as he tried to get to Reyna.

Duncan laughed again. "You're denser than I thought."

"Vampires," I said the word slowly. I knew they couldn't actually be supernatural, but they wanted to be. I'd read about the condition online. People who want to be vampires so bad that they have sharp teeth implanted and stuff. Insane, but these guys totally fit the bill. Fake or not, those teeth could cut Reyna. I held my hands out behind me. "Let her go."

"If we let her go she'll just call for help."

"No she won't."

"You think your friend would leave you for dead?" Duncan asked.

Jeryl tied my wrists. "It doesn't matter. We can't take the risk. We don't need her, but we won't kill her if you cooperate."

"And what does cooperating involve?" I tried to keep my voice strong, but dealing with crazy people for nearly an hour was taking its toll. I was exhausted, and I just wanted to press rewind and be back at East Madison.

"Don't scream or make a scene."

"We're not going down quietly," Chad growled.

"Oh yes, you will." His captors started pulling him forward. Like the rest of us, his hands were tied behind him.

They led us back through the VIP room. The bead curtains seemed more menacing this time.

"Get in."

I blinked in the darkness. "I can't see." That line was starting to get old.

"Sorry." The lights suddenly turned on again, and I saw a long, black bag in front of me. "Uh, what am I supposed to do with that?"

"Get into it."

I glanced around. My friends were situated in front of similar bags.

"You want to put us in body bags?" Shaun said incredulously. "Aren't you going to kill us first?"

"Would you like me to?" Duncan asked. His dead pan voice seemed a whole lot more sinister this time around.

"Duncan. Go find Lloyd," Jeryl barked.

"Now? Aren't you getting ready to leave?" Duncan glared at Jeryl.

"I said to go. He's the only one missing."

"Fine. But wait for me."

"No. We'll see you there."

"You just want her first," Duncan snarled.

"And I will have her first, but that's not the issue."

Have me first? That had better not have meant what I thought it did.

"Why not send someone else?"

"The sooner you leave, the sooner you meet us."

"Don't harm her." Duncan gripped my arm so tight it hurt.

"She'll be in one piece."

One piece? Gee, that was reassuring.

Duncan released my arm and walked through the beads. Really? He was just going to leave? I knew he was in on this, and he'd been the one to bring me in, but still he seemed like the safest bet of all the men around us.

Jeryl pointed to Chad and Shaun. "Either get in your bags, or I kill the girl."

"You just told Duncan you wouldn't." Shaun seemed to have no fear.

"I said I wouldn't hurt Daisy. I said nothing of the other."

"Oh yes, the one who smells of sex," Shaun mumbled.

"Hey!" Reyna yelled.

I wondered if my friends were drunk. They were handling the situation almost too well. I was doing everything short of passing out.

I didn't need Mr. Fangs to experiment on Reyna again so I allowed Jeryl to push me into the bag. I really hoped there were holes to breathe through. "If something happens to any of those three, I will do nothing you ask."

"Relax, Daisy. We'll keep them around for a while." Jeryl zipped up my bag.

The bag partially muffled the voices, but I couldn't have concentrated anyway. I felt like I was suffocating. Were they going to kill me after all?

"Calm down," Jeryl hissed as I felt myself being lifted. "The heavier you breathe, the more air you go through."

I breathed heavier again. I was dizzy and nauseous and my chest hurt.

"I'm here, Daisy." Reyna's voice gave me some comfort. She was one of the few people who knew just how claustrophobic I was. I refused to even take an elevator. "Think happy thoughts." Happy thoughts? Considering I was inside a body bag, happy thoughts weren't easy to come by.

I heard more talking, and then I was put down again on an uncomfortable surface. A door slammed, music blared, and we started to move. We must have been in the back of a truck or van. I tried to pay attention to the turns at first so we'd be able to figure out where we were, but I quickly lost count. Where were they taking us?

"Next time you get mad at me just hit me, okay," Shaun teased.

His bag must have been next to mine.

"If we make it through this alive I'm going to kiss you for standing up for me."

"Kiss me? Is that it?" He was trying to distract me. To keep me calm. The boy changed personality so often it was giving me whiplash.

"Don't push your luck."

"You won't be kissing that human, Daisy." Jeryl's voice pulled me from my momentary peace.

"I'm so sorry, guys." It really was all my fault.

"I'm sorry for being an ass." Shaun really was being a charmer.

"Did Shaun just apologize?" Chad asked.

"Yeah. I guess the thought of dying is making me do strange things."

"Shut up back there," Jeryl yelled.

We listened. Maybe it was the suddenly more intense tone of Jeryl's voice or the realization that we'd been driving long enough that we couldn't have been in New Orleans anymore, but the joking was over.

We drove and drove until I lost all sense of time. Each bump hurt as we banged around in the back. I was terrified, but knowing I wasn't in this alone helped. Still, I knew we'd be lucky to get out of this alive, and by the way Jeryl had been talking and looking at me, it wasn't going to be pleasant. Maybe death would be better than what they had in store for me. I quickly shook off the thoughts, I couldn't afford to panic.

Eventually the vehicle stopped, and my whole body tensed. I hated being inside the bag, but I wasn't sure I wanted to face what would be waiting for me when I was removed from it. *If* I was removed from it, I reminded myself.

"We're only letting Daisy out. I want her to see her new home," Jeryl said from right near me.

My new home? I shuddered. I really hoped Reyna or the guys had told someone where we were, or that someone would track my cell phone. That is if my purse had made the trip. Somehow I didn't think my captors were concerned about my stuff.

I gulped in air as the bag was unzipped. I blinked, seeing the blur of a face in the darkness. "Where are we?"

"Home sweet home." Jeryl took my bound hands and pulled me out. "This is your new castle."

I squinted to see what he was talking about, but everything was pitch black.

We moved forward, and my eyes adjusted enough in the moonlight that I could see men carrying the other bags on their shoulders. I felt awful. I was the one who got us into the mess, and I was the only one walking. Still, I definitely wasn't safe. Who knew what these crazies had planned?

"Here we are," Jeryl said with pride.

I looked up to see a ramshackle old home. "Oh."

"Oh? Is that the only term in your vocabulary? This is your new nest. You should be happy."

"Nest? Happy? The only way I'm going to be happy is if you let my friends and me go. Don't even worry about driving us back. We'll walk."

"Walking works for me too," Shaun agreed from a distance. He was thanked by having his bag tossed on the wooden porch. The bag fell all the way through the wood.

He grunted. "Fuck, that hurt."

"Shaun!"

"I'm alive, baby. Thanks for the concern though."

I let the baby thing go. Considering he'd just been dropped through a wood porch, he was off the hook.

"Isn't anyone going to get him?" I asked.

"Why?"

"Why? Because he's in the dirt and stuck in a bag. Go get him."

"From what Duncan said this boy means nothing to you. Isn't this what he deserves?"

"If anyone gets to punish Shaun it's me. I should have kicked him in the balls, but that was for me to do."

"Thanks for that." At least he was still talking.

"We're going inside. The rest of your friends will wait out here."

"What?" I gasped. "No."

"I already told you, you're the only one we want."

I wanted to argue, but why? They were probably safer outside. I only wanted them with me for my own protection. "Please, just let them go." I knew the request would fall on deaf ears, but I had to try.

"No." Jeryl picked me up and slung me over his shoulder like a sack of potatoes.

I kicked him. "Put me down."

"No. I run this nest and you belong to it. I can do what I want with you."

"No you can't." I fought against him.

"We can make this easy or difficult. One word and your friend dies."

Considering they'd dragged us out here in body bags I didn't doubt the threat, but wasn't he going to do that to all of them anyway? "What do you want with me?"

"I'd be happy to explain everything to you upstairs."

Again with the upstairs? He walked into the front door, and a few men turned to look at us. "We've got a nice Halloween present this year."

"What's that smell?" One of the waiting men asked.

"It's her. I can't wait to see what her blood tastes like."

What my blood tastes like? Were they really all convinced they were vampires?

"Listen, my blood doesn't taste good. Insects don't even like it. I never get bitten."

"Well, that's going to change." One of the guys laughed. "You'll be bitten plenty."

"In lots of places," another added.

I started to shiver. This was getting real. Why were they so fixated on me? A tiny voice in my head screamed the name Kalisa. Did the witch's potion have something real to it? Did she want me dead?

Jeryl placed me on the worn floor of a bedroom. He untied my hands, but completely blocked the doorway. "Why don't you get changed? I'll wait outside."

Wait outside? Was he actually going to give me privacy? "Change into what?"

"Your dress." He gestured to a lace garment lying on the bed.

"Why would I do that?"

"Because I asked you to."

I decided not to argue. This was the first time he was leaving me alone. I needed to use the freedom to my advantage.

"I'll be outside. I want to see your body for the first time when I rip that dress off you—with my teeth."

"Great."

He closed the door, and I walked over to the window immediately. I tried to open it, but it wouldn't budge. I pushed up against it as hard as I could.

"What are you doing in there?" Jeryl called.

"Just getting changed."

"You have thirty more seconds. If you're not changed when I open this door, your friend is going to have a problem."

Damn it. I gave up on the window and picked up the dress. It was a faded white lace dress that looked like it was fifty years old. I stepped into it and started to slip my arms into the sleeves. The door burst open. "What are you doing?"

"Putting on the dress."

"But you are still wearing your other clothes. Take them off first."

"Why? It will fit."

"I want you naked underneath."

"You didn't specify that."

"Then let me make myself clear." He walked over and put his hand over my neck again. By the look in his eyes, I seriously wondered if he was going to let go before he choked me. "I want you completely naked underneath that dress. Not a stitch of clothing. Underwear and bra included. Do you understand me?"

I tried to open my mouth, but I couldn't from the pressure of his hand.

He released me, but I stumbled back. "You may think I'm stupid, but I'm not. You are going to learn to listen."

"Or what? You're going to threaten my friend?"

"Is that not enough of a threat for you?"

He called down the hall. "Bring the girl up. It looks like we will have to do a demonstration."

Panic seized me. "No! I'll do as you asked."

"Good. I'll stay in the room this time."

"What happened to not watching?"

"Watching you do as I command might be just as rewarding. And this way I know what's going to be waiting for me."

I cringed at the thought. Not happening. I slid off my skirt underneath the dress, and I let my underwear follow. I had to pull off my shirt, but I was able to slide my bra off while covering myself with the dress. Unfortunately parts of the dress were nearly see-through.

Jeryl just watched with his arms crossed, so evidently he was ok with me getting around the rules as long as I didn't technically break them.

"You may lay down on the bed now."

"Lay down?" What the hell?

"Yes. I need to tie you down while I take care of some things."

"Tie me down?"

"Do you have to repeat everything I say?" He grabbed me around the waist and pulled me over to the four-poster bed. "Lie down on your back, arms above your head."

"You don't have to do this. You scared me enough, I won't run."

His lips turned into a frightening smirk. "I have better hearing than you give me credit for." He pushed me back on the bed. "Did you really think I'd leave you in a room with a window that opened?"

Yes, but I kept that reply to myself.

"The best part of being in our nest is I don't have to gag you. You can scream all you want, and no one will come for you."

"Why do you want me? I'm not worth all this."

"You're the most irresistible human I've been around in years. Your blood calls to all of us, which means you are meant for us."

"Meant for whom?"

"Us. The nest."

"Wait. You don't mean... aren't there like fifteen or twenty of you?"

"Twenty-three."

"And you expect me too..."

"Have sex with them all? No. Of course not, Daisy. Your body is for me—and Duncan because he brought you in after all, but your blood. Your blood is for the nest."

"Fuck."

"I look forward to doing just that to you, Daisy, but like I said, I have things to take care of."

He grabbed my arms and tied them to the bed posts. "Might as well rest, precious. You're going to need your energy."

"I'm not tired."

"Perhaps this will help." He held up a needle. "It'll make the bloodletting easier, but you'll be conscious before I join you in bed. I promise you that. I want to make sure you get to enjoy every minute with me."

I gazed at him in horror just as he jabbed me. He left the room, and I fought against the restraints. Slowly things got fuzzy, until I couldn't fight anymore, and my eyes fluttered shut.

CHAPTER EIGHT

A loud commotion woke me up. Before I could comprehend what was going on, the pain hit me. Every inch of my body hurt, and stiffness like I'd never experienced made it impossible to lift my head. I gave up trying once I realized it only made the pain worse.

The sounds around me grew even louder. A mix of shrieks, breaking glass, and grunts had me fighting with my eyelids to get them open, but it was no use. I was too weak.

"Help me get her untied," a male voice hissed.

I struggled once again to open my eyes, but I couldn't.

"I'm doing it," another man replied, "She's the last one. We're fine."

The first voice sighed. "But she's lost a lot of blood. The others haven't." I felt the gentle touch of someone sweeping me up into their arms. "We need to get her help."

"Then get her to help. I'll stay around to take care of things here." The second voice was gruff and held none of the concern the first one did.

"If I hadn't seen that vampire she'd been with we'd have been too late."

"But we weren't. I'll see you later."

I heard a scratchy sound, and then more shattering of glass.

I needed to see who held me, so I worked harder to open my eyes as I felt a moment of weightlessness. I forced my eyes open and closed them again quickly. I was dreaming. There was no other explanation for how we were airborne. I'd never dreamed of flying before, but then again I'd never felt so dizzy and out of it before either.

The next time I opened my lids I was staring directly into a set of beautiful blue eyes and we were definitely on the ground. In the moonlight, I took in the strong features and blond hair of the man who held me. Large, black wings spanned out behind him. It was him again. "It's you."

"Don't speak. You can't afford to waste any energy." His words were terse, but not mean. "But you need to stay awake. I'm afraid if you lose consciousness again we might not be able to revive you again."

"Revive me again?"

He still held me securely against him. "There's no time to explain, we need to go. Just relax, we'll get help soon." He sounded like he was saying those words for himself more than me, but I nodded as I hung on to his neck. The action sent another searing pain through me.

The man winced as though he were the one who was hurt. He reached out to touch my face, but he dropped his hand before it could make contact.

"Wait. Where are my friends?"

"They're safe and on their way back to New Orleans. I promise."

I nodded. I had no proof they'd moved my friends, but I had to believe it. Why go through such effort to save me just to leave the others?

"I'm going to shift you slightly so I can take off."

"Take off?" I asked with confusion.

"I'm sorry but it would take too long to get there any other way." He moved me so that my back pressed against his chest, and he wrapped his arms around my waist. "We'll be there soon."

With that he took a few steps forward and then my feet left the ground. We were flying, and I was definitely awake. I'd have added wild hallucinations to the list of weekend craziness, only this couldn't have been one—it was just too real. We moved higher up in the sky.

I looked down at the ground in time to see a big glowing area of red and orange with rising smoke. They'd burned the old house down.

My eyes closed, but I opened them long enough to make sure I hadn't been imagining it. We were flying. I tried to look around me, but I couldn't. I was far too weak. My eyes closed again, and I settled back against his firm chest.

***

"You have to help her." My hero's voice woke me up. He was holding me in his arms, and we were back on the ground. We were inside this time. From the looks of the hallway we were in, it was a house.

"Come, let me see." A low female voice answered.

He started to lower me down, but I clung to him.

The woman chuckled. "It seems she's attached to you, Owen."

Owen? His name was Owen. The name seemed to fit.

"I don't know her."

"You just found her in a vampire nest?"

"I've seen her a few times, and I got suspicious." He exhaled loudly. "None of that matters. Just fix her."

"She's not going to let go, so you'll have to sit with her on your lap."

"That's fine." He shifted us and sat down. I didn't care where I was as long as he stayed. He gave me the only comfort I'd had all night.

Someone touched my face, and I opened my eyes. An old woman's dark, brown eyes locked on mine. "You've been mixed up with a witch too, I see."

"A witch?" Was I right? Did all the trouble start with that potion?

"Yes." She brushed my hair back. "You were bitten by multiple vampires. That's not common. Vampires don't generally share their human prey. I sense a witch's influence on you that is probably the cause."

"I saw a witch in New Orleans, but it wasn't real. It was one of those tourist spots."

"Now that you've been kidnapped by vampires and saved by a Pteron, do you really doubt a witch could be real?" The woman asked.

I didn't answer. I didn't know what to believe. And what the heck was a Pteron?

"The only thing strong enough to cause this would be Seduction's Kiss, and there's only one witch in New Orleans crazy enough to make that anymore. Did you see Kalisa at the Midnight Cauldron?"

"Yes."

"Darn that woman. She thinks she can play matchmaker, but she doesn't realize the other forces at work."

"Matchmaker?" Owen asked.

"Any witch could tell this human is something special. She sensed she was meant for a paranormal and gave it a push."

"A push?" Owen absently ran a hand through my hair. "Is that why I couldn't stop thinking about her?"

Couldn't stop thinking about me? At a time like this I shouldn't have cared that he liked me, but I did. Then I thought about Reyna. "Are my friends okay?"

"Yes. They are all back at home. Don't worry about them." He paused like he was debating whether to continue. "And I might as well just get this out of the way. They won't remember a thing, and neither will you."

"What?" Why wouldn't I remember?

"I'm afraid she'll have to remember, Owen. Letting a witch into her mind could do damage right now. She's weak, and that potion Kalisa gave her is potent." She put a damp washcloth on my forehead. "And to answer your previous question, no, your thoughts have nothing to do with witchcraft. You're a Pteron after all."

An unreadable expression crossed his face. "Oh."

"So if you've been thinking about this human, it's because you like her." The woman laughed.

"A Pteron?" I decided to ask out loud this time.

"Did you notice his wings, sweetie? He's a crow Pteron, aligned with royals."

Owen balled his hand into a fist. "Stop. Don't tell her anymore, Mayanne."

"Don't you plan to introduce her to Levi?"

"No. I don't plan to see her again."

She made a grunt. "Somehow I doubt that."

"But she knows our secrets. What do we do?"

"You don't need to kill me. I swear I won't tell anyone."

"After all the work I've done saving you, I wasn't planning to hurt you." He smiled for the first time. "But can you tell me something?"

"Yes. Anything." I felt like I could tell him anything. There was just something about him that made me want to spill out my life story. I also owed him my life. From the bits and pieces of my memory coming back, I knew that the vampires were close to leaving me for dead.

The witch laughed as she banged around behind us.

"Why were you with that vampire?"

"Duncan? I was trying to stay away from a creep I was staying with. I'm only here because my friend's visiting her boyfriend."

"So you don't live in New Orleans?" There was a note of disappointment in his voice that made my heart soar.

"I live in Atlanta."

"Ok, drink this." Mayanne brought over a cup of something red.

"What is that?" I was skeptical of drinking anything after the night I'd had.

"It's not going to taste good, but it will rid your body of the magic and anything those vampire teeth left behind."

"Go on, drink it. I promise Mayanne wouldn't hurt you." Owen's words were enough. I took a sip. I recoiled, but cleansing my body of those vampires was worth it. I drank the whole thing down.

She smiled. "I'm impressed. I've never seen a human drink that without being forced."

"I've had a rough few days."

"Hopefully some rest will help."

"Rest? But I have to get home." I glanced around at the room. It looked like a kitchen that hadn't been updated in decades. I still had no idea where we were.

She shook her head. "Not yet. You need to stay and rest a few hours. I need to make sure this worked."

"I'll stay with her." Owen started to stand up.

"I would have insisted." She took the empty cup. "I'll get you something else to wear as well."

I looked down at the ripped lace dress, remembering I had nothing else on under it.

She seemed to sense the direction my thoughts were going in. "Do you feel strong enough to clean up?"

I nodded, but then turned to Owen. "Will you still be here when I get done?"

He smiled. "I am your ride home after all."

"Those beautiful wings are real?" I knew they had to be. We'd flown, there was no other explanation.

"You think they're beautiful?" he asked with genuine surprise.

"Absolutely. I've wanted to touch them since I first saw them."

"She's made for a paranormal, Owen. That includes Pterons."

An unreadable expression crossed his face. "I'll wait here."

Mayanne took my arm to steady me as she led me down the hall. She opened the door to a small bathroom and helped me wash off and change into some fresh clothes. "You were very lucky tonight."

"I know. I could be dead right now." The reality of how close to death I'd been was hitting me full force. I'd been living a nightmare.

"And he'll come around." She helped me slip into a soft cotton dress. It felt strange to have someone I didn't know dress me, but I was too weak to argue. Besides, anything was better than that old lace dress.

"Owen?"

"Yes. I can tell your feelings for him run deep."

They did. That reality was an easier one to accept. "I already knew he was attractive, and now he saved my life."

"You really think your interest lies in his appearance? He's a handsome young man—but that's not it." She put some sort of first aid ointment on my shoulder and neck.

"I barely know him."

"And you're going to have to work hard to find out more." She took the old ripped dress. "For right now you need to rest before he takes you home."

I nodded. "Thank you for all the help."

"Of course." She led me down to a small bedroom with a double bed. "Rest here."

"Is Owen still in the house?" I asked.

"I'm right here."

I turned, and he was in the hallway. "I can sit with you if you want."

I nodded. "Please, do."

I lay down on the white and red quilt, and Owen sat down in the chair next to the bed.

"Don't let me sleep too long."

"I won't."

I tried to keep my eyes open so I could enjoy the time I could with him, but my eyes were too heavy. My lids closed.

"What's your name?" He asked in half a whisper.

"Daisy."

"That's a beautiful name."

"Thank you."

"I'm glad you're okay. You scared me. I thought I was too late when we first got there."

"We? So there was someone else there?"

"Yes. A friend." He didn't elaborate, so I didn't push for more. The other guy didn't matter.

"And he's a Pteron too?" Even though I didn't care who the guy was, I did wonder *what* he was.

"Yes, but you need to stop talking about us. You need to forget we exist."

"How am I supposed to do that?" I opened my eyes as best I could.

He was turned to look at me. "I don't know, but talking about us will only put you in danger or get you committed."

"Both wonderful possibilities."

"Great sense of humor."

"What did Mayanne mean by my being meant for a paranormal?"

"I don't know, but you need sleep. Rest up." He turned away.

"All right." I closed my eyes.

"If you need anything let me know."

Need anything? How about want? I decided to be bold, to take one more chance. "Could I get a kiss? Something good to turn this whole weekend around?"

"You want me to kiss you?"

I kept my eyes closed, unwilling to see him laugh.

"If I kiss you, will you promise not to talk about us? To forget about Pterons?"

"I can't forget."

"Will you try? At least promise not to tell anyone."

"I can promise to try."

I felt the bed shift, and I stayed as still as possible. Was he moving closer to me?

His lips brushed against mine lightly, but that small contact set me on fire. I reached up and wrapped my arms around his neck. The action did something to him, because the feather light kiss grew more fevered. I soaked up the salty-sweetness of his mouth. My entire body hummed and responded to his lips. His hands pressed into the bed on either side of me as he hovered over me, and I buried my hands in hair. In those moments I knew one thing. I was forever ruined for other guys. Forget the witch's concoction—this was seduction's kiss.

lure

THE ALLURE CHRONICLES

ALYSSA ROSE IVY

CHAPTER ONE

DAISY

"Are you ready to tell me about your recent dreams?" My psychiatrist, the one my mother forced me to see, watched as I chipped off more of my dark purple nail polish.

"There's nothing worth sharing."

"Are you sure?" she pressed. She seemed to think pushing me made me more talkative. It didn't.

"Absolutely. There's been nothing new for months." My answer was completely true. My dreams hadn't changed. Of course she'd probably want to know that I was still having the same recurring dreams that had filled my nights for over two and a half years.

"You haven't been thinking about that boy then?" She pushed her glasses up on the bridge of her nose.

"I'm seeing someone new. I told you that a few weeks ago."

"Oh, yes. Andrew, isn't it?" She leaned back in her chair.

"Yes. It's long distance, but we'll get to see each other later this week." I was getting really good at giving selective information that didn't require outright lying.

"Are you still planning your trip down to New Orleans?"

"Yes. It's a fantastic opportunity. I need to take the interview." I straightened up on the couch.

"Have you considered what effect this might have on you? Whether it might trigger the dreams and thoughts again?"

"Of course I have." Or rather I'd considered how my family and psychiatrist would respond to me going. I knew it was my only option. It had been two and a half years since I'd nearly been killed, and it had been just as long since I'd seen my rescuer, Owen. Although the fear from the close brush with death had started to fade, my desire to see Owen again hadn't. It had increased. We'd only shared one kiss—but that kiss might as well have been branded on my lips for how difficult it was to shake the memory.

"And you think you're ready for it? Have you considered asking a friend or family member to go with you?"

"I'm meeting Andrew there. It's going to be fine."

She pressed her lips together. "I am glad that you are so confident."

"Why wouldn't I be? I'm completely better now."

"How much does Andrew know? Is he aware of your history of dreams and visons involving the city?"

"He knows everything. One of the best parts about him is how easy it is to talk to him."

"How did he react when you told him?"

"He understood completely. He's just glad I'm better." Only partially true. He did understand completely, but he was the only one who knew the truth. I hadn't given up my obsession.

"Great. It's important that you surround yourself with people who understand. Would you like me to talk to him before you go? Make sure he's prepared for anything you may go through?"

"No!" I replied a little too quickly. "I mean, I'd rather not have you talk to him."

She folded her hands in her lap. "That's your choice."

"Thanks." I put my bag over my shoulder. "It's time, isn't it?"

"It is. I'll see you back after your trip."

"Yeah. I'll see you then." I smiled before hurrying out of her office. I'd already paid my copay, so I walked out of the office and back down to the parking garage. It wasn't until I was in the car that I let out a sigh of relief. Final obstacle out of my way. It was time to return to New Orleans.

***

I signed into Paranormal Obsessed, the online community I'd spent way too much of my free time on lately. The way I saw it, I didn't have much of a choice. I'd tried to tell my friends and family about my experiences in New Orleans, but none of them believed me. Not even Reyna, the one friend who'd gone through it with me. When Owen told me they'd wiped Reyna's mind of the events, he wasn't kidding. The problem was they'd wiped her mind of a lot more. The pre-New Orleans Reyna was more interested in playing matchmaker than going to class. The post-New Orleans Reyna was the president of the community service club. Part of me thought she was a better person now, but I'd never say that out loud.

I had a new message, and I clicked on the link to open it.

AT45: Hey! We're getting ready to hit the road. We still on for Wednesday?

The green "online" icon was lit, so I replied back quickly.

Flowergirl1: We're still on. I just need to finish packing.

AT45: Nice. How'd that appointment go?

Flowergirl1: Fine. Same old.

Andrew knew more about my current life than most of the people who actually knew me. I'd learned pretty quickly that trying to convince people you'd met paranormal creatures can only get you in trouble. I stopped trying when the word "committed" got tossed around. So, on the outside I was back to being the peppy, "normal" sorority girl I was supposed to be. I got decent enough grades in college and went out enough to keep my friends from worrying. I didn't enjoy going out though because I got way too much of the wrong kind of attention, and there was a certain witch to blame for that. At least it wasn't a problem online. Everything was easier when I was just typing.

I tossed my tablet next to me on the bed and closed my eyes. I remembered that Halloween night like it had just happened. I'd learned to block out the bad details. The ones about being kidnapped by vampires and nearly drained to death. The details I didn't let myself forget were the ones about Owen rescuing me from the house and bringing me to be healed. I didn't forget about his beautiful black wings, or the way he said my name. Daisy. And most of all, I didn't forget about the kiss.

"If I kiss you, will you promise not to talk about us? To forget about Pterons?"

"I can't forget."

"Will you try? At least promise not to tell anyone."

"I can promise to try."

I felt the bed shift, and I stayed as still as possible. Was he moving closer to me?

His lips brushed against mine lightly, but that small contact set me on fire. I reached up and wrapped my arms around his neck. The action did something to him, because the feather light kiss grew more fevered. I soaked up the salty-sweetness of his mouth. My entire body hummed and responded to his lips. His hands pressed into the bed on either side of me as he hovered over me, and I buried my hands in hair.

I opened my eyes and sighed. The daydream was over. That was it. After the kiss I'd fallen asleep, and the next thing I knew I was waking up in the passenger seat of Reyna's car. She was pounding on the window asking why I'd spent the night out there. It didn't take me long to discover that she remembered nothing—and that she thought I'd lost my mind.

I heard a ding and checked the tablet screen.

AT45: Oh, and I think I've got a new lead for you. I'll tell you more when I see you.

Flowergirl1: What kind of lead?

The green signed on icon disappeared. Of course. He enjoyed teasing me with stuff like that. It didn't matter. I was finally going back. College graduation was a week behind me, and I had a legitimate reason to return to the Crescent City—a job interview for an internship at The New Orleans Times. I'd never planned to pursue a career in journalism, but after all the time I spent researching to find out every little detail I could about Owen and paranormal creatures, it was a natural decision to switch my major.

I pulled out my go-to black, wheeled duffel bag and started tossing in some clothes. The bag was getting old, but the wheels still worked fine. I tossed in my bag of toiletries and two pairs of shoes. I was trying to travel light, but I needed some nice clothes for the interview.

I opened my door and started to drag my duffel down the hall of my childhood home. I had no intention of making it my primary residence again.

"Do you need help with your bags?" my dad called up.

"No. It's just one."

He ignored my response and met me before I'd even made it three stairs. He pulled the bag from my hand.

"Thanks." I appreciated the help even though the bag wasn't super heavy.

"Of course. I still can't believe you're leaving again so soon. You've only been home a few days."

"This internship could be a great opportunity, and they scheduled the interview."

"I know. I was just hoping you'd be around a little this summer."

"I'm only going to be gone a few days. Even if I get the job, the internship won't start for a month or so." I highly doubted I was going to get the job, which meant every second counted during the interview trip.

"All right. I guess we should get moving if you're going to make your flight."

"Yeah, I don't want to miss it." I tried to keep myself as calm as possible. My dad was acting cool, but I knew he was worried about me going back to New Orleans. My mom was the one who made me see a therapist, but dad still worried in his own way.

Less than three hours later I was buckled in and ready for take-off. This was really happening. In a few hours I'd be back in New Orleans.

CHAPTER TWO

DAISY

I checked the details of my hotel information again to make sure the name matched the building in front of me. The hotel was gorgeous—even more gorgeous in person than it was online. Maybe it was worth the ridiculously high price tag. My mom had insisted I splurge on a nice place to stay. Since I was only staying two nights, I decided to go for it because the location was perfect. It was right down in the French Quarter.

I was immediately hit by a wave of heat as I stepped out of the airport shuttle and headed to the front doors. A bell boy held open the door for me, and I stepped into the absolutely breathtaking lobby of the Crescent City Hotel. My eyes first traveled to a beautiful chandelier with dangling crystals, before I noticed the large travertine tiles covering the floor and the dark wainscoting that framed the room.

I walked over to the front desk, eyeing a beautiful mahogany bar. I'd have to check out the bar later.

"May I help you?" a petite woman asked.

"Yes, I'd like to check in. The name is Daisy Welford."

"One second." She typed something into her computer. "I've got your reservation right here, Ms. Welford. What card would you like to leave for incidentals?"

I slid my credit card across the desk.

"Here you go. You're on the fourth floor. The elevators are across the lobby." She slid a paper envelope across the counter.

"Thanks." I returned my credit card to its spot in my wallet and pocketed the envelope with the room keys before walking over to the elevator. A man dressed in a deep gray business suit was also waiting.

An elevator arrived, and I stepped in. The man didn't move to enter. "There's plenty of room."

"That's fine, I'm going down."

"Uh, ok." The doors closed. What was he talking about? The lobby was the ground floor. The guy must have been confused, but I'd been judged enough the past few years to do the same to anyone else. I pushed the button for the fourth floor.

I found my room and walked in. The room was fairly small with a queen sized bed, but it seemed nice. I set down my duffel and purse on the bed and looked out the window. It looked over an interior courtyard. Not bad. I had nothing planned until my interview the next morning. I needed to find some dinner, and that was a perfect excuse to take a walk around the French Quarter. I made a fast stop in the bathroom before heading right back downstairs to the lobby. I was met with another burst of humid heat as soon as I stepped outside, but I quickly got used to it. Born and raised in the south, that kind of heat wasn't new.

The streets were far less crowded than the last time I'd walked them. Maybe it was the time of year, or because it wasn't Halloween weekend. Either way, it was nice to walk around without worrying about the crowds. I was able to better appreciate the architecture and the sights and smells of the city. It reminded me of the quiet morning I'd spent downtown last time.

At first I just wandered down Chartres Street, but as the sun started to set, I headed over to Jackson Square. It looked nearly identical to the last time I'd walked through, and most of the vendors were the same.

I took a deep breath before heading over to Royal Street. This was my chance to try to find some of the people I'd met my first trip to New Orleans. I wanted to start with the small photography studio. It seemed safer than the Voodoo shop, which had been way more real than I'd originally thought. I stopped in front of where the photography shop should have been. I wasn't all that surprised to find the store now housed a new artist. There was a lot of turnover in the art world, particularly when it came to maintaining a high priced store front.

"Can I help you?" A guy who was probably in his mid-twenties asked from the doorway.

"Oh. Sorry. I was just looking for someone who used to have a store here."

"Oh. My dad's had this place for two years now. He got it at a steal because the guy who had it before him up and left without paying the rest of his lease. "

I thought about the photographer. He didn't seem the type to dash out. Either way, it meant one thing. There was no way I was going to find him now. It wasn't the end of the world though. The real person I needed to see worked at the Voodoo shop. "Thanks for your time." I started to walk away.

"Wait."

I turned back. "Yes?"

"This is going to sound a little bit forward, but I'm going to ask anyway."

Ugh. I decided to meet his question head on. "Sorry, I'm seeing someone."

His face fell. "Oh, would he really mind if we went out for coffee one time?"

"He wouldn't, but I would." I walked away quickly. I never knew when the after effects of the magic concoction I'd been given my last time in town would kick in. A witch had tried to remove the remnants of it from me, but she hadn't been completely successful. I definitely attracted way more attention than I had before, and some guys (and girls) were more affected than others. By the footsteps I heard behind me, this guy was one of them.

"Wait!"

I didn't turn. Hopefully he'd get bored and leave me alone.

"Wait up. Please."

The desperation in his voice made me feel sorry for him. I stopped.

"Hey, I didn't mean to scare you off. You're just the most beautiful girl I've ever seen, and I didn't even get your name."

"I'm not the most beautiful. If you take a few deep breaths and think about it, you'll realize that."

"What?"

"Try it. Really look at me. Am I really that attractive?" This usually worked. It let people see through the magic to who I really was. I wasn't ugly, but I wasn't a knock out beauty either. I fell somewhere in between.

"That must be the lamest way to get rid of a guy I've ever heard." He stuffed his hands in his pockets. "I bet you were making up the boyfriend too."

"I don't look any different to you?"

He looked at me seriously. "Nope. But maybe you will after coffee, or drinks, or dinner, or *anything* else you want to do."

"Anything? Like if I wanted to have sex right here on the sidewalk you'd be down for that too?"

He grinned. "I'd definitely be down for that, but I've heard the jails here suck."

"I've got to go." I turned around.

"Where are you going?"

"Shouldn't you be watching your dad's store? You left it open."

"Good point. Wait here."

I didn't reply. Hopefully I'd lose him. I'd dealt with clingy guys on a regular basis since being given the magic paste appropriately called Seduction's Kiss, but this guy actually appeared to be nice, which made it worse. It was easy to ignore jerks, but this guy didn't seem like one. I picked up my pace hoping he'd go back to the store.

"You really won't wait?"

"I told you, I've got to go."

"Fine." He pulled out his phone. "I'll text my dad and tell him to come by and lock up."

I rolled my eyes. "Are you listening to yourself? You'd risk your dad's stuff just to follow me?"

"Sure. He'll understand. This is fate."

"Fate?" I raised an eyebrow. "Nice try."

"You don't agree?"

I wanted to tell him the truth, it was magic, but the only thing that would accomplish would be making him think I was crazy. Wait. That could work. "You want to know what it is?" I stopped walking.

"What?"

"Magic. It's magic."

"Like there's magic between us?"

"No, magic is making you think I'm more desirable than I am."

He laughed. "You really do have the best excuses."

I groaned. "Seriously? Don't you think I'm crazy?"

"Not any crazier than me." He grinned sheepishly.

"Goodbye, whoever you are." I started walking again. I needed to lose this guy before I reached The Midnight Cauldron, the Voodoo shop where I got the stupid paste.

"I'm Evan. And you are?"

"No one you need to remember."

"Come on. Do I have to guess your name?"

"What part of goodbye don't you understand?"

"Those two words have nothing on fate, and this is fate."

"You need to get laid or something. You're a little bit pathetic." I wasn't one to make fun of people, but this guy had moved quickly from nice to annoying.

"You could help me with that, you know."

"Ugh. Shut up." I started speed walking.

"Hey, you're the one who suggested sex on the street."

"I wasn't being serious." I stopped and glared at him. "Leave me alone, ok? This isn't fate. I have things to do, and you're going to get in my way. Nice meeting you and goodbye."

I rounded the corner, and The Midnight Cauldron came into view. Evan was still following me.

"I'll leave if you give me your number and your name. A real number. Not a made up one."

"You sound like an obsessed stalker."

"If it helps at all, you're the first girl I've done this to."

"Gee, great."

"So? What's your name?"

I needed to get him off my back. There was only one way to do it, throw him a bone. "I'll meet you at Old Absinthe House for a drink at nine."

"Really? You'll actually be there?"

"Sure. Just please let me do what I need to do."

"How do I know you'll actually show up?" He shifted his weight from foot to foot.

"You don't."

"That's not good enough."

"It's all you're getting. The alternative is I scream really loud and get you in trouble."

"Fine, I'll trust you'll really be there, but how about your name?"

"It's the name of a flower." I took a few steps.

"Daisy?"

"Do I look like a Daisy?" I asked without turning around.

"Yes."

I shook my head. "See you later."

"Can't wait."

I looked over my shoulder. He was actually walking away. Phew. I had no desire to have a drink with the guy, but it at least bought me time. I'd have to figure out what to do later. First I had to survive my next encounter with the witch.

CHAPTER THREE

DAISY

I waited until Evan had disappeared around the corner before stepping through the open doorway of The Midnight Cauldron.

The smell of incense still filled the small space, transporting me back to the Halloween that changed everything. Every little detail of the store looked the same. Candles lined the window sills, and the racks displayed the same little gifts and novelties. There was some comfort in the sameness. At least this place hadn't changed.

When I reached the counter I noticed a few differences. The rack of vials had disappeared. It had been replaced by keychains and other knickknacks.

I hit the bell on the desk. I wasn't thrilled about seeing Kalisa again, but I hoped she'd lead me in the right direction. She owed me after all the trouble she'd caused.

"Hi, can I help you find something?" an older woman asked. She was dressed in a flowing floral dress and had her hair tied back.

"Hi. I'm looking for Kalisa."

"There's no one here by that name."

"She owns this store. At least she did a few years ago." I tried to ignore the panic setting in. What the hell was going on? How did this woman not know the name of the owner?

"I've owned this place for over two years now, and it was sitting empty when I bought it."

Another store sitting empty? Nothing was adding up. "Are you sure? This store was open when I was here about two and half years ago."

"Maybe you're thinking of another Voodoo shop." She gave me a funny look I immediately recognized as the 'you are crazy' gaze.

I needed to stop before she tried to get me help. "Oh. That's got to be it. Sorry."

"It happens, but I'd be happy to help you find anything you need. Maybe a Voodoo doll? Or a frog's leg?"

"No thanks." I hurried out of the store. Either that woman was lying, or Kalisa was long gone. Had she screwed over other innocent tourists and been run out of town, or was there something else at work?

I broke into a near run as I moved on to the next place I'd seen that Halloween. I wasn't actually going to step foot into the vampire bar, Gravediggers, but I needed to know it was still open.

I stayed on the far side of the street, confused when I noticed a crowd congregating outside the open doors. The last time I'd been there the place had been dead—no pun intended.

I tentatively walked over. A pretty girl dressed in a tight black dress smiled at me. "Two for one martini night tonight."

"At Gravediggers?"

"Uh huh. Want to come in?"

"That's okay."

"Are you sure? You can take shots off me."

"Uh, no thanks." The Seduction's Kiss paste was working at full force that night. Maybe being back in New Orleans made it stronger.

"Are you sure?" She batted her eye lashes.

I watched as a large crowd of girls all wearing matching t-shirts that said 'Amy's Bachelorette' walked in. There was no way these girls were going into a vampire bar.

I took a deep breath before stepping inside. Despite watching the other girls enter, I half expected a vampire to grab me from behind. Instead I found trendy twenty-somethings sipping martinis. It wasn't a joke. Gravediggers had become a martini bar.

"You okay?" The girl touched my shoulder when I walked outside.

I shrugged away from her touch as politely as I could. "Fine." I wasn't fine. Not at all. Either everything had changed in two and a half years, or I was losing my mind. It couldn't be. It had all happened. Owen had happened.

I headed back toward the hotel. I couldn't stomach any more time out in the quarter, and I wasn't in the mood for dinner. I wasn't in the mood for anything. Except a drink. I could definitely use a drink to help me relax.

The hotel bar was hopping, but I managed to find a stool all the way at the end. The bartender, a guy probably in his early thirties, walked over. "What can I get you?"

"A Rum and Coke please."

"Captain's okay?"

"Yeah." Paying for top shelf liquor wasn't in my recent college grad budget.

He slid the drink across the bar. "Should I open a tab?"

"No thanks." I put a ten down on the bar. If my drink cost more than that I was in trouble.

"What brings you to New Orleans?" Despite the crowd, the bartender was chatting with me. I hoped it was out of boredom. I couldn't take much more of the crazed Seduction's Kiss response.

"A job interview." Having a cover story was convenient. It helped with my parents and with anyone I met while down there.

"Oh yeah? Anything cool?"

"An internship at The New Orleans Times."

"Oh cool. Good luck with the interview."

"Thanks." I picked up my glass. "It's tomorrow."

"Is this your first time here?" He opened a beer for another customer and handed it to him.

"No. I was down here for Halloween a few years ago." I sipped my drink. Between the alcohol and the light chat, I was starting to relax. I wasn't crazy, there had to be an explanation for everything.

"Halloween, eh? Pretty crazy, right?"

"It was a crazier weekend than you would ever believe." My stomach growled. I really needed to eat eventually.

"Are you staying here?"

As much as I was careful about sharing any personal info with people, I figured it couldn't hurt. "Yeah."

"Cool. I was asking because you should try the room service then. The food here is great."

"My stomach was that loud?"

He laughed. "Kind of. If I was getting off soon I'd offer to take you out somewhere, but I have to be here until five."

"Five a.m.? Are you serious?"

"This is New Orleans."

I took another sip of my drink. "I guess so."

He smiled. "If you're still up, come back by."

"Considering I have an interview at nine, I better not be, but thanks." I smiled. All right, not a clinger. Maybe age helped dispel some of the magic's effect.

The bartender walked off, and I started to people watch. One of the best ways to get your mind off things is to focus on what other people are doing. Most people have lives that are interesting to everyone but themselves.

"Hey, man!"

I turned to see the new arrival to the bar. He was an incredibly attractive guy with brown hair. He was probably a few years older than me, and I recognized him. It took me all of thirty seconds to place how, and my whole body froze. He was one of Owen's friends that were with him when I first saw him. He was my first clue. My first proof that what I'd remembered happening that weekend had actually happened.

I waited. He was surrounded by people. The bartender evidently knew him because he immediately made and handed him a drink. "I assume you wanted your usual?"

"Thanks, Alex." He accepted the glass of something brown. Probably whiskey.

I finished off my drink, still waiting for an opportunity to talk to Owen's friend. What could I say? There was no way he'd remember me, but I couldn't let this opportunity pass me by. Maybe Evan was right about fate—although it had nothing to do with me and him. This was about finding Owen.

I took a few deep breaths and walked over to where the guy stood with some friends. "Excuse me?"

He looked at me. "Can I help you with something?"

"I was wondering if you could tell me where to find your friend Owen?"

"Owen?" His eyes widened. His other friends looked at me funny.

"Yes." I kept my expression neutral. I had to play this calm even though I felt anything but.

"Do you know him?" he asked.

"Yes."

He nodded to his friends. "I'll be right back." He walked away, and I followed.

"I'm sorry to bother you, but I really need to find your friend."

"What's your name?" he asked.

"Daisy. What's yours?"

He laughed. "I don't get that question a lot. I'm Levi."

"We met once before, but it's been a long time."

"You look vaguely familiar." He seemed to be contemplating something, as though he was trying to place me.

"Glad I was memorable."

He laughed again. "Nice sense of humor. I wish I could help you, but Owen left town."

"What?" My chest clenched. "When?"

"It's been months now."

"Oh."

"Sorry I couldn't help." He started to turn away.

"Wait." I looked at him closer. He had to be a Pteron. He had the same look as Owen. "I know what you are."

"Excuse me?"

Maybe I was going to get myself in trouble, but I was desperate and unwilling to give up on my only lead.

"I know you're a Pteron." Saying that word out loud felt good. So natural despite how little I understood it. The only thing I knew was that these creatures were strong and hiding a substantial set of wings. I'd kept the name to myself for years, not even sharing it with Andrew. Owen had emphasized the importance of keeping it secret, but now that I knew he wasn't even in the same city I didn't care. He saved my life, but that didn't mean I was going to keep his secrets forever. If they wanted me to shut up, they were going to have to explain why.

Levi looked over his shoulder at his friends before returning his attention back at me. "I don't know what you're talking about."

"Yes you do. Owen told me, and I've seen his wings. I know he's one too."

Levi shifted nervously. "I really don't know what you're talking about."

"Please stop. I've been waiting years for answers. I'm tired of waiting."

He leaned over and stared into my eyes. "Listen, I don't know who you are, but you need to stop. You're only going to get yourself in trouble."

"I'm already in trouble." I sighed. "Please, just tell me I'm right. I need to know I'm not losing my mind."

He ran a hand through his hair. "Fine. Let's say hypothetically that you're right. What do you want? Why are you looking for Owen?"

"I need to thank him." My reply was far too simple. There were so many reasons I wanted to find him, but thanking him again seemed like a start.

"Thank him for?"

"For saving my life."

His eyes widened slightly again. "Listen, there isn't much I can do. Owen's gone."

"Can't you get a message to him for me then?"

"I haven't heard from him in months. He needed a break and went off the grid."

"Off the grid?" I eyed him skeptically. "Somehow I doubt that."

"It's true."

"Fine. Thanks for your time." I turned away.

"If it helps, I'm sorry I can't help you more."

"It doesn't help, but thanks." I should have headed for the elevator, but I didn't. Instead I headed outside.

CHAPTER FOUR

OWEN

I thought moving to the mountains would give me some peace and quiet, but I was wrong. It seems I was a magnet for people as desperate for company as I was to be alone. They say when you're lonely the best thing to do is to surround yourself with people, but that's not true. The more people I was around, the lonelier I felt. It was only a reminder of how I was still single and in the same place while everyone else in my life had moved on.

I'm not human. Maybe I should start there. The reason I was single—and as a result lonely—was because of that fact. I'd only shown two girls what I was. The first one ran away and broke my heart, and I never gave the second girl the chance. Her kiss, the heart stopping kiss that left me hungering for more, was the only warning I needed. It was too dangerous. I needed to run from her before she could do the same.

It had been over two years since I'd kissed a girl. I know that sounds pathetic, but really what was the point?

Sex for the sake of sex gets old when there's nothing to back it up. My best friends had never agreed with me. They'd spent their time sleeping with any girls they could, but even they'd settled down.

"Owen?" Clyde called as soon as I stepped outside my front door. You'd think living five miles from the nearest town would make visitors scarce, but I wasn't that lucky.

"Hi. Is there something you need?" I tried to keep the edge out of my voice. I didn't need to make enemies. I was trying to blend in.

Clyde laughed and adjusted the rim of his cowboy hat. He was a Montana boy who'd left his parents' ranch to rough it in the Colorado mountains. He might have given up the ranch life, but that cowboy hat was still always on his head. "It's always great to see you, man. Such a great sense of humor."

"I'm on my way out."

"Out where? You aren't even wearing a shirt."

He was completely right. A shirt was only going to get in the way for what I was heading out to do. "Who says I need a shirt?"

"Pretty much any store or restaurant. That is where you're going, right? Into town?"

"No, I'm going for a hike."

"With no shirt? And no water?"

"You sound like my mom. Is that the point?" I wasn't used to guys like Clyde. I'd grown up alongside the royal members of The Society, the highest paranormal elite there was. None of them worried about water or proper clothing choices.

"I'm here with an invitation."

"An invitation?" I arched an eyebrow.

"An invitation to a whole new world, man. I'm telling you, this is the real deal."

"It sounds like you're offering me drugs or a prostitute. I don't want either."

He laughed. "Good one. That's a good one, man."

"Does that mean the invitation is for something else?"

"Let's just say I have some capital for an investment that can't go wrong."

"Oh yeah? An investment that can't go wrong? Sounds likely." I crossed my arms. I was getting impatient.

"What does Coleville lack?"

"Good seafood."

"Come on, seriously. What don't we have that every other town out there has?"

"Get to the point, Clyde. I don't have all day."

He shifted his weight from foot to foot. He was wearing cowboy boots. As if the hat wasn't enough. "A bar."

"We have a bar. It's just not running."

"Exactly. We need to reopen it."

"And you want my help?"

"Yes. You don't have to contribute any money. Like I said, I have the capital."

"Then what do you need me for?"

"Your presence. You know how much everyone in town loves you. They'll sign anything if you're in on it."

"I see. You want my influence."

"Maybe." He shoved his hands in his back pockets.

I looked at the kid. He wasn't technically a kid at twenty-two, but he seemed so young. I was only a few years older, but I'd been through enough to make those years seem a hell of a lot longer. "What's in it for me?"

"Free booze, access to the hottest spot in town, and of course the money."

"There's no money in Coleville. We both know that."

"There's some, and we'll bring in more. We need to make Coleville the hottest tourist destination this side of Denver."

"The only way to make Coleville that way would be to develop a ski resort. I doubt your capital is going to get you that far."

"This is only the start."

"I need to think about it." I didn't. I wanted nothing to do with his little bar, but I also wanted to get on with my day.

"All right. That's fair. Call me when you're ready."

"Sure thing."

He tipped his hat. "See you around. Looking forward to doing business with you."

"I never said I was going to."

"No. But I'll make that maybe a yes." He hurried off back to his truck.

He wasn't a bad kid, just over eager, I reminded myself as I walked back behind the cabin. I waited until I heard his truck pull out toward the road before transforming. I always felt better with my wings out.

I took off into the sky, my long black wings taking me higher than the tree line. Luckily altitude sickness doesn't bother Pterons. We once shifted into crows, but evolution had different plans. We've been spotted a few times, and people seem to think we look like fallen angels. We aren't angels—fallen or not.

There was nothing that could compare to the feel of flight; the wind rushing around my wings, the sensation of weightlessness, and the knowledge that all of my troubles and worries were miles below me. I'd been flying since I was a kid, but I knew I'd never get tired of it. My wings were part of me. They represented my strength. In a perfect world I'd never have to hide them, but this world wasn't perfect. Not by a long shot.

I landed down by a small stream high in the mountains. I left my wings out. There was no one around for miles.

I started walking with no destination in mind. I usually didn't have one. Maybe getting involved in Clyde's plan wasn't a bad idea. I needed something to do, and a reason to keep me from going back to New Orleans. I wasn't ready to face my real life yet.

I noticed a pop of color on the other side of the stream. I walked around the long way.

I bent down and touched the stem of the pretty purple flower. "A daisy. A wild daisy." Just saying the name of the flower brought me back to the kiss again, back to my Daisy. At least that's what I thought of her as. I didn't know where she was. She could have been married by now for all I knew, but I'd still always think of her that way.

I'd never told my friends about the kiss. They made fun of me enough. I didn't need to add fuel to the fire, but I got the sense that my friend Jared knew that the girl meant something to me. It would be easy to find her if I'd bothered to ask for her last name, but finding her again had been the least of my worries that night. I had needed her to promise to stay quiet and keep our secrets.

I released the flower. There was no reason to pick it just so it could die. I turned and headed back the way I came still thinking about Daisy and one long ago kiss.

CHAPTER FIVE

DAISY

Owen was gone. The realization hit me like a ton of bricks as I wandered around the quarter. I glanced at my watch. It was eight-thirty. Technically I still had time to meet Evan for drinks. I debated with myself. I had no interest in seeing him, but my conscience wouldn't let me completely stand him up. It wasn't the poor guy's fault he'd fallen victim to magic. I knew the feeling. After a few minutes of deliberation, I decided to leave him a note. That was the polite yet smart thing to do.

I hesitated for a moment before stepping into the Old Absinthe House. There was always the chance he was there early. My escape plan was to get lost in the crowd. I'd probably attract more attention, and I'd get away that way.

Someone knocked into me on their way into the bar, so I finally walked inside. I pushed through the crowd, looking down to avoid catching anyone's eyes and headed straight for the bar.

I pulled out a pen and scrawled a note on a cocktail napkin. I waited for the bartender to notice me.

"Can I get you something?" the female bartender asked with a smile.

I handed her the napkin. "If a guy comes in looking for a girl named Daisy, could you give this to him?"

"Sure." She read over my sloppy note. "Poor guy."

"Nah, he's luckier this way." I headed for the door.

"Leaving already?" A male voice asked from behind me.

I groaned internally. Of course he'd show up early. I turned around slowly and came face to face with Evan. "I left you a note."

"Looks like you won't need it."

I sighed. "Would you do me a favor?"

"Sure," he replied way too eagerly.

"Could you let me off the hook? I'm having a bad night, and I have a big day tomorrow." If I could avoid having to use the escape plan I'd prefer it.

"Instead of letting you off the hook, why don't I help make things better? I'm a good listener."

"No thanks."

"Come on. Just have a drink with me." His eyes were hungry, and his voice had lost the lightness from earlier.

"Leave her alone."

I glanced around the dark bar for the source of the female voice. The only person looking at me was a girl wearing a hoodie sweatshirt with the hood up. She was sitting at a nearby table with two guys. One had a hood on as well. The other had on sunglasses.

I glanced from the girl in the hoodie back to Evan. "I'm going to go."

He touched my arm. "Just one drink."

"She said no." The girl in the hoodie stood up and headed toward us. She pushed off her hood when she reached us. I blinked a few times. This girl was gorgeous. Her long black hair fell down her back in waves and her brown eyes were surrounded by lush, almost impossibly long eyelashes. She was the kind of gorgeous that makes movie stars look plain. She looked to be in her early to mid-twenties, maybe a year or two older than me. "I'd love it if you could leave her alone."

Evan's face went blank, and he started nodding. "Okay." He backed away from us.

"Thanks." I looked over my shoulder to where Evan was hightailing it from the bar. That had been far too easy. I guess the words of a drop-dead gorgeous girl could cut through the effect of Seduction's Kiss.

"No problem." She smiled lightly. "He seemed to be coming on pretty strong."

"I tend to attract those kind of guys, but I'm sure you deal with it even more." A girl who looked like that would have to be used to it.

"I have my share." She seemed to be studying my face. "Come join us. We don't come on too strong."

I followed her gaze to the table she'd just left. The guys were now looking at me. Neither had a hood or sunglasses on anymore.

"We've got a pitcher we don't mind sharing."

"Oh that's okay." I replied while squinting to get a better look at the guys now that they were showing their faces. They stared back at me with broad smiles. They each had that same ethereal beauty that she had—although more masculine with those chiseled features that make a man classically handsome.

The girl pulled my attention back. "There's nothing in the pitcher if that's what you're worried about."

"That's not what I was worried about." I was concerned about that, but the simple answer would be not to drink. I just wasn't sure whether I wanted to socialize with anyone.

"Hugh, come over here please," the girl said in a sing song voice.

One of the guys stood up and walked over. He had light brown hair that he wore slightly long. He'd been the one wearing the sunglasses. "Hi there."

The girl turned to him. "She doesn't want to sit with us."

Hugh narrowed his eyes at me. "Why not? You don't think we're worth your time?"

"It's not that," I found myself explaining quickly. "I was getting ready to leave."

"Just come sit for a few minutes." Hugh reached out and took my hand. "I promise we don't bite."

There was something hypnotic about the way he spoke that made it impossible for me to say no. I nodded. "Sure. I can do that."

Hugh pulled out a chair for me at the table. "Roland, this is…? What did you say your name was?"

"Daisy." I snapped out of my trance after my name left my lips.

"Pretty name. It looks like we have another flower, Violet."

"Your name is Violet?" I looked closer at the dark haired beauty.

"Uh huh. We do have names in common."

What was I doing? Why was I sitting here chatting with these people? They had some strange pull on me that made me immediately nervous. Now that I knew non-humans existed, I was wary of anyone who made me feel strange.

"Where are you from?" Roland asked. "Wait. Let me guess."

"Okay…"

"Milwaukee."

"Nope."

"Hmmm. How about Cincinnati?"

"No, listen to her accent. She's southern." Violet patted my arm. "Is it Alabama?"

"I'm from North Carolina."

"Oh, I was going to guess that next." Roland pushed out his chair slightly.

"Where are you guys from?"

"Originally?" Violet asked.

"Sure." I didn't notice a trace of an accent on any of them so far.

"I barely remember anymore."

"I guess you move around a lot?" Either that or the girl was being overdramatic.

"Constantly. Who wants to stay in one place?" Hugh leaned back in his chair. "No matter how great a city or town is, it always gets boring."

"Even the best people eventually get boring." Roland sat up straight. "But not you. I bet you never get boring."

"I do. Trust me."

"What's your story?" Violet turned to me.

"My story?"

"Yeah. Why are you attracting guys like that? What kind of witchcraft are you mixed up in?"

My body froze for the tenth time that day. "You can tell?"

"Yes." Violet smiled. "Of course we can."

I was right. There was something strange at work. I should have known by the way she'd sent Evan running from the bar. I'd managed to survive a vampires' nest. How much worse could these people be? "You're the first people to get that."

"That's because we're not average people." Hugh smirked.

"Meaning?" I tried to keep the nerves out of my voice. I had to play it cool. This might be my only chance to find out more about Owen.

"We can't talk about it here."

"Why not?" I looked around. No one was paying attention to us at all.

"We can't, but maybe you could tell us why you have magic on you."

"Not until you tell me how you know."

Violet sighed. "You're upset. I could tell from the moment you walked in. Is it all because of that guy?"

"No." I shook my head. "And I'm fine."

"Let it go, Violet." Roland crossed his arms. "If she doesn't want to talk about it, she doesn't have to."

"But then we can't help her." Violet narrowed her eyes.

"We can help her later. Right now we can talk about something else." Roland slid his chair slightly closer to mine.

"What else do you want to talk about?" As strange as this meeting was, I found I was fascinated by them. The thought of walking away from the table seemed like an impossible task. Besides, they were willing to acknowledge a paranormal world existed. They might be more willing to help than Levi.

"You." Roland looked right at me. "Let's talk about you."

"That's not going to be a particularly interesting conversation."

"Sure it is." Violet crossed her legs. She was wearing boot cut jeans that fit her like a glove.

"It isn't. If you knew the half of it you'd think I was crazy." Had I just said that out loud?

"Then tell us all of it. If half the story would make us think you were crazy, the full story might just convince us that you're sane. That's the problem. People never wait to hear someone out before making judgments." Roland sipped his beer.

"That makes sense. Kind of."

"You'll get used to Roland." Violet leaned in. "He likes to think he's deeply philosophical."

"Who says I only think it?"

"Everyone who matters. Even the girls who hang on your every word are only doing it because of your pretty face," Hugh taunted.

"Daisy sees me for more than that." Roland put a hand on the table in front of me. "Don't you?"

"Oh yeah sure."

Violet laughed. "I was right. She isn't affected!"

"I think she is a little, but not like other people." Hugh refilled his cup. "It's like she can turn it off when she wants to."

"Are you affected?" Violet touched my arm. "Just a little?"

"What are you talking about?" I stared blankly.

"You didn't seem surprised when we hinted we weren't average people, does that mean you could tell we were different?" Violet asked.

"You're hard to stay away from."

"But you're talking to us coherently." Hugh leaned in.

"Yeah, but her eyes got hazy a few times," Roland added.

"I did feel like I was in a haze before, but then it went away." I went with honesty. I wanted answers from them, and hopefully if I showed some of my cards they'd show some too.

Violet pursed her lips. "So it affects her initially, but she can get rid of it. Interesting."

"Maybe we should experiment," Hugh said excitedly. Someone should not get excited when talking about experimenting on another person.

"No thanks."

Roland laughed. "Don't worry, we're not going to hurt you."

"No offense, but you saying that doesn't change anything. I don't know you guys."

"Are you attracted to us?" Roland asked.

"Oh. You guys are definitely attractive, but I'm not ready to jump you or anything."

Violet clapped her hands. "This is fantastic! The initial fogginess you described will go away. I'm sure of it."

"This is a new level of low. People are clapping because I don't want them."

Roland laughed. "And she even has a great sense of humor. Perfect."

"What's perfect?"

"Don't mind Roland." Hugh refilled his glass with beer. "Are you ready to tell us more about why you were upset?"

"How did you know about the magic?" I needed to know what they were. Knowing they were more than human wasn't enough.

"We can sense it."

"Can you sense other paranormal things?"

Violet looked over her shoulder. "We should get out of here if we're going to talk about this."

"Where can we talk?"

"I'll show you." She stood up. "Sorry you never got a drink."

"Don't worry. I didn't need one."

She laughed. "I like you."

"That's good… I think."

"It is." She stood up.

"That doesn't mean I'm leaving with you." I wanted information, but I wasn't a complete idiot.

"You have to."

"I don't have to do anything." I crossed my arms.

Violet leaned over. "Do you want to know what we are?"

I nodded.

"Then come. We're not going to hurt you."

"How do I know?"

"You don't." Hugh shook his head. "But what's the alternative? You reek of boredom and misery."

"Gee, thanks."

"What he means is that we can tell you want answers. We might have them, but you're going to have to trust us."

"Trusting people never works out well for me."

"Suit yourself." Hugh turned his back.

I knew I should have stayed exactly where I was, but what if these people could help me find Owen? I'd already spent two years going mad looking for him. How much worse could things get? "Fine."

"Good choice." Violet grinned. "I'm glad you made it."

"I hope I feel that way tomorrow."

We walked out of the bar and onto Bourbon Street. "Will you at least tell me where we're going?" Walking off with people I didn't know who were more likely than not non-human probably wasn't the brightest idea, but I needed to put what happened that Halloween night to rest once and for all.

"That depends." Violet linked her arm with mine. It was such a friendly gesture for someone I'd just met, but somehow it didn't bother me. Her touch immediately put me in a good mood.

"Depends on what?"

"Whether you're ready to tell us what was wrong. And what you're doing here."

"Here, as in New Orleans?"

"Yes." Hugh turned around to look at us.

"I have a job interview."

"That's not why you're *really* here." Roland took my free arm.

"It isn't?"

He laughed. "Oh, Daisy. You're too much."

"How would you know why I'm here?"

"We know you've got magic on you, but you're a human."

"How do you know I'm human?" I was uncomfortable being sandwiched between them. The intimidation factor picked up.

Roland leaned over. "The same way you know we're not."

His words both terrified and excited me. "Are you going to kill me?"

"Kill you?" Violet stopped. "Is that why you almost didn't come? Why would you think that?"

"I had a run in with vampires last time I was here."

"Seriously?" Hugh asked. "As in real blood suckers? Not humans pretending to be them?"

"I thought they were fake at first, but they nearly killed me… I had the misfortune of being taken to a nest."

"How'd you survive?" Roland still held onto my arm.

"Someone saved me."

"Oh." Violet started moving again. "This is where the story is going to get interesting."

"This is where the story gets pathetic." My obsessive searching was embarrassing already, the thought of saying it aloud made it worse.

"I'm sure it's not pathetic." Violet pulled me even closer. "Don't be so hard on yourself."

"It is pathetic, but I'm so desperate to find him that I'll tell you."

"Him. That answers one question." Roland leaned in so close I could feel his breath on my face.

"What question?"

"You like men."

"Did you doubt that?" I had no problem with anyone thinking I was into girls, but it still surprised me.

"You seem very comfortable with Violet."

"Ever think that's why she's comfortable with me?" Violet leaned over me to Roland. "She can be herself with me because she isn't concerned with wanting me."

"You don't have to be concerned with wanting me. I want you too if it makes you feel any better." Roland grinned.

I pushed away from both of them. "Ok, that's creepy."

Violet clapped. "This is awesome! She really can resist us. We've found our fourth!"

"Your fourth what?" They were excited that I didn't want them, so I assumed they weren't talking about anything involving sex.

"We'll tell you everything once we get home."

"Home?" I was still standing in the middle of the crowded street watching them. Everyone walking by stared at us.

"Our temporary home. Like we said, we move a lot."

Going home made me think of the nest. My body tensed. "I can't. I should get back to my hotel."

"We're not going to hurt you, and we may be able to help."

"Help with what?"

"It's pretty obvious. You're looking for the guy who saved you."

"And you think you can help?"

"There's only a few types of creatures that could have saved you from a nest of vampires. None of them are human."

"And you've got connections in the paranormal world?"

Hugh laughed. "We've got plenty of connections."

"I have my interview tomorrow. Can I find you again after that?"

Violet closed the space between us and put her arms on my shoulders. "Do you really want to go to that interview?"

"No, but I need to. I have to find a job."

"Would you rather find a job or find the guy who saved you?"

"Can't I do both?" I needed the job if I wanted an excuse to spend any more time in New Orleans.

"Just answer. Which is more important to you? Right here. Right now." She looked right into my eyes, and I couldn't turn my head. The fog was back, but it was different this time.

"Owen." I let his name slip.

"Owen?" Roland came to stand next to Violet. "Tell me more about Owen."

I tried to blink, but I couldn't. "Stop!"

"Sorry." Violet let go of me. "Sometimes I can't help myself."

"What did you do to me?"

"I wanted to see if touch made you more impressionable. It does, but you can still fight it."

"I'm going home."

"But what about Owen?" Violet asked lightly. "Ready to give up on him?"

Why had I used his name? I knew it wasn't by choice, but I wished I could have let something else slip. Anything else. "Do you really think you can help me?"

"How did he save you? How did he get you away from the vampires?" Violet asked gently.

"He flew." She didn't persuade me to speak this time. I willingly said the words.

"We can help you," Hugh answered. "Or we can at least find someone who can."

"You know what he is?"

"Come home with us. We'll talk there." Violet linked arms with me again.

"Only on one condition."

"What?"

"You don't use that weird thing on me again. You talk to me person to person."

"Deal." She smiled.

"And please don't kill me. I'm only twenty-two."

"Do you really think we're going to hurt you?" she asked again. "Is your trust in us that weak?"

"I don't know. I don't know anything anymore. Every place I went today proved I was crazy."

"But we proved the opposite, didn't we?" she asked.

"Somewhat."

"And we'll further prove it."

I hoped she was right. "I told you why I'm upset, now you tell me where we're going."

"It's going to be so much cooler if we just show you." Hugh grinned. "We won't blindfold you though, that would probably mess with the whole trust thing."

"Considering I was put in a body bag last time I was here, I'm hesitant to accept a blindfold."

He nodded. "And don't forget you still have to explain the magic. That wasn't from the vampires, or your hero."

"No. It was from a witch."

"You're a magnet for paranormal creatures, aren't you?" Roland reclaimed my other arm.

"I have been told I was destined for a paranormal."

"I can see that." Violet picked up her pace. "But that doesn't mean you have to be with one. Destiny is the kind of thing that can be changed."

"Most people say the opposite. That you can't change it."

"We're not most people."

"I'm realizing that."

"Let's go find a car." She looked toward the road.

"*Find* a car?"

"Yeah. We left ours somewhere. I can't remember."

"You left your car somewhere, and you don't remember?" Maybe they were crazier than I originally thought.

"Don't worry, we'll get a ride." Violet stepped away from the curb on Canal Street and held up her hand like she was hailing a cab.

A blue SUV pulled to the side. "That's not a cab," I hissed.

Violet walked around to the driver's side. The driver rolled down the window, and she leaned in. "Hi there, mind if we borrow this?"

"Of course not. I'd be happy to let you borrow it. It's all yours." A middle aged man got out of the car. He had a huge grin plastered on his face that appeared out of sorts with his dazed expression and glossy eyes. "Have a nice night."

"What?" I watched the man's retreating figure. "Did he just give you his car?"

"Sure. People do that a lot for us." Violet got into the driver's seat.

"What are you?"

Hugh slipped into the passenger's seat. "We're your new best friends. Hope you don't mind I'm taking shotgun. I get a little car sick in the back."

"Bullshit." Roland coughed.

"I'd be an idiot to get in this car with you." But idiot or not, these people offered me something no one else had—information.

"What's your alternative?" Violet called over. "Go back to your life of searching? Does that seem like a better plan?"

"No. It doesn't." I slid into the backseat and Roland followed.

"Good choice, Daisy." Violet stepped on the gas, and we sped away from the curb.

CHAPTER SIX

DAISY

Violet was an awful driver. Maybe she'd be considered good if she were driving in the NASCAR circuit, but from my position in the back seat of the SUV she was awful. My stomach started doing flips as she sped around corners and dodged between cars.

"Violet, you're scaring our guest." Roland put his arm behind me on the seat. He'd taken the middle seat which made me uneasy. These people were far too touchy feely, especially considering the effect their touch could have.

Violet waved her hand as if to brush off his words. "She's fine. I bet she likes speed."

I said nothing. I was too busy grabbing hold of the oh-my-god bar as she sped through the city streets.

Hugh looked back at me. "Looks like we rendered her speechless."

That got me talking. "Does she always drive like this?"

"Yes," Hugh and Roland said at once.

"I'm a great driver." Violet accelerated as she wove through the traffic. "It's everyone else on the road that's bad."

I closed my eyes. "How far are we going?"

"It's less than twenty minutes."

"Good. With your speed we'll be there in no time."

Roland laughed. "Daisy, where have you been all my life?"

"Somewhere far away from this crazy driver."

"Don't be so melodramatic, Dais." Violet laughed. "You'll get used to it."

Dais? Was she really using a nickname for me? I opened my eyes. Having them closed wasn't helping. "I wouldn't count on it."

Eventually the city streets disappeared, and we pulled onto the interstate. "We're leaving the city?"

"We're not going far. Relax." Hugh turned back again. "Roland, take care of her."

Roland wrapped his hand around the back of my neck, and I could feel a wave of relaxation flowing over me. I felt my protests slipping away. "The touch thing does work, Violet."

She took her eyes off the road to look at us. "It's convenient."

I sat forward. "Stop! None of that. You guys promised."

"Sorry." Roland put his hands in his lap. He didn't look sorry at all.

I closed my eyes again, feeling my stomach lurch as she turned off the interstate. I really should have eaten something.

Violet suddenly stepped on the breaks. I opened my eyes. We stopped inches in front of a towering chain link fence. I reluctantly stepped out of the car after some coaxing from the others.

"Where are we?"

"You'll see." Roland hopped out and grabbed my hand.

I peered through the gate and saw a large abandoned grandstand that was literally falling down. In front of it was what looked to be abandoned turnstiles. "What is this place?"

"Guess." Violet started to climb the fence. "Think you can make it or need us to find another way in for you?"

"She can make it." Roland put my hand on the chain link fence. "Just watch."

"Uh, I didn't sign up for illegal activity." I pointed at the large no trespassing sign attached to the fence.

"Trust me, we won't get in trouble." Violet hopped down on the other side of the fence. "Haven't you noticed we have a way with people?"

"I really don't want to get arrested."

"Stick with us, and you won't."

"You aren't really living here, are you?"

Hugh sighed. "Stop talking. The longer we chat out here the more likely someone will see us."

"I thought you said we won't get in trouble."

"We won't." He glared. "But that doesn't mean I feel like dealing with the cops."

I took a deep breath. I'd come this far. Was an abandoned property any worse than a vampire's nest? Then a scary thought hit me. What if there were vampires here? "Is anyone else here?"

Roland put a hand on my shoulder. "Nope. Don't worry. We're not feeding you to the vamps or anything."

I shuddered. "Don't even joke about that."

"He won't. None of us will." Violet peeked at me through the fence. "Come on. The sooner you climb in here, the sooner we talk about Owen."

The mention of his name got me moving.

Hugh chuckled. "We know how to motivate her now."

I carefully climbed up the metal fence. The touch of the metal below my fingers brought me back to middle school when my friends and I had to climb a similar fence after getting locked in a park after hours. If my parents only knew the trouble I'd gotten myself into. I hopped down on the other side. The guys followed.

"You're a natural." Violet smiled.

"A natural at breaking into places? No thanks." I had enough trouble in my life already. I didn't need to create more of it.

"Come on." She took my hand. I used my other hand to fish out my phone from my pocket. I turned on the flashlight on my phone. The farther we walked from the road, the darker it got.

We walked toward the turnstiles that I'd seen earlier, and I caught a glimpse of what looked to be an old town with a wide road and buildings on either side. Since a town wouldn't require turnstiles for entrance, it had to be something else. "Wait. Is this an old amusement park?"

"And we have a winner." Roland put an arm around me. "Didn't take you long."

We walked around the ramshackle turnstiles and through a wide opening. "This is crazy."

"The whole park was covered by water for days after Hurricane Katrina. The owners pulled out and left everything here."

"Unreal." I shined the flashlight in front of me so I could peek in at the dilapidated buildings that I assumed were once souvenir shops. "But why do you guys live here?"

"We're always looking for unique places to stay when we travel. Hotels get so old."

"But you could stay anywhere. I mean the way you got that guy to give you his car."

"We'll return it, don't worry."

"How? How are you going to return it?"

"His information will be in the glove compartment. We'll even fill it back up with gas, or we'll have someone else do that."

"You don't pump your own gas?" I eyed the guys.

"We do. It's the delivery we like to avoid. It can get awkward." Hugh scrunched up his face.

"I wonder why it would be awkward to see the guy who you stole a car from?"

"Stole? Is that how you see it?" Violet linked her arm with mine again. I seemed to always be sandwiched between her and Roland. Hugh kept more of a distance.

"The guy didn't want to give you his car. There's no other way to see it."

She leaned over. "You'll see it another way when you get to know us."

"Ok, back to the original question. Why are you staying in this post-apocalyptic wasteland?" I gazed around at the crumbling buildings.

"You don't feel it?" Violet asked.

"Feel what?"

"That feeling."

"Uh…"

"Close your eyes." Roland spun me so I was looking at him. "Concentrate on nothing but the moment."

"Ok."

"Don't talk, just concentrate." He squeezed my shoulder once before letting go. "What do you feel?"

"Fear. Intrigue. Some excitement."

"Places like this are breeding grounds for mixed emotions." Violet's voice came from right next to me. "This site holds such happy, joyful memories. So many happy screams, kids with ice cream cones, couples kissing, but now it's a dark place. It's a reminder of a terrible storm that took countless lives."

I opened my eyes. "Emotions are important to you."

"Emotions are everything to us." She turned and started walking.

"What does that mean? In what way?"

"Think about it. I want you to figure it out yourself."

"How am I supposed to do that? I don't know anything about this stuff."

"Two years of searching and you haven't learned anything?" Roland remained by my side as we walked.

"I still don't know what you are."

"What do you think we are?"

"I told you I don't know." I gritted my teeth. Why were we always going around in circles?

Roland leaned in to whisper in my ear. "You should know what we are, considering you have some of us in you."

"What?" I jerked away. "What are you talking about?"

"It's time for you to tell us where you got the magic." They all circled me.

"Whoa. You told me you weren't going to hurt me."

"We're not. We'd never hurt you." Violet's eyes got big. "We just want you to be honest with us. If you're honest, we'll tell you everything you want to know."

I swallowed hard. "You swear you're not going to hurt me?"

"Those vamps did a number on your trust."

"Not enough evidently. If they did I wouldn't be here with you." I knew I was crazy, but I was also desperate.

"Yes you would." Violet ran a hand through her hair. "You'd have always been drawn to us."

"And us to you." Roland smiled.

"What do you want me to tell you?"

Violet glanced up at the dark sky. After a moment she returned her gaze to me. "Where did you get that magic? Who gave it to you?"

I sighed. I needed to come clean. I didn't have any other choice. "A witch named Kalisa. She owned this Voodoo shop just off Bourbon Street called The Midnight Cauldron."

"Owned, as in past tense?" Hugh asked.

"I went by there earlier tonight, and the person there had never heard of her." My stomach growled.

"We've got to feed her. Her stomach's been doing that all night." Roland gestured to me. "All I have is a box of cookies. Do you guys have anything better?"

"Nope," Hugh replied. "We always eat out."

"I'm fine. Let's finish this talk so I can go home. I'll get food at the hotel."

"Where are you staying?" Hugh asked.

Considering they had me at their mercy, I figured it couldn't hurt to tell them. "The Crescent City Hotel."

Violet laughed. "You're not serious."

"I am. I know it's pricy, but I got a good deal."

"You happen to be searching for a Pteron and are staying at the Crescent City Hotel?" Hugh arched an eyebrow.

"Pteron... you do know." Despite my precarious situation my heart soared.

"Of course we do." Violet took a step toward me. "We need to know everything. What did the witch give you?"

"She made some sort of paste and put it on my forehead. She called it Seduction's Kiss. And I think it should have been called Seduction's Nightmare. After she gave it to me I started attracting the wrong kind of attention."

"Seduction's Kiss?" Violet asked. "She called it Seduction's Kiss?"

"Yes." I remembered that detail vividly. "This other witch that helped save me told me no one but Kalisa would be crazy enough to make it."

"Of course not!" Hugh yelled. His face twisted in anger.

I glanced at the other two. They didn't look quite as angry at me, but they were definitely upset.

"Is there something about it I don't know about?"

"It's not her fault. She's innocent. Don't take out your anger on our new friend." Violet watched me, but it was clear she was talking to Hugh.

"Please level with me. I told you the truth. Now you tell me why you're flipping out."

"That concoction she gave you, Seduction's Kiss, it had to have been made from our essence. She'd had to have killed one of our kind to get it."

"What?" My chest clenched. What kind of trouble had I just stepped into?

CHAPTER SEVEN

OWEN

"Open your eyes, Owen." Her soft voice woke me up from a deep sleep.

I listened to her quiet command and broke into a grin. "Hi there. I didn't hear you come in."

"I'm sneaky like that." She snuggled into my side as though she'd been in my bed all night.

"Let me look at you." I rolled her over onto her back and hovered over her. I always liked the view of her lying beneath me.

"How do I look?"

"As beautiful as always. I just needed to make sure you hadn't gotten any new freckles or anything since I last saw you."

"How can you tell? I'm still wearing clothes."

"I can change that if you want." I grinned again. Teasing Daisy came so easily. I was myself with her in a way I hadn't been in years.

"You probably shouldn't."

"Why not?" I ran my lips along her neck. "Why don't you ever let me really touch you?"

"I can't stay. You know that. It's going to make it worse when I leave."

"I can handle it." I started to pull the strap of her cami down her shoulder.

"But then you'll know."

"Know what?" I looked into her eyes. "What don't you want me to know?"

"That you didn't actually save me." Her eyes closed and her hands fell to her sides.

"Daisy?" I shook her. "What's wrong?"

Her body was cold. Icy. "Daisy! Answer me!"

I continued to shake her and nothing happened.

I woke up with a start. Another dream. Exactly the same again. They were becoming more and more frequent now. I'd have thought leaving New Orleans would have had the opposite effect.

I gave up trying to rest. There was no chance of it happening now. It was a good thing I only needed a few hours of sleep.

I fixed myself a quick snack before I heard the sound of a car outside. I headed to the front of the cabin and opened the door.

The sight of the jeep out in front could only mean one thing—trouble. Trouble in the form of a red head who had been making my life complicated since the day she was born.

"Hey, brother!" Hailey jumped off my front porch and headed for me. She pulled me into a hug before I could react. "Great to see you."

"What are you doing here?" It's not that I didn't like my little sister, but her presence hadn't been requested.

"You gave mom your address in case of an emergency."

"And what's the emergency?" My mom was usually pretty trust worthy. She understood my need to stay under the radar for a while.

"I'm dropping out of school."

"What?" I stepped back. "Are you crazy? You only have one more year of college left!"

She laughed. "I'm not really dropping out. I just told mom that so she'd tell me where you were."

I groaned. "Next time I'm not telling her anything."

"Relax. Levi still has no idea."

"Don't pretend you understand why I'm here." I hated to run off on my best friend the way I did, but when your best friend is also the king of a paranormal society things aren't always easy.

She put a hand on her hip. No matter how old she got, she still held on to the same mannerisms she had as a kid. "I know why you're here. It's the same reason I'm here."

"Oh yeah? Enlighten me then. Why am I so lucky to get this visit?"

"I need a break from it all, like you."

"Nothing about your situation is like mine."

"Why not?" She narrowed her eyes. "I'm an advisor just like you."

"An advisor to the queen. Not the king."

"And that matters?" She glared. "Do you realize how mad Allie would be if she heard that?"

"If you're so worried about Allie's opinion, then why are you here?"

"I told you. I need a break."

"And?" There was always more with Hailey. I loved her, but she always had a hidden agenda. You just had to figure out what that was.

She looked down. "I was worried about you, and I missed you."

"Are you getting sappy on me?"

"No. It's normal for a sister to miss her brother."

"Is that so?" I raised an eyebrow. "What kind of trouble are you in?"

"None." She still avoided my gaze. "I shouldn't have bothered you."

"Tell me what's going on."

"I'm going to go." She turned.

"No. You can't come out here and worry me and then just leave."

"Isn't that what you did? You just left?"

I sighed. "Is that what this is about? You're mad at me for leaving?"

"It's not like you. You always put everyone else first."

"Which is why I left. I needed time for myself."

"And that time had to be out here? Living all alone in the boonies?"

"I like it. It suits me." The small Colorado town kept growing on me. I loved the peace and quiet, and the slow pace.

She rolled her eyes. "When are you coming home?"

"I'm not sure."

"Levi's going to have to pick a new advisor if you don't come back soon."

"I assumed he had already. Besides, I thought Toby was helping out while I was gone."

"You really think Levi wants to listen to him? Toby might be his brother-in-law now, but he is still Allie's ex-boyfriend."

"Either way, I didn't leave him alone."

She leaned back against the railing of the porch. "He's taking it hard."

"He'll get over it."

"You almost sound like you're considering staying away forever."

"Forever is a long time."

"Ok, this is really awkward, but Jared isn't around so I'm going to say it."

"If it's what I think you're going to say, don't." The mention of my friend Jared sent up red flags.

"You need to get some, Owen. How long has it been?"

"And on that note, Hailey, I'm going inside." She'd crossed a line. Brothers and sisters did not discuss each other's sex lives or lack thereof.

"Come on. We're both adults now. We can talk about this stuff."

"Nope. Never. We will never talk about this stuff."

"Stop being such a baby, Owen."

"Are you planning to stay here for a while?" I wasn't sure how long we could go without hurting each other in my tiny cabin meant for one.

"Should I? Or are you going to be grumpy the whole time?"

"Stay." Despite how annoying she could be, she was still my sister, and I knew there was more at work than her worrying about me. She'd gotten herself into some kind of trouble, and she needed my help. Hopefully she'd open up to me in a few days.

"Is there anything worth seeing in town?"

"A few shops and a diner. It's the scenery that's the draw. Want to go for a flight?"

"Sounds good, but I need to eat something first. I've been driving all day, and I'm starving."

"I can't believe you drove all the way out here. What if I'd moved on already?"

She shrugged. "Then I would have had a scenic tour of the U.S."

I laughed. "All right. Let me take a quick shower. Help yourself to anything in the kitchen."

"All right." She headed for my tiny kitchen, checking out the room on her way.

"How are you living here? You don't even have a TV?"

"Think you can handle staying here?"

"At least I have my phone." She pulled it out as I walked toward the bedroom. Life was about to get a whole lot more interesting.

CHAPTER EIGHT

DAISY

"Excuse me?" I struggled to come up with words. What did they think I'd done? Did they blame me?

"We're going to have to tell her what we are." Roland took my hand as though Hugh hadn't just said what he obviously said.

"Let's go inside before we do." Violet looked up at the sky. "It's going to rain."

"It's not supposed to rain tonight." I'd checked the weather report that morning before I left home.

"It's going to rain." Hugh said. "Violet is always right."

Roland tugged on my hand. "Come on. I think you're going to like our place. We've been here a few weeks so we set it up nice."

"A few weeks?"

"Yeah. We already told you we move around a lot."

"How far away are you guys staying?"

"It's through here." Violet turned around to look at me. "You can relax. You're safe with us."

"I thought Hugh was going to attack me." My heart was still beating erratically, but my rational side said they could kill me where I stood just as well as anywhere else.

"Sorry about that." Hugh smiled sheepishly. "I shouldn't have been taking my anger out on you."

"Anger is kind of his thing." Roland smiled, and I knew I was missing some sort of inside joke.

"Great. It isn't mine."

"That's good because we couldn't handle more of that." Violet didn't turn around this time.

"I'm not going to just walk off with you guys." I stood my ground. "You pretty much accused me of killing one of your kind."

"No we didn't." Violet turned. "We accused the witch of it. I believe you're innocent."

"You do, but can you say the same for Hugh?"

"I believe you're innocent too. At least you seem to be." Hugh looked up at the sky. "Let's go. I don't feel like getting wet."

I thought about my options. Either way I was probably already screwed. "Fine, but please don't kill me."

Roland leaned in. "I'll protect you."

"But you are one of the ones I'm scared of so that doesn't count."

I followed them through the main area of the amusement park. We walked underneath the remnants of an old rollercoaster. I glanced up, nervous that the wooden track could fall at any moment. The sky darkened, and we'd passed the empty Ferris wheel when a few minutes later the sky lit up with lightning. "Looks like you were right, Violet."

"I'm always right about the weather."

"Only the weather?" Roland asked. "I thought you were always right about everything."

"She's trying to act humble for Daisy." Hugh pushed some of his light brown hair behind his ear. "The thing is she's going to see the real Violet eventually."

They kept talking like I was going to be seeing a lot of them. I wasn't planning on it unless it was going to bring me closer to Owen. That was why I was doing this. Wasn't it? Although I also wanted to know about the magic. Nothing had been the same since I was given Seduction's Kiss.

We wove through the old amusement park, past old rides that now hung by the barest wire in disrepair. My heart hurt a little looking at the old big swings, now with just the strings hanging down. The seats were long gone. It was always my favorite ride when I was a kid.

"We're here." Violet turned into a dilapidated building right as the rain started. I hurried behind her, eager to get out of the cascading water.

I glanced around. Old ride cars stood empty in front of what looked like a stage. "You're living in a ride?" I peered through the growing darkness. My phone's flashlight wasn't providing nearly enough light.

"It's got a really cool feel." Roland was once again standing right next to me.

I carefully stepped over the bent metal pieces as I followed Violet down a long, dark hallway.

She stopped suddenly. "Here we are."

Violet turned on a light switch. It took my eyes a moment to adjust as I took in the furnishings that appeared like they belonged in a swank apartment. Satin fabric was laid over antique furniture. Two lamps sat atop side tables, and hammocks hung from the ceiling. To top it off, the floor was covered with a plush rug.

"Where are you getting that power from?" I pointed to the lamp.

"A generator. We always travel with a few." Hugh made it sound like my question was silly, as though everyone carried a spare generator with them when they traveled.

"Wouldn't it be easier to rent an apartment or something? I know you're tired of hotels, but come on. Isn't this extreme?" Their little place was such a contrast to the ruin of the amusement park we were in.

"I already told you, it's all about the emotions."

"I see." I looked around. My hunger and exhaustion were catching up with me, but I wasn't sure if sitting was such a good idea.

Violet seemed to read my mind. "You're safe. You need to relax. Take a seat."

I nodded absently and found a seat on one of the antique couches even though safe was the last thing I felt. "What are you guys?"

Violet took a seat next to me. She gestured for Roland to sit on my other side. Why did they always do that? Hugh sat across from us on the other couch. "You know about Pterons, witches, and vampires, which means you shouldn't have a hard time accepting there are other types of creatures."

I nodded. "It's always going to seem strange, but yes, I believe it."

"We're one of the oldest beings in this world, or any world for that matter."

"Uh, any world? Are we talking aliens?"

She shook her head. "Not in the way you're thinking, but we can discuss that later."

"Ok." I wanted her to continue. The suspense was getting harder to take.

"Normally we wouldn't tell a human what we are, but you already have our essence as part of you. Really, you are lucky we're the ones who found you first. Others of our kind would have asked questions later."

"Meaning they would have killed me?" I started to rethink my decision to leave with them. Were they even more dangerous than I thought?

Violet looked away. "Remember, I said others. Not us."

"So what are you?"

"We're Allures." Roland shifted next to me. "I'm guessing you haven't heard of us before?" He seemed to be waiting for my response.

"No…"

"We're the basis for lots of myths, but otherwise we've managed to keep our presence a secret from humans."

"Kind of like Pterons? No one knows who they are?"

"I don't particularly like being compared to a bird shifter, but I'll take it."

"A bird shifter?" I sat forward. "That's what Owen is?"

"What did you think he was?"

"I don't know… at first I thought Pteron could mean angel."

Violet smiled. "They're not angels. What color are his wings?"

"I thought you said you knew him."

"We never said that. We said we could help you find him." Hugh crossed his legs at the ankles.

"Black. His wings are black."

"Makes sense since you met him here." Violet unzipped her boots. "He's crow, so aligned with the Laurents."

"The who?"

"The Laurents. They're the family running The Society now."

"So someone else did before?" I asked.

"Many years ago," Violet continued, "But for as long as anyone you know has been alive the Laurents have ruled."

"That's interesting and all, but you never told me what an Allure was."

"What do you think we are?" Violet curled her feet up under her.

"How would I know?"

"You've been around us for a few hours. That should have told you something."

"You can control people's minds."

"You're getting warmer, but it's not mind control."

"You have the ability to make people do things that you want them to do. If it's not mind control, what is it?" I thought of the guy with the SUV, and about how Evan had walked away so quickly.

"We're not controlling their minds. We're controlling their feelings." Violet smiled. "But we can only use and play with the feelings they already have."

"You lost me."

"Remember when I told you why we're staying here."

"You like how many emotions have been felt here?"

"Exactly."

"I'm sorry but you've lost me already."

"It's hard to explain without showing you, so let's use the example of the guy who so graciously lent us his car."

"Okay." I watched Violet uneasily.

"How do you think I convinced him?"

"You used magic to make him do it?"

"No. Not magic. Close your eyes and remember what happened. What words were exchanged?"

"You asked him if we could borrow the car and he said of course, he'd be happy to."

"Exactly. He'd be happy too."

"I'm still not following."

"He was happy to give me the keys. I made him feel that way."

"You made him feel so happy he turned them over?"

"Essentially. It kind of works on you, but not as well. That's why I have to touch you. If you were a full Allure it wouldn't work at all."

"I know you said you sense an essence on me, but I can't convince people to feel so happy they turn stuff over to me."

"You can't willingly manipulate emotions because you aren't truly one of us. You just have our appeal—our allure. We use that to get access to someone's emotions."

"Oh." I was startled by the wave of disappointment that hit me. It's not like I wanted to be an Allure—whatever they actually were. "You say you can use people's emotions, does that extend beyond happiness?"

"Of course. Happy feelings are too fleeting. I prefer anger." Hugh sat forward. "But you already knew that."

"You use a person's anger to make them do something? How?"

"May I show you?"

"No thanks."

"Come on. Give me your hand, I have to touch you to make it work."

"Fine." I held out my hand more out of curiosity than anything else.

At first nothing happened, but then I noticed a candy bar wrapper on the floor right outside their little space. Who would litter like that? Were they crazy? Didn't they have anything better to do? Anger boiled inside me, and I couldn't stop it.

Hugh dropped my hand. "Wow, I don't think I've ever met someone who hated littering so much."

I grimaced at him while I tried to calm my fast beating heart. I hadn't been that angry in ages. "I prefer Violet's happy."

Roland laughed.

I looked at him. "I already know what your preferred one is."

"Do you?" He looked at me funny.

"It's easy. Relaxing, soothing feelings."

All three of them looked at each other. "Uh, what?"

"Wait. He doesn't do that to everyone?"

Violet laughed. "Roland? Roland relaxes you?"

"Maybe…"

"I'm glad I do, but the only emotion of yours I've touched is excitement. I used it to keep you in the car." He winked.

"Then why do you relax me? Is that weird?"

They all exchanged looks again, and I knew they were hiding something.

"Come on. What is it?"

"I'll let you know when I figure it out." Violet pulled her legs up under her. "We've never met someone who's been given our essence before, so this is all new."

"The only thing the essence has done is helped me attract attention: the bad, I want to jump you, kind of attention."

"Were you always that way, or did it start when you got that paste?"

"When I got that paste."

"Are you sure?"

"I guess I've always attracted some creepers…" I thought about Shawn. He was roommates with Reyna's crush, and he'd come on to me before I took the stuff.

"Have you ever manipulated people with it?"

"Used their attraction? No. I run from it."

"We'll have to see what you can do." Violet grinned.

"Uh, no thanks." I moved to standing. I wasn't doing any more experimenting.

"Why not? Might as well use what you have. If it is going to make you a target, why not get something out of the deal?"

"That's okay." Hopefully I'd find a way to get rid of it.

"Is it really okay? What would have happened to you if Owen hadn't saved you?" Roland asked. "Would you want that to happen again?"

I shuddered. "I've been safe for over two years."

"Nothing weird has happened?"

"Besides the random weird stalkers?"

"That's not normal you know."

"It's just been life. It was the only thing that made me think I wasn't as crazy as everyone thought."

"Sit back down. Tell us about it. Why did everyone think you were crazy?"

I stayed standing. I felt stronger that way. "When you tell people you were kidnapped by vampires and saved by a hot guy with wings, they kind of think you've lost your mind."

"You're spending your time with the wrong kind of people." Hugh leaned back on the couch. "We don't think you're crazy."

"Because you're not human."

"So stay away from humans."

"I want to find Owen." That was the only reason I was in New Orleans anyway.

"We'll help you."

"How?" Now we were getting somewhere.

"We'll have to do some research. There can't be too many Pterons named Owen in the city."

I considered telling them I knew he wasn't in town, but I changed my mind. Maybe I could use this as a test. If they came to me and pretended to have found him I'd know they were making things up. I silently praised myself for the quick thinking before belatedly replying. "Why are you going to help me? What's in it for you?"

"In return you help us track down that Kalisa. She has to answer for her crime." Violet's hand balled into a fist at her side.

"Although I still don't get how she did it. No witch can subdue one of us." Hugh seemed pensive.

"I already told you I don't know where she went."

"But you also said you met another witch. The one the Pteron brought you to. She could help. We're not asking for miracles, only some help."

"I'll try, but I don't know where that witch even was. Owen flew us there."

"So Owen knows." Violet ran her hand over the satin fabric. "Another reason to find him."

"Help me find Owen, and I'll do my best to find Kalisa."

"Deal." Violet held out her hand.

I shook it hoping I wouldn't end up regretting my decision, but I'd have done almost anything to get closer to Owen. I was tired of wasting my life away.

"Great, now what should we do the rest of the night?" Violet stretched out on the couch.

"Tonight? I have to get back to my hotel. It's getting late, and I'm completely unprepared for my interview tomorrow."

"You aren't still planning to go on that interview, are you?" Roland asked.

"Of course I am."

"Doesn't that seem pointless?"

"I need a job. Unlike you guys I can't just get people to give me money."

"You have your whole life to get a job if you want, but trust me, it's over rated." Violet stood up. "Sure it might be exciting at first, but it's going to get boring fast."

"I'm not worried about that now."

"Where's the interview at?" Hugh asked.

"The New Orleans Times."

"So you want to be a journalist?"

I shrugged. "Sort of."

"Let her do the interview. We can wait." Roland smiled. "What time will you be done?"

"It's a nine a.m. interview. I'm not sure."

"Nine a.m.? We need to get you back to your hotel then." Roland jumped to his feet. "I'll drive you."

"I'll take her," Violet offered. "I don't mind at all."

Hugh stood up. "I'll take her. I need to run an errand downtown anyway."

"No making her mad to test the limits," Violet narrowed her eyes.

"Would I ever do that?" Hugh asked with puppy dog eyes.

"Yes. You definitely would." Roland glowered. "And you better come back tonight. No staying over with her."

"Uh, no one's staying with me." There was only one paranormal creature I was interested in sleeping with...

Hugh laughed. "I'm immune to your love potion, Daisy. Don't worry."

Violet tossed him the keys. "Be safe. We'll see you tomorrow. Good luck with your interview."

"Thanks." I followed Hugh out through the makeshift living room and back into the abandoned park. "At least it stopped raining." I once again used the flashlight on my phone to light our way. The light wasn't nearly enough to get rid of the creepy factor.

"That's what we call a New Orleans rainstorm. It stops and starts quickly."

"No complaints. I thought we were going to get soaked."

"Worried about ruining the upholstery in the borrowed car?" He laughed.

"Are you trying to make me annoyed?"

"It's a bad habit. I can't help it. I like riling people up."

"Try harder to help it." We walked at a brisk pace through the amusement park. It was even more eerie this time with a layer of fog surrounding us. I wished I was wearing more than flip flops as I stepped in a deep puddle.

"Want me to carry you?"

"Please tell me you're joking." I started walking even faster. I was hungry, tired, and ready for a hot shower.

"I'm just offering. You're wearing the wrong shoes, and you look pale."

"You can't see that I look pale."

"I can see better than you can in the dark."

"Great." Spending time with paranormal creatures reminded me of how human I was. Seduction's Kiss or not, all I could do was attract unwanted attention. I couldn't do anything useful.

"Are you excited or nervous for tomorrow?" He dropped the carrying offer quickly. I was glad. The thought of him picking me up didn't sound appealing even though I was close to falling over with exhaustion.

"For the interview?"

"What else would I mean?" He smirked.

"How would I know?"

"You're fun."

"Fun?" I wrapped my arms tighter around myself. Despite the warm night, I was cold. Maybe my wet feet and damp hair had something to do with it.

"Yeah. You're sarcastic and you say what's on your mind. Not enough people do that."

"Do you?"

"Mostly."

"Do you ever do good things with anger? Use it in ways that don't cause trouble for people?"

"Sure I do. It's called passion. Have you ever been so mad at someone you've wanted to kiss them?"

"Nope. Can't say I have."

"Are you mad at Owen?"

"Why would I be mad? He saved me."

"But didn't he ditch you? That is why you're searching for him, right?"

"Yes." To be honest I had been mad at Owen. I'd cursed him many times over the years for making me want him so bad when I couldn't possibly have him.

"But when you see him, are you going to still want to kill him? Maybe you'll slap him first, but then you'll kiss."

"If he'd kiss me."

"It's pretty inconvenient that Pterons are immune to mental magic and persuasion."

"Is that why he didn't want more?"

He laughed lightly. "Didn't want more? As in he wasn't dying to get in your pants?"

"Exactly," I mumbled.

Climbing over the fence was even more nerve wracking the second time. There's a different feeling when you're breaking out of somewhere rather than sneaking in. I got a flash of a mental image of trying to break out of some sort of prison. Hopefully it wasn't a premonition of the future. I was beginning to feel like anything was possible.

Hugh waited for me at the bottom. "Can you go any slower?"

"Can you be any more impatient? We're not all super human."

"Maybe."

"Unlike you, I don't frequently climb chain link fences."

"And that's where you're life has gone wrong." He got in the driver's side and started the car.

I jumped right into the passenger seat. I wouldn't put it past Hugh to speed off without me, and there was no way I was climbing back over that fence to look for the others in the ghostly amusement park.

In all of my planning and thinking about my trip to New Orleans, meeting a group like the Allures had never crossed my mind. I still wasn't sure I could trust them, but if they could get me closer to Owen, I had to give them a chance.

CHAPTER NINE

DAISY

I groaned, rolling over and away from my cell phone. The incessant buzzing of my alarm was giving me a headache. I could have sworn I'd only had one drink the night before. So why did I feel hung over? I reluctantly rolled back to my phone and shut off the alarm. I needed to get up. Otherwise I was going to be late for the interview.

Less than an hour later, I was showered and dressed, but I wasn't ready to go. At least not mentally. Even though it felt like I'd spent so much time planning the trip, very little of that time was spent preparing for the interview. Luckily I was usually pretty good at thinking on my feet, but I had no idea what kind of questions they'd throw my way. This wasn't the only job out there I reminded myself. I wasn't the kind of person who thrived on stress. Instead I preferred to view events as what they were, stepping stones in a much broader journey. Of course there were some exceptions. My near death experience felt a lot bigger than a stepping stone.

I hopped into a white cab outside the hotel and headed toward my interview. I'd gone through the route on my phone a few times already, so I knew it shouldn't take more than thirty minutes even with some traffic.

The driver was quiet once I gave him my location, so I pulled out my phone and checked out the paranormal forum. I had a message from Andrew. *We still on for tonight? You doing all right?*

I'd forgotten all about meeting Andrew. It's like my time with the Allures had made me forget everything else. I replied. *Yes. See you as planned. I've gotten some leads, but nothing concrete.*

That seemed fair enough. Hugh had given me his phone number. For all I knew it was fake. I couldn't worry about any of that now. I had to keep my head in the game. In another few hours the interview would be over, and I was free to worry about anything else.

I slipped my phone into my black bag. It was my version of a brief case, and it matched the black skirt suit I was wearing. Both the suit and bag were graduation gifts from my parents. They were eager to see me find a job and move forward with my life. They didn't need to worry. Even if I didn't get this job, I wasn't planning to live at home. Whether they voiced it or not, they still thought I was crazy. I refused to spend my life living with people who didn't think I was all there. I guess that was the good thing about the Allures. They didn't think I was crazy because they were even crazier.

"You got an appointment?" the driver asked, breaking me out of my thoughts.

It took me a moment to respond. Thinking about Violet and her friends made it hard to concentrate on anything else. "An interview. I have a job interview."

"You going to work for the paper?"

"That's the hope."

"Now, why would you want a job like that?" He glanced over his shoulder.

"Excuse me?" I prepared my women power rant. We belonged in the workforce as much as men. We could do more than pop out babies and make dinner.

"Wouldn't you want to do something more fun? See things? What fun is it to report on the news when you can live it?"

Wow. I wasn't expecting that one. "Live the news? I'm not sure if that's a good thing."

"Sure it is. Not all news is bad. That's only what gets reported the most."

"You're right."

"I know I am. I've learned a lot driving around this city."

"I bet you have, but even if this isn't the most ideal job, I still need it."

"And I understand that. You've got it."

"How do you know?"

"Just a sense. You seem like a woman that can get what she's after."

"Thanks." I looked out the window as we passed office buildings. This was definitely a different part of the city.

"Here we are." He pulled up along the curb in front of a large concrete building. "Good luck."

"Thanks." I handed him the fare. "Keep the change."

"Thank you."

I got out and closed the door behind me. I could do this. It was only a job interview.

I walked through the glass doors and over to the reception desk.

"May I help you?" a young man asked.

"I'm here for an interview with," I pulled out my phone. Had I really forgotten the name? I found the email. "With Monica Vines."

The man smiled. "Take the elevator up to the third floor."

"Thanks."

I used the elevator ride to smooth out my skirt and hair, and to read over the details of the job.

When the doors opened, a woman was standing by the doors smiling. "You must be Daisy."

"Yes." It took me a moment to compose myself. I hadn't expected to be greeted so quickly.

"I'm so glad you were able to make it." She held out her hand.

I tentatively stepped out of the elevator. "Are you Monica Vines?"

"Yes, that's me."

I accepted her hand. "Nice to meet you."

"You have impeccable timing. That's something I love in an employee." She hurried off down the hall, and I followed behind.

I glanced at my watch. I was two minutes early. "I try to be punctual."

"You couldn't have picked a better day to come in."

I hadn't been the one to pick it. They'd assigned the interview date, but I kept that detail to myself. "Great."

She gestured for me to walk into her office. I did so and took a seat.

She sat down behind the desk. "How do you feel about travel, Daisy?"

Talk about getting right to the point. I'd been expecting some getting to know you questions first. "I don't mind it."

"Great. Then you're hired."

"Excuse me?" I narrowed my eyes. Was this some sort of joke?

"Considering you come so highly recommended by the editor you'll be working with, you shouldn't be surprised."

"Aren't you the editor I'd be working for?"

"Not directly. We hired someone new for our youth travels section."

"Youth travels section?" As far as I knew the paper had nothing of the sort.

"Of course. Everyone has one, and I was happy to add one to our Sunday edition."

Happy to? Wait. It couldn't be. "Who did you say the editor I'd be working with was?"

"Violet of course. Isn't she just fabulous?"

There was a knock at the door.

"Oh, come in! We were just talking about you."

I turned, knowing full well who would be standing there.

"Hi, Daisy. I'm so excited we're going to be working together."

"Me too, but I must admit I'm a little bit surprised. I had no idea you were a newspaper editor." I didn't go light on the sarcasm.

"I'm one of the highest rated youth travel correspondents."

"I'm sure that's a very competitive category." I didn't know what to think. Had she gone through the charades and made up a fake newspaper section just to mess with me? Why did Violet care at all about what I did?

"She said she's fine with the travel, so we'll just fill out the paperwork."

"Terrific. I'm sure this is the beginning of a wonderful partnership."

Monica beamed. "Could I see your Social Security card and license to make copies?"

"Uh, sure." I handed them over. I needed time alone to speak with Violet anyway.

As soon as she left I turned to Violet. "What is this? What's the game here?"

She smiled. "I don't know what you're talking about. You said getting a job was important. You have a job."

"A real job. Not one that involves writing for a fake column."

"It's not fake, and let's say it like it is, Daisy. You didn't come to New Orleans for this job. You came for a man. Now you have the cover to continue searching for him."

"Cover? How did you know I viewed things that way?"

"I didn't know, but now I do." She smiled that all white teeth breathtaking smile of hers. "How long are you supposed to be checked into the hotel?"

"Through tomorrow. My flights is in the morning."

"There's no way we'll be done by then. Call your parents and tell them the internship starts immediately."

"I told you I have to check out tomorrow, and I don't have an apartment lined up or anything."

"You're staying with us."

I shook my head. "Uh, no I'm not."

"We've got room."

I glanced over my shoulder to make sure no one was listening. "There is no way I'm staying at that abandoned amusement park."

"We can talk about it tonight."

"No we can't. I have plans."

"Change them. We've got to start the search."

"I thought you were going to do that alone."

"Why would you want to miss the fun?" She headed toward the door. "We'll be by to get you at eight."

Monica reappeared with more paperwork before I could say anything else. I groaned to myself. Now what?

CHAPTER TEN

OWEN

"I love this place!" Hailey yelled far too loudly as we sat at a center table in the busy diner at lunchtime the next day.

Several customers turned to look at us, and I just smiled.

"I mean it's so authentic old west. I didn't know they had places like this anymore."

"They do. The whole town is like this."

"It's cool." She took a bite of her burger.

"Can I get you anything else?" Marta, the bright eyed blonde waitress asked. She was one of the first people I'd met in town.

"We're great, thanks." Hailey smiled.

Marta smiled right back. "So nice to meet some of Owen's family. I knew he couldn't be a complete loner."

"Nope just a loser." Hailey didn't get the rise out of me she probably expected.

"Forgive my sister. She's still adjusting to the altitude."

Marta laughed. "I have a little brother you know. I get it." She walked off.

"Would you look at that!" Clyde called from the entryway. It hadn't taken long for him to notice me. He sauntered over and held out his hand to Hailey. "I'm Owen's friend, Clyde. Are you the sister I've heard so much about?"

"Owen's talked about me?" Hailey didn't hide her surprise.

"Actually I heard you were here. Word travels fast in this town." Clyde nodded over his shoulder to the street.

"I see." She took a sip of her water, looking a little less excited about the authentic nature of Coleville.

"Mind if I join you two?" Clyde pulled over a chair.

"Sure," I answered even though he'd already sat down.

He hung his hat off his chair and turned to Hailey. "I didn't catch your name."

"It's Hailey."

"A beautiful name for a beautiful woman."

I laughed and tried to turn it into a cough. Clyde's lines weren't going to work on my little sister.

"Thanks."

"Did you travel out here all alone?" He rested an elbow on the table so he could lean in closer to her.

"Yeah. It wasn't too bad."

"That's crazy." He watched her intently, hanging on to her every word.

"Not really."

"Are you staying here long?"

"Just a few days. I've missed my big brother."

Clyde turned to me. "I bet."

"So what do you do, Clyde?" Hailey asked.

"Right now I'm helping out over at the Black Creek mine, but I'm interested in developing some businesses. I'm hoping to make your brother a partner."

"My brother? A partner in a business?" Her eyes widened. "You have to be kidding."

"Why not? He's a real people person."

She burst out laughing. "Owen? A people person? He's so anti-social it's sickening."

"Sure he keeps to himself, but everyone loves him. Besides, he's got that business savviness."

"Are you really doing this, Owen?"

I shook my head. "No. I've already got a job."

"You said you'd consider it."

"Hi Clyde." Marta walked over, thankfully interrupting the partnership discussion.

"Hi, Marta." He smiled at her. "Could I get the usual?"

"Absolutely. Want a Coke with that?"

"I'll just have water today."

"Great. I'll get that right away." She smiled at him again before walking away.

"So what do you do, Hailey?" Clyde turned his full attention to her.

"Uh, I'm in college and work part time."

"Part time doing what?"

"I'm a consultant?" she asked more as a question. She was going to have to get better at making up cover stories.

"Oh." If he was suspicious of her answer he didn't show it. "Where are you in school?"

"Tulane." She sipped her water again.

"Cool."

I zoned out on their conversation. Hailey could handle Clyde's harmless banter for a while.

Before I knew it the check came.

"I can get it." Clyde grabbed the bill.

"That's okay." I pulled it away. I didn't want Clyde thinking he was doing Hailey any favors.

"Okay. Thanks, man." He nodded at me before pivoting toward Hailey again. "Are you going to be here a while, or heading back to see anyone?"

"Are you asking me if I'm single?" Hailey could be blunt.

"Yes, yes I am."

"I'm single, but it's by choice." She stood up. "I'm going to walk around for a bit. See you in a few."

Clyde watched as she disappeared through the door. "You've got a beautiful sister."

"Emphasis on the word sister."

"Message received loud and clear." He picked up his hat and headed for the door.

***

"Leaving already?" I watched as Hailey tossed her mess of belongings into her duffel.

"Not that I wouldn't love to stay in this thrilling town with you forever, but I promised Cade I'd stop by to see him."

I groaned. "Cade? Really? Do you have to get mixed up with that guy?"

"That guy is a king. Aren't you the one who usually reminds me to be polite to royalty?"

"That's when we're talking about Levi. The real king." Hailey should have known better than to get me started on Cade. He'd only gotten the title because the queen had made an unfortunate deal.

She shook her head. "Whatever. If you decide to head back to New Orleans in the next few weeks meet me at Cade's. I'd love the company for the drive back."

"I'm not going back that soon."

"Fine." She walked outside to her Jeep. "Tell Clyde I said goodbye."

I laughed. "The poor kid's going to be depressed."

"He'll get over it. Maybe he'll finally give that waitress a chance. They'd make a good couple."

"That's very un-Hailey of you."

"What? I like seeing people happy."

"You're not into matchmaking."

"And this isn't matchmaking, I'm just wishing them well."

"You still never told me the real reason you're here."

"Sure I did. I was checking on you and taking a break."

"I'm going to find out eventually." There was no way Hailey came just to check on me. There was always another reason.

"If you want to get all conspiracy theorist on me then do it. It's not my problem."

I went with one last hunch. "You haven't talked about Allie much."

She looked away. "I've got to go."

"In other words you guys are in a fight."

"I'm leaving. I don't have time to talk about it."

"If you had time to come all the way out here, you have time to talk."

"Not necessarily."

"Hailey. Out with it."

"We got in a ridiculously stupid fight over nothing, and now everything's awkward."

"Awkward how? Like you haven't apologized?"

"Me apologize?" She put a hand to her chest. "Why would you assume I'm the one to blame?"

"She's the queen."

"So?" Her eyes narrowed. She was getting ready to let me have it. "This is about friend Allie, not queen Allie."

"They're the same thing." I'd dealt with the same situation myself. Being best friends with your boss wasn't always easy to handle.

"I'm sick of it."

"Doesn't mean you shouldn't apologize."

"There's nothing to apologize for. It's not like that."

"No?" I rested my hand on the hood of her Jeep. Surprisingly she didn't yell at me for it. She was annoying protective of her car. "Then what kind of fight was it?"

"No making fun of me."

"Now you have to tell me." I smiled. It took a lot to get Hailey embarrassed.

"She wants me to be a godmother."

"But you're not even religious…"

"That's what I said, but she explained she meant more in the 'be the person the kid can go to for help and stuff.'"

"Ok, sounds reasonable. What was the fight?"

"I said no."

"Why?"

"Why? Because I'm not the kind of person kids should come to for anything. I can barely figure out my own life, and there are so many better people for that job."

"But she picked you."

"You're no help. You moan and groan about your life, but then you think everyone else's life is so simple."

"You're scared. You were too scared to say yes and so instead you insulted her by making it seem like you didn't want to be involved with her family."

"That's so stupid!"

"Is it?" I treaded lightly, but I knew at the bottom of all of this was Hailey's insecurities. She had no doubts about her physical strength, but that's where her confidence ended. She didn't understand that she was strong emotionally too.

"Why do you always do this?"

"Do what? Make you face reality?"

I expected her to continue to rant, but instead she hugged me. "When did life get so complicated?"

"It's always been complicated, but you've been sheltered."

"And what about you?"

"Less sheltered, but living in a bubble. Everything changed when Levi became king and then Jared left." It also changed when I met Daisy. I just hadn't realized it at the time.

"You need to come home eventually." She stepped back to give me space, but her eyes stared into mine. She was turning the tables and getting ready to lecture me. "Running away can't solve everything."

"I didn't run away. I'm taking a break."

"Fine, then I'll come back and get you in August. I need to be back before school starts."

"I might need a longer break than that." I wasn't sure when I'd be ready.

"A longer break than that isn't just a break." She gave me a knowing look.

"Drive safe."

"I will. Uh, live safe."

"I will."

She got into the driver's seat, and I closed the door.

She rolled down her windows. "Find yourself a girl, Owen."

"Say hi to Cade."

She laughed before pulling out of the driveway.

I was alone again, and I didn't know how I felt about it.

CHAPTER ELEVEN

DAISY

I'd just stepped out of the shower when I heard a knock on the door. The Allures were early, and I was far from ready for them.

"Coming!" I called as I hastily threw on clothes. Part of me had hoped they wouldn't stop by, but I knew that hope was unrealistic.

I wrenched open the door without taking the time to brush out my hair. I had a problem with leaving people waiting.

"I like the natural look." Violet stepped right into the room. "It suits you."

"You're early." I grabbed my brush and did my best to get rid of the tangles.

"Time isn't really our thing." Roland sprawled out on my bed.

"Glad you're making yourself comfortable." If they planned to spend time with me, they were going to have to get used to my sarcasm.

"Thanks. I'm very comfortable."

"I wasn't serious."

"Yes you were." He smirked. "Either way, we have to find something fun to do tonight."

I resisted the urge to snap at him for laying on my bed. It wasn't worth the argument. "You mean you don't want to spend it enjoying your fabulous ghost amusement park pad?"

"Was that sarcasm I heard?" Hugh laughed. "I'm enjoying your personality more and more."

"I already told Violet I have plans for tonight. I'm not quite sure why she still brought you here."

"What kind of plans?" Roland leaned up on one elbow.

"I'm supposed to meet someone."

"Who are you supposed to meet?" Roland sat up completely. "You don't know anyone in New Orleans."

"The bigger question is why you're so concerned, Roland?" Hugh crossed his arms. "Does it matter if Daisy knows someone in this city?"

"It means she might be holding back on us. Maybe she knows more about this Seduction's Kiss business than she's letting on." Roland sounded uncharacteristically bitter and skeptical. Hugh was the one who usually gave me a hard time. It was funny how I was already getting used to the Allures only a little over twenty-four hours after meeting them.

"This has nothing to do with that. Trust me." I sighed. I was hoping to avoid having to tell them about Andrew.

Now that I'd found paranormal creatures again, it seemed even more pathetic.

"Then who is she?" Roland asked.

"She?" Violet laughed. "What makes you think it's a girl?"

"If she's so crazy about the Pteron, she shouldn't be meeting boys." Roland watched me careful. "Right?"

Violet rolled her eyes. "Who is it?"

"A guy I met online."

"Online?" Roland's eyes bugged out. "Don't you know it's dangerous to talk to strangers like that?"

"Is it any more dangerous than spending time with you guys?"

"She's got a point." Hugh leaned against the back of a chair.

"And it's not like I met him on a dating site. We've been talking on a paranormal forum for a few years."

"A paranormal forum?" Hugh asked. "That would be…"

"A place where humans talk about paranormal creatures and how to find them." As I'd already predicted it sounded even more pathetic when I said it out loud. At least they didn't know I'd been telling my therapist we were seeing each other.

Hugh laughed so hard he almost fell over. "Please tell me this is a joke. You aren't chatting up boys on weirdo boards."

"I wasn't chatting him up. He was just someone to talk to." I looked down. "He believed me when no one else did."

Violet put a gentle hand on my shoulder. "I'm not laughing. It's human instinct to search for companionship, and it must have been nice to have found someone who believed in you."

"Did you guys have online sex?" Hugh grinned.

"No! It's not like that. He's in love with some girl. All we talk about is paranormal stuff."

"Then how do you know he's in love with some girl?"

"Because he doesn't think she's human."

"Oh…" Violet pursed her lips. "Interesting…"

"Yeah. We have stuff in common."

"Where are we meeting him?"

"We're not meeting him." I shook my head. "I am."

"Why?" Roland asked. "Why can't we come?"

"Because he's going to freak out if I show up with a bunch of people. Besides, I don't want you messing with him."

"We won't mess with him." Violet waited next to me. "We'll be on our best behavior."

"I don't like this idea."

"You know we'll follow you if you don't take us with you." Roland didn't beat around the bush.

"Seriously? Did you mean to say that out loud?"

"Yes." He narrowed his eyes. "You've got Allure in you. It's our right to make sure you're not up to anything bad."

"In other words he wants to make sure you don't try to screw your internet friend." Hugh smirked.

"She's in love with a Pteron. She's not going to screw a human." Roland wrinkled his nose.

"Ok. That's it. That's enough talk about my sex life."

"What are you going to wear?" Violet asked, moving the conversation away from what was becoming seriously awkward.

"This." I glanced down at my dark jeans and pink tank top.

"Great." Violet smiled in a way that seemed genuine, but I wasn't sure. I didn't know how to read any of these Allures.

"Daisy would look good in a paper bag." Roland smiled. "But I prefer what she's wearing."

"I'm not concerned with how I look."

"I was only making sure you weren't going to wear something sexier. I know your conversations with this guy have been platonic, but did you forget something, Daisy?"

That's when it hit me. "Seduction's Kiss."

"Exactly. How old is he?"

"Around my age."

"And it seems like it works the strongest on men in their most virile state. What Roland really meant," she glared at him, "was it's not safe for you to go alone."

"I've been out around men my age plenty of times in the past two years."

"Yeah, but did you see that kid yesterday? What would you have done if I hadn't walked over?"

"Something about being back in New Orleans is making it worse," Hugh said under his breath.

"So if I leave, it will die down again?"

"Maybe. Maybe not." Violet looked thoughtful. "We still don't really understand what the witch gave you. Theoretically you've set it off, and it's going to get worse and worse."

"Or not." I couldn't believe that. My life was crazy enough.

Roland's eyes widened. "Yeah, we're going with you."

"I can take care of myself."

"I get that, but don't you want to make sure you live long enough to see Owen again?" Violet asked. She knew how to play to my concerns.

"Fine. You guys can come, but please try to be nice to him. He's the only one who believed me, and because of that he's important to me."

"Where are we meeting him? If it's a busy place we'll have plenty of other emotions to manipulate." Hugh's eyes danced.

"At Fritzel's down on Bourbon."

"Great." Violet ran a hand through her hair. "Let's go meet your friend. What did you say his name was?"

"I didn't. It's Andrew."

"Ok. Let's meet Drew then." Hugh headed toward the door.

"He doesn't go by Drew."

"Now he does." Hugh winked.

I groaned. "You guys can be very annoying."

"But the loveable kind of annoying, right?" Violet asked.

"Uh, mostly." If either of the guys had asked, I would have had a very different answer. "Wait. Why aren't you guys wearing hoods tonight?" I hadn't seen them do it since the first time I'd seen them.

"Because we have no problem getting noticed tonight." Hugh winked.

"Great." So much for them not causing trouble.

The lobby was crowded, but everyone seemed to notice us as we stepped off the elevator.

Violet linked her arm with mine as we walked briskly across the lobby toward the front door.

"Is it always like this for you?" I asked as we stepped outside. A man nearly tripped over himself trying to get another look at us.

"Pretty much. Now you know why we often wear hoods and sunglasses."

"I wish I'd have thought of that idea."

"I still don't believe you didn't get a lot of attention before you got the magic."

"I didn't. I got almost none."

"I find that hard to believe." Roland took his usual spot on my other side.

"It's true. I pretty much blended in."

"There had to be something there for that potion to have worked so well." Violet winked at a guy walking past. His face lit up like a light bulb.

I rolled my eyes. "Do you have to play with people?"

"What? He's going to be in a good mood all night."

"Because he thinks you like him. You don't."

Roland looked over his shoulder. "She has a point, Violet. He's following us now."

She sighed. "Fine." She released my arm and turned around. "Hi, why don't you go turn back the way you were?"

"I'd be happy to." He smiled and started walking the other way.

"It's an easy fix."

"I wish I had that ability. It's like I have an on switch but no off switch."

"We can fix that," Roland mumbled.

Violet glared at him. "Let's focus on finding Owen first. But of course right now we need to find Andrew. Do you know what he looks like?"

"Yes. He added me as a friend on his other social media so I'd know he was who he said he was."

"Oh. That was smart, unless that social media was fake too."

"It seems real. He even has baby pictures up."

"Could still be fake." Roland shrugged.

"Then it's a good thing I have you to protect me."

"I'm just saying, how do you know he's even human? For all you know he's one of the vampires who kidnapped you, and he's been waiting for a chance to get you in his claws again."

"Roland!" Violet snapped. "That's enough."

I shivered. "That's not true."

"But you don't know. You're such easy prey."

"You're right." I turned to him. "I don't know. I also don't know if you guys are luring me to come with you so you can kill me."

"I already assured you, we're not going to hurt you." Violet pulled our linked arms in closer to her as we walked down the street. "We mean you absolutely no harm."

"But I can't know that."

"Yet, you're still coming with us." Hugh glanced over his shoulder. "Interesting."

"The thing is, you never know anything in life. You never know who or what to trust." I'd learned that the hard way time and time again.

"And you really want to find Owen, isn't that part of it?" Hugh was very good at getting at what I was really feeling.

"I've already wasted two and a half years of my life. I don't need to waste more. I need to find him and get this over with."

"And you will." Violet sounded resolute. "Oh, and we're here."

She stopped in front of a brick building with a wrought iron balcony above it. It fit right in on Bourbon.

Jazz music poured out the front door, beckoning us in. I was glad Andrew had chosen a place that would give us a break from the typical club music. New Orleans was known for jazz, and I'd been excited to finally experience it.

We walked inside, and Violet and Roland stood glued to my side. I wasn't sure what they planned to do if there was a problem, but if you could manipulate emotions, you could probably do a lot to protect someone.

"Daisy!" someone called from across the room. Miraculously I could hear it over the loud jazz music being played by a live band. At another time I'd have been up there dancing to their intoxicating beat.

I turned to see Andrew waving. He looked exactly like his pictures, kind of cute in that nerdy sort of way.

"That's him." I nudged Violet.

"We assumed." Roland rolled his eyes, and we headed over to where he stood.

"Uh, I guess you didn't come alone either." Andrew smiled sheepishly in greeting.

"Who are you here with?" I searched around. Did he bring friends too?

"Me." Levi stepped around a small group of people. "Great seeing you again."

My chest clenched. What was going on? Was this a trap? I was suddenly glad to have the Allures with me.

"Uh…" I had no idea what to say. I was moving into panic mode, a mode that I was getting more and more used to.

"Andrew is my brother-in law. He mentioned he was meeting a friend, and when I saw your picture I remembered you. You're the old friend of Owen's, aren't you? It's been far too long." There was a warning in his tone. He was lying about when he last saw me, but he didn't want anyone to know. I didn't want them to know either. I'd purposely kept our meeting from them.

I was overwhelmed by a mix of confusion and anger. What was I supposed to do? Roland squeezed my hand and brought me back to reality. "Nice to see you again too. These are my friends."

"I see." Levi held out his hand to Violet first. "Have we met before?"

"Not formally."

"Oh." He studied her. "I see."

Andrew cleared his throat. "This whole introduction stuff is great and all, but we're only here so Daisy and I can meet."

Levi nodded. "I'm sorry if we're intruding on your little meeting. Why don't you two sit down and chat."

Violet glanced at a nearby table and caught the eye of one of the girls. "I can tell that the people sitting there would be happy to give up their seats. They were ready to leave."

And just like that the table vacated. They smiled at us. "It's all yours. We hope you enjoy the seats!"

Andrew's eyes bugged out.

"Uh, great timing," I stammered.

Roland glowered at Andrew. "Maybe I should keep them company. It's always tough to make conversation when you've just met."

"We'll be fine. Daisy and I know each other well." Andrew winked.

Roland looked at me. "We won't be far."

I nodded before taking a seat at the small table. Andrew sat down next to me. "That was weird."

"It was."

"And you look different than your pictures."

"Different?" I asked. This was the moment of truth. How affected was he by Seduction's Kiss?

"I guess you're not photogenic." He held up his hands. "No offense, because you're wow. Just wow."

"The pictures are accurate." There was my answer.

"Who are those guys?" He gestured to where the Allures stood with Levi.

"First, tell me why you lied to me." Now that I was alone with Andrew, my anger had surfaced. "You've been playing me like a fool."

"No I haven't!" Andrew appeared stricken by my accusation. "Of course not."

"Levi knows Owen. You heard it with your own ears. Your *brother-in law* knows Owen."

"That's the lead I was talking to you about. I really don't remember much from my step-sister's wedding, it's all fuzzy for some reason, but the other night it hit me. I knew an Owen that fit your Owen's description."

"You just suddenly remembered this?" I crossed my arms. I wasn't convinced.

"I'm telling you the truth. And he's Hailey's brother! How crazy is that?"

"Hailey? As in the girl you're obsessed with?"

Andrew looked over his shoulder and then leaned in. "Keep it down. I'm not public with that. My step-sister, Allie, would kill me if she knew I wanted her best friend."

"Why? Why would your step-sister care?"

"She doesn't want me near her friends."

Was he even weirder than I thought? I shrugged it off. It didn't matter. What mattered is he might know more than I did about how to find Owen.

"My step-sister told me I was crazy when I suggested it, but I don't think Levi is human either. My guess is he's the way you describe Owen, and this means I was right about Hailey. She's not human either. She probably has wings too." His face lit up with excitement. "Isn't that awesome?"

"Your step-sister is human though?"

"Yes. Very. We went to high school together."

"Let's say for a minute I believe you..."

"You do believe me, don't you? I really wasn't lying to you."

"Let's say I do. Did Levi tell you anything about Owen? Where to find him?"

"Only that he's not here. Hailey isn't either. I just missed her." His smile faded. "But that's all right. At least I know what she is. Or sort of. You never did tell me what Owen is exactly."

I looked down. I guess I hadn't been completely forthcoming. "I'd ask Levi. He'd be able to tell you a whole lot more than me."

"He's not going to admit it to me."

"Then what did he tell you?"

"I'm staying with them, and I mentioned you and how you were looking for this guy you're kinda obsessed with." He gave me another sheepish smile. "Then Levi got all weird and said he was coming."

"None of this makes sense. We're obsessed with siblings, and your brother-in-law isn't human."

"Pretty much sums it up." He smiled. "So now it's your turn. Who are those people you are with?"

"Some new friends." I still didn't know what to say or not say to Andrew. I believed him, but it all seemed too strange to be true.

"Daisy? Are you ready?" Violet walked over. "It's getting late."

It wasn't late. It wasn't even nine thirty, but there was something in her voice that had me nodding my head. "Sure. It's been a long day."

"And just like that you're leaving?" Andrew gripped his bottle of beer. "We have so much more to talk about."

"I'm sorry. We can try to meet up again later."

"Another ten minutes?" His eyes pleaded with me, and I knew most of it was coming from Seduction's Kiss. That made it even easier to stand up.

Violet smiled at Andrew. "You guys can talk again soon. I have some important stuff to talk to Daisy about."

I had to make a quick decision. Did I stay and make sure Andrew didn't know more than he was letting on, or did I go with the Allures who may have learned more from Levi?

I stood up. "Sorry, Andrew. I have to go."

I really hoped I was making the right decision.

CHAPTER TWELVE

DAISY

"You have some explaining to do." Violet held onto my arm as we wove our way through the crowds on the street.

"I could say the same to you. What was all of that about? You only gave me a second to talk to my friend."

"Your friend?" Roland sneered. "Either you've been lying to us, or he's been lying to you."

"I should have told you I met Levi." I elbowed my way through a large group of drunk tourists that wouldn't move.

"You think?" Hugh's icy tone had me glancing up in time to see his frown. "Do you really not know who he is or are you playing stupid? For your sake it had better be the former."

"Who who is?"

"Levi." Hugh signed with frustration.

Violet glanced over her shoulder. "Let's shelve this conversation until we get out of town."

"Out of town?" I stopped short. "Who said anything about that?"

"Owen left which means there's no reason to wait." Hugh watched me impatiently.

"Levi told you?"

"Yes. Wouldn't it have been convenient to have told us that before? What were you planning to do, sit around hoping he'd come back?"

"I hadn't thought that far ahead. I was more focused on the interview." I was also determined not to give them any more information than necessary until I knew they could be trusted.

"The interview is over. You've got the job." Violet fell back to walk next to us.

"I've got a fake job."

"Does that matter?" Violet asked without any inflection in her voice. I couldn't tell if the question was serious or not.

"Probably not."

"My point exactly." She stepped toward the curb. "Let me get us a ride."

"You mean steal another car? I'm not going anywhere with you unless I know where we're going."

"We're going to find Owen."

"Even his friends don't know where he is. Why would you?" I stuffed my hands into the back pockets of my worn-in jeans.

"We have to tell her who he is. This is getting ridiculous." Hugh sighed.

"We'll tell her in the car." Violet stepped into the middle of the road. A luxury sedan squealed to a stop right in front of her.

"I'm not going anywhere with you." I turned away. Maybe if I looked away I wouldn't be as much of an accessory to the crime. Who was I kidding? I was. Just like I was going to go with them. I had no other leads, unless I counted Andrew, and who knew whether he was any more trustworthy than the Allures, or any safer.

"What the hell are you doing? Get out of the road!" The driver screamed.

Violet walked over to the driver's side window and leaned in.

She started to speak, and moments later she walked back over to us. "We're all set. You drive the first leg." She tossed a set of keys to Hugh.

"Fine with me." Hugh walked over to the driver's seat.

"Do you want shot gun?" Roland held open the passenger door.

I shook my head. "Tell me where we're going."

Violet glanced back the way we came. "Not yet. We need to make sure we weren't followed."

"Of course we were followed," Hugh said through the open door.

"By Levi and Andrew?"

"Get in the car." Hugh wasn't asking a question.

"You're really going to help me find him?"

"How many times do I have to tell you before you believe me?" Violet gritted her teeth.

"We've got to go." Roland pulled on my wrist and launched me into the car. He followed in behind me and slammed the door. Before I could make sense of what was happening, Hugh hit the gas and we sped away. He was an even crazier driver than Violet.

"What the hell?" I struggled to buckle my seatbelt. If I was going along for this ride, I was going to do everything possible to survive their insane driving.

Roland gave me an apologetic look. "Sorry, doll, but I saw the king. We don't need him slowing us down."

"The king?" What was he talking about?

Roland made a clicking sound with his tongue. "Levi. He's The King of The Society. It's a giant paranormal organization, and he doesn't like you sniffing around for lover boy."

"King? That guy is a king?" They had to be kidding.

"And your boy Owen is his chief advisor." Violet turned to look at me. "Good, you're in shock."

"The thing I'm in shock over is you guys kidnapping me, but why is it good?"

"Because it means you're telling us the truth about something. I wish you hadn't hid your conversation with Levi from us. Now we're going to have to be more careful."

"It's not like you guys have given me all that many reasons to trust you. I mean you did just force me into a car."

"We are protecting you." She leaned her elbow on the center console.

"From what? You really think Levi would hurt me?"

"Not him directly, but others. An Allure essence is strong and others will want it for themselves. They might do desperate things to try to extract it from you."

"So you say."

"We more than say it." Roland wrapped his hand around my wrist. It was the second time he'd grabbed my wrist, and he was making me nervous.

"Just get it out of me then. Get it out of me, and we can go our separate ways."

I held onto the seat as Hugh continued to weave through traffic.

"You can't just get rid of it. It's part of you. It's why no magic could remove it."

We turned onto the interstate, and Hugh stopped cutting in and out of cars so much, but that change was overshadowed by his crazy speed.

"Great." I leaned back. "At least I know I'm not crazy."

"You already knew that." Roland's voice was friendly again.

"Where are we going? You can at least tell me that."

"We're seeing a friend out in California."

"California?" I sat up straight. Hugh had finally slowed down to driving a normal pace.

"Yes. Just outside L.A. We know another Pteron that seems to know everyone. He's got ways of tracking people down who want to stay hidden."

"Wouldn't a king have that ability too?"

"Of course, but he also has honor."

"What does honor have to do with anything?"

"Does a man of honor track down his friend and confidant against his wishes?"

"No." I leaned back. "Does that mean I don't have honor?"

"Honor has nothing to do with it. You need closure."

"It's more than closure," I said half to myself.

"It's closure." Roland scooted closer to me. He'd never bothered with a seatbelt. "Don't let yourself think it's more because you'll only get hurt."

"And maybe both of you will," Violet said quietly.

"I'm not worried about getting hurt."

"Whatever you say." Hugh changed lanes. "It's going to be a while before we stop."

"Wait. We can't leave yet."

"We're already ten miles from the city."

"I thought you were only getting away from Levi."

"If he'd wanted to follow of us, he could have, but we didn't need to deal with another confrontation."

So all the crazy driving was for fun? "Whatever. I have to get my stuff and check out of the hotel."

"I've already contacted the hotel. They'll move your stuff and put it in storage."

"When? When did you contact them?"

"I went outside to make a quick phone call while we were back at the bar."

"I didn't know."

"I guess you were too distracted by your date." Hugh laughed.

"It wasn't a date."

"If it was it was a short one." Roland brushed his hand against my neck. I shrugged him off.

"You say that now, but you wouldn't have said it earlier." Hugh glanced back at Roland.

Roland shrugged. "I don't know what you're talking about."

"What are we going to do for clothes? I have nothing on me. I'm missing important things."

"What kind of important things?" Violet asked.

"Things." I was grasping for straws, but I wasn't ready to leave the city yet. I needed my bag, and I needed to slow things down. Everything was happening too fast.

"Don't you have your birth control in your purse?" Violet turned around again.

"Who said anything about birth control?"

"It makes sense that you'd be concerned about that, but don't you have it?"

"I do. But that doesn't matter."

"I have condoms." Hugh winked. "I have you covered."

"This has nothing to do with birth control or condoms!" I screamed.

"We can get everything we need on the way. Just enjoy the ride." Roland scooted back over to his side. I appreciated the space, I could barely breathe as is.

I took a few deep breaths. "What's going to happen when we find your friend?"

"We ask him about Owen."

"And if he doesn't know anything?"

"We keep searching."

"That's going to take time."

"We have all the time in the world." Roland grinned.

"Is that your way of saying I have no life?"

"No." Roland leaned in. "It's my way of saying you're going to have one hell of a life."

CHAPTER THIRTEEN

DAISY

"We aren't really going to drive all the way to LA just to find your friend, are we?" Once the shock of it all wore off, it was time to ask some questions.

"Not directly, no." Violet turned around in the passenger seat. "We'll make some stops."

"Stops as in hotels? No offense, but I'd rather not sleep in another abandoned amusement park."

"What she's trying to say is she wants to get us in a hotel room with her." Even without seeing him, I knew Hugh was smirking.

"It's not going to work. You're not going to make me mad."

"I wouldn't challenge me if I were you." There was a warning in his tone that should have scared me, but I was feeling so overwhelmed it was starting to make me numb.

"Hugh, don't you dare. There are far better ways to entertain ourselves on this trip."

"Like what?" He changed lanes, narrowly avoiding a tractor trailer. Staying entertained wasn't my highest priority.

"We can play a game." Violet turned back to the front.

"Why does the thought of playing a game with you guys scare me?" I asked.

"It shouldn't scare you more than being in a car with us." Roland stretched out his legs beside me in the cramped car.

"You've got that right."

"Ok, great. What game should we play?" Violet's constant good mood was nice, but it bordered on annoying. Did she have to be peppy all the time?

"How about truth or dare?" Hugh smiled at me in the rear view mirror. "Ever play that one?"

"Of course I've played it, but how do you play that in the car?"

"The same way you'd play it anywhere," he challenged.

"What kind of dares can you do in the car?"

"Fine, if that concerns you we can keep it simple and play truth."

"Meaning the only option is to answer a question?" This game didn't sound fun if I had to answer, but I wouldn't mind asking the Allures some questions of my own.

"You up for it?" Roland asked.

"As long as you don't get too personal with the questions." I had to protect myself somehow.

"Why?" Roland rested his arm behind me on the seat. "You afraid to share your secrets with us?"

"The whole point of a secret is that it's just for you. You're not supposed to share."

"Are you too scared to play with us?" Hugh asked. "You don't think you can handle it?"

"I don't want to play. It has nothing to do with fear." I didn't need to give them any more ammo against me. As far as I was concerned, they already knew too much.

"Well, we have to do something. Either come up with your own game, or we play that one."

I thought it over. "I'll play." I didn't want to share anything more than I had to with the Allures, but really, they already knew the embarrassing stuff. If I could learn more about who they actually were from the game, then it was worth it. "Who goes first?"

"I will." Violet's quick response put me at ease. Of the three of them I'd rather face her questions. "Daisy, truth or truth?"

"Why bother asking it as a question if it's not one?"

"I'm trying to still make it feel like a game."

"Ok, fine. Truth."

She kneeled on her seat to look at me.

"You could get killed that way."

"I'm fine."

"With Hugh driving, I really wouldn't do that." He was even worse than Violet was.

"It's not a problem." She brushed her hair off her shoulder. "Ready for your question?"

"Sure." I swallowed hard.

"Does your name suit you?"

"My name?"

"Yes. Does the name Daisy suit who you really are."

"I've never thought about that before."

"That means it's a great question." She grinned. "You can take a second to answer."

"It doesn't."

"Why not?" Roland asked.

"I'm not delicate like a flower. I'm not girly pretty either. I'm much rougher around the edges." Or rougher all over now. I'd changed a lot since that fateful Halloween night.

"Flowers aren't always delicate. They're strong, and who says you aren't pretty?" Violet stared into my eyes so intently I felt like she could see my soul.

"My turn."

"Okay, who are you asking?"

I debated who would be the most forthcoming. Violet had played fair with her question, so I didn't want to make things too crazy. "My question is for Hugh."

"For me?" He chuckled. "All right. Let's have it."

"How long have you known Violet and Roland?" I needed to get a sense of how far back their friendship went.

"I've known Violet the majority of my life. I've known Roland for less time." He smirked at me in the mirror.

"That doesn't answer the question."

"Sure it does. I've known Violet for the majority of my life, and I haven't known Roland as long."

I groaned. "Fine. How many years have you known Violet?"

"You already asked your question," Roland playfully pushed my arm. "It's my turn."

"Let me guess, your question is for me too?"

"Yes. This one's for you." He crossed his legs at the ankles. "Why are you so determined to find Owen? And no bullshit response about wanting to thank him or something. I want the real answer."

"What does it matter to you? You're only helping me so you can get to the witch."

"We still want to know what's motivating you," Violet said softly. "You haven't told us much yet."

"Was that the point of this whole game? To get information from me?" I realized the hypocrisy of my question. I was doing the same thing to them.

Violet shook her head. "No. The point was to pass the time."

"Yeah, right." I rolled my eyes.

"Are you going to answer?" Hugh asked.

"Sure. Why not? Because of how he made me feel. No one's made me feel that way. And that kiss."

"This is all over a lousy kiss?" Roland's mouth fell open. "Seriously?"

"Partially."

"Describe it," Violet ordered in a surprisingly strong tone.

"What? The kiss?"

"The kiss, the feeling. All of it."

"Why?"

"Just do it. Okay?" There was something almost desperate in Violet's words that got me talking.

I closed my eyes. "The kiss was magic. Not the artificial magic of the witch, but an all-encompassing out of body experience that left me wanting and needing everything yet nothing."

"More. Tell us more," she begged.

Once I started recounting it, I didn't want to stop. "I can still feel his hands, his lips. Hear his voice. It's like he seeped into my soul."

"Wow."

I opened my eyes to see Violet kneeling on the seat staring at me.

"Ok, I know that sounds sappy."

"Not sappy. Wonderful." Violet smiled sadly. "Hold onto those memories. Hold onto them and never let them go."

"I don't plan on it." I stared out the window at the seemingly endless interstate. We'd crossed into Texas at some point, but I hadn't noticed.

"Do you want to go Hugh, or should we quit?" Violet asked.

"We can quit."

"Already?" I had so many more questions to ask. "But no one's asked Roland anything."

"Fine." Hugh changed lanes. "Roland, what's your favorite color?"

"Blue, but you already knew that."

"It's my favorite too." I eagerly grabbed hold of something I had in common with him. They seemed so different than me that any common ground helped.

"I knew you had good taste." Roland smiled.

That tiny tidbit in common gave me the confidence to push for more information. "So I know the game is over, but could I ask another question?"

"Ask away," Violet answered without turning around.

I let out a deep breath before diving in with my question. "Were you ever human, or were you born Allures?"

"Really? Is that the best you can do?" Hugh asked.

"What questions should I be asking then?"

"None. You should just worry about finding your precious Owen." Roland spoke without looking away from the window. "You'll have time to worry about us later."

"Whatever." I'd had it. Even Roland was being a jerk to me? What was with the whole mood swing? Hadn't Violet told me to ask away? I waited for her to say something, but she remained silent. Instead of pushing my luck further, I sent a quick text to my mom to let her know I was hired by the paper and wouldn't be coming home as planned. I knew she'd have a million questions, but I didn't have any answers for her yet. I pocketed my phone and closed my eyes. I needed to do something to make the time go faster.

***

I blinked to get rid of the fogginess. The sky was dark, but a fluorescent light shone into the car through the windows. We were parked at a small gas station. "Where are we?"

"We're at a gas station." Roland smiled. Was he back to himself again at least?

"Other than the obvious?"

"We're somewhere in New Mexico. I haven't seen the name of a town in a while."

"Already? How long have we been driving?"

"You were sleeping for hours."

"For hours?" I knew I was exhausted, but I'd never fallen asleep in a car like that before.

"We're trying to make good time. Violet's taking this shift, and then I'll take the next."

"Do I get a shift?" I glanced at the empty front seats. I didn't see either Hugh or Violet outside. Where were they?

"I'm not sure if we should let you."

"I've seen how Violet and Hugh drive. I assure you I'm not any worse."

"Yeah, but you're too emotional."

"What does emotional have to do with driving a car?"

"You might make rash decisions."

"You sound ridiculous."

"I know." He smiled.

"Where are they? How long have we been parked?"

"They're taking care of some things."

"They're stealing something, right? Manipulating someone to get us stuff?"

"It's not stealing."

"Yes it is. It's stealing."

"You'll get it one day."

"You guys keep saying that, but I don't think I will. I'm never going to agree that it's okay to take advantage of people and take what isn't yours."

"You will."

I sighed. "Do I have time to go inside and use the bathroom?"

"Is that your way of asking me to come with you?"

"Why would I want you to do that?"

"Because you're nervous of being left behind."

"Why would I be? You guys forced me into the car. Why would you just ditch me at a gas station in the middle of New Mexico?"

"You have time."

"Great." I unbuckled and opened my door. Once outside I stretched. I'd been sitting for far too long. I also immediately realized that my need for the bathroom was far greater than I originally thought.

"Daisy!" Violet called as soon as I pushed open the door to the convenience store.

I waved before heading straight for the restroom.

I used the restroom and washed my hands. I took in my reflection in the mirror. I should have looked exhausted and rumpled, the way I always looked on a long car trip, but I didn't. I just looked like me. The nap must have helped.

Violet was waiting for me outside the door. "What's your favorite kind of candy?"

"Why? I don't need any."

"You'll want some sugar. What do you like? Chocolate or non-chocolate?"

"Twizzlers."

"Interesting choice."

"Why?"

"That's Roland's favorite too. You guys can fight over it."

"I'm fine. I'm just going to get some water."

"Already have it." Violet held up a plastic bag. "I wanted to make sure I didn't need to grab more candy."

"Are we really driving this straight through?"

"We're making one stop to see a friend."

"Oh. Roland didn't mention it."

"That's because Hugh and I just decided."

"Oh. Roland wasn't part of the decision?" I was still trying to figure out the dynamics between the three.

"He wasn't purposely left out, but he was in the car."

"Okay." I eyed the door. "Should we go back to the car?"

"Yeah, but Daisy?"

"Yes?"

"Everything is going to be okay. It might get crazy and terrifying, but it's going to be better."

"Uh, and you want me to get back in the car with you?"

She touched my arm. "You don't have a choice."

"Sure I do."

"Wow. That was fast." Worry lines marred her forehead.

"What?"

"Nothing." She looked out the glass window of the store.

"No. Just say it."

"Even my touch doesn't work well for you anymore."

"You were trying to mess with my feelings?" I whispered. The clerk was watching us. Who knew what she'd already done to him?

"Yes. Just to test it."

"I told you not to." I put a hand on my hip.

"You don't have to worry about that anymore." Without a word she started toward the door. After a moment's hesitation, I followed.

CHAPTER FOURTEEN

OWEN

I never thought I'd say it, but I missed my sister. At least I missed her company. She'd only been there for a few days, but I got used to the conversation, and even her nagging had started to seem less annoying.

I'd been fine by myself before her visit, but after she left I was reminded of how life used to be. I'd only lived alone for a few years after college, and even then I spent more of my time working or with my friends. Isolation was a new experience, and it gave me far too much time to reflect on my past and the possibilities that had never come to be. Inevitably those thoughts always went to Daisy, the girl I knew I could never have, but who had trusted me so much. I'd never shared a kiss quite like the one we'd had, and I always wondered what would have happened if I hadn't put on the brakes so quickly. Nothing would have happened, I always reminded myself. When the reality of what I was caught up with her, she would have run and never looked back.

A few days after Hailey left, I found I welcomed the arrival of Clyde's truck when it pulled into the gravel in front of my cabin.

I walked out to greet him.

He hopped out of his truck with a huge grin on his face. "You're wearing a shirt today."

"I am."

"Does that mean I didn't catch you before another hike?" He raised an eyebrow.

"This is pretty good timing."

"I heard your sister left."

"She did."

"That's too bad. I was going to talk to you about asking her out."

"I had a feeling you were." I bit back a smile. Whether I wanted to admit it or not, Hailey had grown up, and men were definitely noticing.

"Have you put any more thought into my proposal? I'm willing to give you a share with no upfront investment if you'll help with the leg work."

"I'll help."

"Yeah?" Surprise covered his face. "I was expecting to have to fight you harder."

"I could use something to do."

"Want to come into town with me? I was going to meet with Earl Miller to see if he's ready to talk about selling the place."

"Sure, I've got nothing else going on." I got into the passenger's side and waited for Clyde to pull back out onto the dirt road connecting my cabin to the main drive into town.

"Sorry, it's a mess. I don't have people in here often." There was something lonely about Clyde I didn't quite understand. What had driven him out to the mountains? Part of the reason he tried so hard with me was that we were some of the only outsiders. Nearly everyone else had been born and raised in Coleville.

"The mess doesn't bother me."

"We can get some lunch while we're in town if you want."

"Let's meet with Miller first, then we can worry about the rest." As much as I welcomed the company, I didn't know how much of him I could handle in one day.

"All right, sounds like a plan."

Clyde chatted on about some random town news as he drove, but I wasn't really listening. Instead I watched a bear poke its head out from the forest line. Something about the bear was off. It was too big.

"You okay over there?" Clyde asked.

"Yeah, I'm fine." I tore my eyes from the bear to speak to Clyde. "Sorry." By the time I glanced back the bear was gone. That wasn't good. I was going to have to follow up on my hunch later.

We reached town and Clyde found a spot along the curb outside of the hardware store. The same man who owned it also owned the one, now closed, bar in town. Hopefully for Clyde, he wouldn't play hardball to a willing buyer since it was currently making him nothing.

The bell over the door rang as we walked into the store, and we headed right for the counter. Usually Miller was working the cash register himself. The counter was empty.

"You back there, Miller?" Clyde called. He was much more comfortable with the locals than I was. He lived in town, which may have been part of it. He also wasn't hiding a secret. I'd never fully gotten used to developing friendships with humans.

"I'll be right out!" Miller yelled.

I decided to peruse the aisles while I waited. This was more Clyde's conversation than mine anyway.

"Hi, boys. What can I do for you?" Miller walked out to the counter looking more harried than usual. He ran a hand across his forehead. I hoped he wasn't ill.

"We were hoping to talk shop if you had a few minutes." Clyde wasted no time.

"Is this about buying the bar?"

Clyde nodded. "Yes."

"You got a real offer for me?" He watched Clyde from over his wire rim glasses. "Not an insult like those kids who tried to buy it?"

"What kids?" Clyde asked suspiciously. "I wasn't aware anyone else was interested."

"The new ones who got here this week. They tried to buy this store as well, but they were offering me peanuts."

"What did these kids look like?" He had my attention. As far as I knew no one new had come to town that week except my sister. The coincidence had me suspicious especially after seeing the bear.

"Real tall like you." He gestured to me. "One with fiery red hair and another two with brown. They looked rough, but not much worse than a lot of the kids here."

"Did they leave a card?" There was no way I was going to let this slide.

He shook his head. "No."

"Ok, thanks."

Clyde looked at me funny. "You think you know them?"

"Nope. I just like to know our competition." That sounded like a plausible excuse.

"They're not your competition if you two have a real offer. First, they offered me a pittance, and second, I don't know them from a hole in the wall. You're both pretty new, but you've been here. The town likes you. Marta likes you." He grinned.

Clyde adjusted his hat. "You do have a lovely daughter, Miller."

"I know I do. Maybe you should tell her that some time."

Hailey was right. Marta was into him. I didn't want to tell her that though. It would go to her head.

"We've got a real offer." Clyde pulled a business card out of pocket and slid is across the counter. "How does that look to you?"

Miller put on his glasses. "That's a place to start."

"How much higher are we talking?"

I turned toward the door as I sensed someone watching. All I caught was a figure dashing from the window. "Clyde, do you have this? I need to check something out."

"Sure, that's fine." He waved me off.

"I'll catch you later." I hurried out of the store, hoping the figure hadn't gotten too far ahead.

CHAPTER FIFTEEN

DAISY

"This friend of yours, is he or she an Allure too?" We'd been back in the car for hours already, and we'd fallen into what was, at least for me, an uncomfortable silence. I could pretend to know what they were thinking when we were talking. The silence was making me paranoid.

"Yes. He's an Allure." Violet kept her eyes on the road as she answered. I wondered if she'd taken a nap when I did because she didn't seem tired at all.

"And how is he going to feel about you bringing me there? I'm guessing he is going to sense the Seduction's Kiss as well."

"How many times do we have to reassure you that we're not trying to kill you?" Hugh glared at me. He'd taken the back seat this time. I didn't mind since Roland hadn't been particularly friendly either.

"You are the ones who told me that if the wrong Allures had found me I'd been dead."

"We're not taking you to meet one of *those* kind of Allures. Louie is our friend. He may even be able to help you."

"Help me how?" I knew she wasn't talking about finding Owen.

"To help us figure out exactly what's going on with you. We need to know what was in the paste the witch gave you, and what effect it's had on you beyond what we can see already."

"You think there's more than we already know?" My chest tightened as panic set in.

"Of course there is. You know it as well as we do." Roland turned slightly in his seat to look at me. "Don't you? Don't you feel it?"

"I'm not sure what I'm supposed to feel."

"Don't push it. We'll talk to Louie when we get there."

"What if I don't want to talk to another Allure?" I barely trusted these three, and I wasn't particularly keen on meeting another.

"I'm going to insist on it." Violet turned off at a barren exit. By the looks of it, we were in the middle of the desert. We were surrounded by cactuses, and I was waiting to see some tumbleweed blowing by.

"Are we that close? We're getting off the interstate already?"

"Has this trip seemed fast to you?" Roland asked.

"Roland, stop," Violet snapped. "I'm not going to warn you again."

"Fine," he grumbled.

His question hadn't seemed like one worth jumping all over him about, but I'd given up understanding the dynamics of these three. "What kind of place does Louie live in?" I sincerely hoped it wasn't anything as creepy as that abandoned amusement park.

"A cemetery," Hugh said calmly.

"A what? I thought you guys liked emotion, not dead people."

Violet laughed. "Hugh's kidding. He lives in a house. A large, old, and rather opulent house, but a house none the less."

"Does he know we're coming?"

"Yes and no."

"Meaning he knows you guys are coming."

"We didn't want to get him unnecessarily excited," Violet explained. "It's fine. He'll treat you well."

"What if he doesn't?" I needed more than Violet's assurances to put me at ease.

"Would you prefer we drop you off on the side of the road and let you face your fate on your own?" Hugh scoffed. "Let you wander around the desert as you struggle to understand why you feel the way you do?"

"I don't want to be dropped on the side of the road."

"Being stranded would be the least of your problems. You can trust me on that."

"Why? What aren't you guys telling me?"

"Let's get to Louie's house. We'll talk more there, and he'll hopefully be better able to shed some light on everything."

"Or so you say."

"Have we done anything to mislead you so far?" She drove through what appeared to be a small town. All I saw was a church, a restaurant, and a few stores.

"No."

"Then why are you questioning us?"

"I don't know," I answered honestly. "Suddenly I'm overwhelmed with anger and annoyance, and I don't know what to do with it." I looked at Hugh. "This isn't you, is it?"

"Do you see me touching you?"

"Touch doesn't work anymore anyway," Violet said softly. "I realized that at the last stop."

"Really?" Roland turned around. "Not at all?"

"Can I try?" Hugh asked. "We need to know."

"I'm so angry already, I don't see how it could hurt this time." I held out my hand.

"Nothing. Absolutely nothing." Hugh dropped my hand.

Violet turned off on a side street. "We're almost there."

I tried to relax, but I couldn't.

"Daisy, you need to calm down." Roland turned around from the passenger seat. "You're stressing me out, and you're not even sitting next to me."

"Why? So I can be forced into more situations I don't want to be in?"

"I'm going back there." Roland climbed over the seat into the middle. "Give me your hand."

"Why? Touch doesn't work anymore, remember?"

"Just give it to me." He picked up my hand, and I took a deep breath. I could do this. I was so close to finding Owen. I let out a sigh of relief.

"None of this makes sense." Hugh scooted away slightly from Roland. "Our touch does nothing, yet Roland's still works in the opposite way it's supposed to."

"Actually it makes complete sense; you guys just don't want to believe it." Roland smiled.

"I'm ridiculously confused, but I feel better than I did a few minutes ago so don't move." I closed my eyes and leaned back against the seat.

"I wasn't planning on it."

Out of nowhere an idle thought hit me. "How long does your effect last? Won't the guy who owns this car call the cops to report it missing? Won't they be searching for the license plate?"

"Nope. He still thinks he lent it to a friend."

"What about his wife? She's never going to believe him."

Hugh laughed. "I'd love to see that conversation."

"You guys are so mean."

"We're fun, not mean." Roland patted my leg. "Get over it. There are way more important things to worry about."

Violet turned once more and stopped in front of a large wrought iron gate. She rolled down her window and pressed the button for an intercom.

"You've arrived!" a male voice yelled. "Come on in!"

The gates slowly opened, and Violet drove us down a long, winding drive that seemed to continue on forever.

I was almost sick with nerves by the time Violet pulled to a stop in front of an enormous home.

Hugh opened the door and got right out, followed by Roland. I took a deep breath before following them.

I'd barely made it two steps before one of the large front doors at the top of a steep set of brick stairs burst open.

"Welcome!" A man dressed in what could only be described as a bright white leisure suit called down. "Welcome one and all!"

What the hell was this? This couldn't be for real. He took a few steps down, and it got worse. He had his shirt unbuttoned revealing his chest.

"Louie is a fan of the seventies," Roland whispered as he clasped his hand with mine.

"Violet, wonderful to see you." Louie, a man who appeared to be in his early thirties, took her hand and brought it to his lips. "Hugh, nice to see you, and Roland, I see you brought a new friend."

I held on to Roland's hand for dear life. Hopefully he wasn't about to go into his anti-social mode on me.

"This is Daisy." Violet took her usual spot on my other side. "She's why we're here."

"I see." Louie eyed me up and down, but he definitely wasn't checking me out. It was more like he was trying to solve a puzzle.

Violet cleared her throat. "I'm sure you already understand by the very fact that we brought her here, but she came into her condition by no fault of her own."

"I'm sure." He studied my face. "Daisy, is it?"

I nodded, still too nervous to speak.

"I'm Louie."

"Hi," I squeaked out.

"No reason to be nervous." He smiled revealing two rows of perfectly white teeth. All of these Allures had perfect teeth. "You're among friends here."

I said nothing and stood stock still.

"Let's go for a walk, shall we?" He held out his hand.

I looked at Violet with panic. Walking off with this guy wasn't part of the plan.

Much to my horror Violet nodded. "Go ahead. We'll be waiting inside."

Roland started to let go of my hand, but I held on tighter.

Louie took a step toward me. "It's all right, child. I'm not going to hurt you."

"The last person to call me child did this to me." At the time I'd never imagined how much my life would change because of her.

"I assure you I won't do the same."

"Can't we talk here?" My whole body started to shake uncontrollably.

Roland squeezed my hand, and my body calmed. "Stay calm. He's going to help you."

"I don't need help."

"You don't?" He released my hand and the shaking restarted.

"What's going on?"

"You're petrified." Louie spoke slowly.

"I'm not that scared."

"Come with me. We'll walk the gardens."

"Go with him, Daisy." Violet pushed my arm. "I swear it's okay."

Louie smiled reassuringly. "Would you feel better if we had a chaperone?"

"Chaperone?"

"I assume you're frightened to be alone with me?"

"Roland relaxes her for some reason." Hugh spoke for the first time.

Louie turned to Hugh. "Now that's interesting, isn't it?"

"It is." Roland kept his eyes fixed on Louie.

"Would you walk with us as far as the garden gates? You can wait for us there. You'll still be within shouting distance which might put our friend at ease."

"Absolutely," Roland answered quickly.

I found myself nodding. I had to get this over with. The sooner I did, the sooner I'd get to see Owen.

I reluctantly accepted Louie's outstretched hand, and he led us around to the side of the house. A large gate that matched the one out front opened to an expansive garden. "Shall we?"

"Sure." I glanced at Roland who was nodding emphatically for me to go on.

The garden was older, as evidenced by the aging planter beds, but the flowers and plants it housed were spectacular. The colors were what I'd have expected in a much more tropical setting. "Wow, this is beautiful."

"Isn't it?" Louie walked beside me, thankfully leaving a socially acceptable amount of space; the type of space Violet and Roland never seemed to leave.

"Have you lived here long?"

"Longer than you know." He smiled lightly.

"Okay…" Of all the questions I had, that one wasn't the most pressing.

"Are you ready to tell me what happened?"

"There isn't all that much to tell. I went to a Voodoo shop in New Orleans, and a witch gave me a paste called Seduction's Kiss that seemed to garner me a lot of attention."

"I'm sure by now you understand what was in that paste."

"Yes and no."

"Honest. Sometimes a nice trait."

"Sometimes? Isn't honesty always best?"

"You know that's not true as much as I do. If your friend has gained a few pounds, would you tell her she looks fat?"

"Of course not."

His lips twisted up into a smile. "Then you understand. In this case honesty is good. I can't help you unless I know everything."

"Why is everyone so convinced I need help? I was fine before I met Violet and the guys."

"Were you?" He raised an eyebrow. "I would think coping with the increased attention of everyone you meet would be difficult."

"It wasn't as bad before I returned to New Orleans."

"It would have happened eventually."

"How do you know?"

"Because what is meant to happen, always happens." Unlike Violet, Louie didn't seem to believe in defying fate.

"Will it eventually wear off then?"

"Wear off?" His brow wrinkled. "What have my friends told you so far?"

"Not much. They seemed hell bent on me talking to you first."

He sighed. "But of course."

"I take it this isn't good news?"

"It depends how you view it, I suppose. Would you prefer to sit down or continue walking?"

"Walking. If I sit down I'll just get more antsy."

"Good choice. I prefer movement myself."

We continued weaving our way around the well-kept garden. My eyes lingered on the ivy and the section of bushes all cut into animal shapes.

"I'd prefer some honesty right now."

"I'm not sure how much of it you're going to be able to handle."

I stopped short in front of him. "Considering everything I've been through, I think I can handle it."

"Ok, then let's start from the top. I don't even fully understand what's happening to you."

Disappointment and relief hit me all at once. "I thought you were supposed to be the expert."

He laughed. "An expert? No. I'm just really old."

I looked at him. "Yeah, real old."

"Looks can be deceiving."

I didn't quite know what he meant. Did Allures age really slowly? Violet hadn't said anything about that. "What can you tell me?"

"I can tell you that the paste you were given likely would have had one of two effects."

"Which are?"

"It could have done nothing but make you irresistible for a few nights."

"Or?" That first option didn't apply to me.

"Or your body would embrace it and accept it for what it was."

"Meaning, what?"

"Meaning exactly what I said. Your body accepted it. You're going through a lot of changes."

"This sounds like a puberty talk."

Louie laughed. "Not quite, but important changes nonetheless."

"What does that mean? What does this have to do with me being less and less affected by the Allures?"

He stopped suddenly. "Explain what you mean by that."

"At first Violet and the guys could influence me a little when they touched me, but that doesn't seem to be working now, although Roland relaxes me still."

"But he's not trying to relax you, so that's different."

"Different? Why does everyone think that's weird?"

"Let's start with the bigger question. Why has their touch stopped affecting you?"

"Ok. Fair enough. Why? Why has it?"

"I don't know."

"How helpful." Louie seemed to have more questions than answers. "But you do know how to stop it?"

He shook his head. "No. And here's where you might want to sit down."

"I'll stay standing."

"You may not be able to stop it. Take some time and let that sink in."

"That's not the kind of thing you can just let sink in." I wanted to be sick. There had to be a way to get rid of it. "Another witch helped. Maybe there's more that she could do."

"In theory, sure, but it's doubtful. If her magic worked, the paste would be losing its effectiveness, not gaining it. All she accomplished was to temporarily dampen the effect and to slow down the process. The one possibility I can think of is finding the first witch. What was her name?"

"Kalisa. She worked at the Midnight Cauldron in New Orleans, but now it's like she never existed."

"If she exists, we'll find her." His eyes darkened. "I'm not confident she can help, but we can try."

"It's possible she can help though. That's something." I said mostly to myself. I refused to believe there was nothing I could do. Everything could be changed. Didn't Violet say that?

"Did Violet tell you anything about how we are born?"

"No." I wrapped my arms around myself. I wasn't sure I really wanted to know.

"First tell me, what are your plans? What brought you in contact with Violet and her companions?"

"I was searching for a guy. A Pteron." There was no reason to bother with the job interview cover now. "He saved me from vampires that wanted me because of that stupid Seduction's Kiss stuff."

"And did you find him?"

I shook my head. "No. Violet said they'd help me find him if I could help them track down Kalisa."

"Do they know where he is?"

"They have a friend that might know."

"You love this Pteron?" Louie held his hand out as if to feel the light breeze moving through the garden.

I shrugged. I wasn't in the mood to make anyone else think I was crazy. "I don't know what it is, but I have to find him. I've been obsessed for years, and I need closure." I repeated Roland's words, even though they didn't come close to covering how I felt about Owen.

"Then you need to go. Find him, and then return here. This talk can wait."

"Wait... that's it? This big important talk was just that?"

"I want you to find Owen first. You'll be able to concentrate better later." He turned and started heading for the gate. "You'll thank me later."

"Will I?"

He glanced at me over his shoulder. "Either that or you'll curse me for it, but I believe you need this opportunity. You deserve it."

Roland straightened up from his spot leaning against the garden wall. "Everything okay?"

Louie nodded. "You need to find Violet and Hugh and go. Find her Pteron, and then bring Daisy back here."

"Are you sure?" He watched us both.

"I'm positive. It's better this way."

Roland nodded. "I'll go get Violet." He ran off.

"I look forward to getting to know you, Daisy."

"Why? Not that you're not a fascinating person and all, but why waste your time with me at all?"

"Because I've never met anyone quite like you."

"Because of the paste? Because of how I was affected?"

"That's part of it." He held out his hand in a semi-wave before walking away.

I thought about calling after him, saying goodbye, but I didn't. What was there to say? He was giving me what I wanted. He was getting me to Owen sooner.

CHAPTER SIXTEEN

OWEN

I had to find the guy who'd been spying on us. No matter how much I wanted to run away from my life in New Orleans, I couldn't turn off my sixth sense, or my instinct to keep paranormal creatures in line. I knew there were plenty of bear shifters living in Colorado, but why did these guys show up right when Hailey did? And why were they spying on me? Something wasn't adding up.

I hurried down the main stretch of town, but quickly headed up to the mountains. If he was a shifter, he was going to feel more comfortable in the wilderness. I hadn't tracked someone in ages. I'd spent most of my time worried about advising the king, and it felt good to use my core instincts again.

I tried to focus on the scents in the air: the poignant evergreens and the slightest hint of a deer. I focused deeper on the smells until I could faintly detect a bear shifter, or as they liked to be called, an Ursus. Given the direction of the wind, he was likely less than a mile away.

Even after I found his trail, I hung back. I didn't want to spook him. Despite how easy it would be for me to keep up, there was no reason to turn it into a chase if I didn't have to. I only needed to find out who he was, and whether his presence had anything to do with me.

He was clearly moving away, and I followed him deeper into the forest, really hoping he didn't turn into a cave. Caves were pretty much the only place he'd have an advantage on me. Pterons and caves don't mix well together.

I shed my t-shirt and released my wings before flying up to the top of a tall tree. I tried to stay hidden behind the evergreen while I looked for him. After a moment I spotted him and took off toward him. I landed near where he was hiding. "You might as well stop trying. I'm going to find you."

He stopped. I couldn't see him, but I could hear him.

"Come out and show yourself." I waited. If he didn't come out in thirty seconds, he was going to make things much worse for himself.

"I'm coming, I'm coming! Don't get bent out of shape."

I watched as a stark naked guy with red hair walked out of the trees. "Can you at least wait for me to find my pants?"

"Yes please." Looking at a bear's junk wasn't exactly high on my list.

I waited carefully. I wanted him dressed, but I also didn't want him slipping off. Lucky for him he made the right decision. He walked out of the woods holding his hands up in front of him.

"Who are you?" I kept my wings out. They added to the intimidation factor.

"I'm Adam."

"And what the hell are you doing here, Adam?"

"My buddies and I are looking to invest in some prime real estate."

"Prime real estate in Coleville? Right."

"Isn't that why you're here?"

"No."

"Then why were you in there talking to that Miller guy? You were talking about buying his property too."

"I was doing that to help a friend." Friend. Was I really going to call Clyde that?

"Then why are you out here? Aren't you supposed to be in New Orleans?"

"So you admit to knowing who I am?"

"Sure. I'd rather avoid going through a Pteron interrogation."

"Did you know I was here?"

"I followed your sister. She's cute you know."

"Should I kill you now or later?"

"I'm only joking."

I glared at him.

"Ok, I'm not actually joking, but I get she's off limits."

"Why did you follow her? And who else are you with?"

"Just two of my clan mates. It was this or spend three months doing community service in Shreveport. It was an easy choice."

"Wait. A choice? Who sent you?"

He smiled. "You really don't know?"

"I do, but I want you to say it."

"The king. He said he had a hunch your sister was heading for you."

"Why would Levi have told you to come here? He knew I was taking time off."

The bear shrugged. "I don't know. I was just doing what I was told."

"Then why all the theatrics with trying to buy from Miller?"

"We heard you were trying to, and we figured there was a reason. The king's advisor wouldn't do it for no reason."

"I'm not buying property here."

"We didn't know that. We heard your friend talking about it. He made it sound like you were in on a deal with him."

Clyde talking about it? No surprise there. The kid didn't know when to shut his mouth. "You can leave now. You found me."

"We have to call the king first."

"Call him. Tell him he's an ass."

"Yeah… I'm not telling the king that."

I laughed dryly. The bear at least had some smarts. "That's fine. I'll do it myself."

"Does that mean I can go now?"

"It means you and your friends are going to leave Coleville right now."

"Why? You don't own this place."

"You were sentenced to community service for a reason. You did something wrong. That kind of trouble isn't something Coleville needs. Besides, I came out here to get away from paranormal crap. You are paranormal crap. Got it?" I stepped toward him to give him the message that I wasn't messing around.

"Got it." He scurried away.

I took off. I was flying home. It would be much faster than walking.

***

As soon as I got home I pulled out my phone and put in the SIM card I'd taken out months before. I immediately called Levi.

He picked up after two rings. "Well hello there, Owen."

"You've got some explaining to do." I may have told Hailey to be polite to Levi, but sometimes even a king needs to be put in his place.

"I'm guessing you found the bears."

"Of course I did."

"I figured that. Why do you think I sent them?"

"You wanted me to call."

"Exactly. Worked like a charm." He laughed, and I could picture the smirk on his face. He was proud of himself.

"What do you want? I thought you were cool with me taking a break."

"I am, or I was until a girl showed up."

"A girl? What the fuck Levi? You're married and a father."

"I'm not talking about that kind of thing, idiot. It's about a girl who's looking for you."

"You sent bears out here because a girl is looking for me?"

"She's not just a regular girl. I can't put my finger on it. Plus, she's hanging around with these people that I can't place. They have to be paranormal, but I don't know what. Oh, and she's been obsessed with you for years."

"Uh, I'm not sure what part of that was the weirdest."

"I kind of remember her, but I can't place her. Her name is Daisy."

"Daisy?" My body froze at the mention of her name. "Where did you see her? What was she doing?" Was it possible after two years she was looking for me?

"I take it you know her?"

"Answer my questions first." I paced the back porch of the cabin. What was going on?

"She was at the hotel. She recognized me and begged me to tell her where you were. She said something about you saving her. Is this the girl from that Halloween? The one you saved from the vamps?"

"Yes." I could barely speak. What was Daisy doing back in New Orleans? My mind flashed to an image of her face. Even after two years I could still remember the taste of her lips, and the way her mouth had eagerly welcomed me in. Then darker thoughts set in. Was she in trouble?

"How did she look? Why was she looking for me?" I couldn't get out the questions fast enough.

"She looked good, I guess. I don't know what to compare it with. She said she wanted to thank you, but she seemed kinda desperate. It turns out she's been chatting with Allie's nerdy step-brother online for years about you."

"Uh, what?" I remembered Andrew from Allie and Levi's wedding. There wasn't much memorable about him, but he didn't seem bad.

"I know, a little bit too much of a coincidence. Allie won't let me interrogate him fully, but he seems as surprised as I was."

"Where is she?" It looked like I was going back to New Orleans sooner than expected. I needed to see her even if it was only for a minute.

"She left town quickly with her friends. She didn't even get her stuff."

"She gave up." I was disappointed. I shouldn't have been, but I was. Selfishly I wanted her to be searching for me. It made the way I felt about her make sense. She wanted to thank me. I wanted to make sure she was okay. That was all it was. It had to be. One conversation with her would give me the closure I needed, and then I could move on.

"Maybe, maybe not. Like I said, I don't know who those people are."

"She could be in danger." That reality had me twisted in knots.

"I don't know what she's into, but something was weird. I questioned everyone I could, and the humans seemed to have thought she was the most beautiful girl they'd ever seen. She's cute and all, but come on."

I remembered the magic on her when we first met. Hadn't that been the affect? Intense attraction? Had Mayanne left some trace amount behind? "Daisy couldn't have been in New Orleans just to find me. Does she live there now?"

"Nope. She was in town for an interview at the New Orleans Times."

"I'm guessing you already talked to someone there?"

"Yes. I'm telling you something weird is going on. Too bad I don't have my advisor to help me."

"You have Toby."

"Shoot me."

"Come on, he's good."

"He's great. He's thorough, works hard, and he's got skill. The problem is he's sleeping with my step-sister, and he used to sleep with my wife."

"Not when she was your wife."

"Obviously. He'd be dead otherwise. But that's not the point."

"Then what is the point?" I could barely think straight. I needed to stay focused.

"I need you back. I get you need space. Take some time, but promise you're going to eventually come back. I don't want to have to find someone else."

"Do you think Daisy's in trouble?"

"Something's going on. What, I can't tell you, but my gut is that she might need help."

"And my gut is you knew if you said that I'd have to agree."

"Look, don't come home today. Let me see what I can find out. I have someone in security running a more thorough background check on her. If there's anything there we'll find it."

"You know I can't just sit tight on this."

"What is this girl to you?"

"Does that really matter?"

"Maybe." He breathed heavily into the phone. "It may help us figure this out. Maybe she really is just a human girl looking for you because she wants to say thank you."

"But you don't believe it."

"No. First she's obsessed, I mean obsessed. I made Andrew turn over his Paranormal Obsessed account for me to search."

"Paranormal Obsessed?"

"Yeah, it's an online forum for people who are obsessed with finding paranormal creatures. It's pretty ridiculous."

"How do you know she's obsessed?" It was more than curiosity asking.

"She's spent time researching winged creatures, guys named Owen, New Orleans college students. It's not all her though. Turns out Andrew's got an obsession of his own."

"With who?"

"You don't want to know."

I groaned. "What is it about Hailey? Does she have to always attract the weirdos?"

"We can say the same thing about you now too."

"Daisy isn't a weirdo. She just wanted to find me." I didn't hesitate before jumping to her defense.

"Maybe she isn't. I knew you'd worry about the security risk with her, but the fact that you're worried about her makes me happy."

"It makes you happy?"

"Yes. You never care about anyone."

"Yes I do."

"Ok, I'll rephrase that. You never care about girls."

"You never did before Allie." He'd been an emotionless player before he met her.

"And that's exactly my point."

"Keep me posted." I needed to know she was okay.

"I will."

"That doesn't mean send more bears after me."

"I won't if you don't go off the grid tomorrow."

"I'm staying put for a few days."

"Good. Talk to you soon." He hung up.

I didn't know what to think. Was Daisy ok? Did she still have magic on her? Why was she looking for me after all these years? I couldn't sort through the questions. There were too many. The only thing that was going to help was seeing her, and I had absolutely no idea how long it would be before that happened.

CHAPTER SEVENTEEN

DAISY

The hours blurred together as we continued our cross-country journey. Roland took his turn driving, and I retained my spot in the back. There were no more games, and even Hugh had stopped trying to bait me. Instead he sat in the front seat staring out the window. For her part, Violet tried to initiate conversation a few times, but even she eventually accepted the uncomfortable silence.

It was with relief that we entered California. I'd never been to the state before, a fact I kept to myself as we traveled. I didn't need to give Hugh any other reasons to make fun of me. I'd done my fair share of traveling along the east coast, but the west coast had always seemed so far away.

Eventually I couldn't take any more of the silence. I had to ask one of the many questions swirling through my head. "Who is this Pteron exactly? The one you're friends with?"

"His name is Cade, and he's the king of California," Violet replied simply.

"Isn't he actually the king of the whole coast?" Hugh added.

"Does it matter?" Roland asked. "The leadership changes all the time."

"I thought it stayed in the same family for years?"

"Years are relative," Roland said mostly to himself.

"Does Cade answer to Levi?"

"Yes and no." Violet slipped her boots back on. She'd had them off for the last leg of the trip.

"Meaning?"

"Meaning everyone knows Levi is the one who's actually in charge."

"Okay." I filed away that piece of information. It was always important to know who was actually running the show. Like with the group I was with. Violet was in charge. I wasn't sure how or why, but the others listened. Roland listened to Hugh too. There must have been some sort of pecking order.

"Cade's a nice guy. Kind of crazy at times."

"Kind of?" Roland interrupted. "Try very."

"Crazier than Louie?" I asked.

Hugh laughed. "You thought Louie was crazy?"

"Maybe not crazy…"

"He's a little intense at first, but he grows on you."

"Is he the leader of the Allures or something?"

"Not the way you're thinking. He just garners a lot of respect."

"There's so much about your world I don't understand."

"We could say the same about you." Hugh tossed a hacky sack and caught it.

"Where'd you get that?"

"The glove compartment."

"You searched through the glove compartment?" I shook my head. Obviously stealing the car was the big part, but rifling through the owner's stuff seemed like even more of an invasion.

"Why not? We took the guy's car and that's what you're worried about?"

"I'm also worried about how you're going to get the car back to him. Plus all the mileage."

"What do you want us to do, Daisy? Ship it back?"

"Yes. No. I don't know. I'm a bad person."

"You're not a bad person." There wasn't much energy in Violet's words.

"Are you guys in a bad mood because you haven't played with people in a few hours?"

"We're not in a bad mood." Violet plastered a smile on her face. "Why would you say that?"

"You're acting grumpy."

"Not any grumpier than you."

"I'm not grumpy. I'm overwhelmed. That's different."

"Overwhelmed?" Roland changed lanes. "What would you have to be overwhelmed about?"

"Nothing. Nothing at all." I rolled my eyes.

"We're going to find Owen."

"We think. We have no clue where he is. We might be driving the opposite way for all we know." My positivity had run out.

"And if he's in Maine we'll fly there. Does that make you feel better?" She rested her hand on the seat between us.

"Will we steal someone's private jet to do that?"

"Did you want to fly commercial?"

"You guys are unbelievable."

"You've made your feelings on the subject crystal clear." Hugh huffed.

"Let's stop to get something to eat." Roland didn't wait for anyone to answer. He moved over to the right lane. "I don't want to show up at Cade's hungry."

"He won't have food?"

"He will, but only the healthy stuff."

"Isn't he a paranormal shifter?"

"Yes."

"And he eats health food?"

"He lives in LA," Violet said like it explained it all.

I laughed. It felt good. "Where are we stopping then?"

"I know of a place around here." He turned off at the next exit.

"You've stopped at a random exit ten miles outside of LA before?" I found that hard to believe, but I probably shouldn't have. What hadn't these guys done?

"This country isn't that big."

"Yes it is. I've never been this far west." I let the truth slip out.

"This is your first time out here?" Violet asked.

"Yup."

"You should have told us! We've passed so many must see tourist attractions!"

"That's fine. Maybe on the way back."

"Where else haven't you been?"

"Shouldn't you ask where have I been?" Might as well admit it.

"Ok, if you prefer that."

"I've been to almost every state on the east coast."

"What about Europe?"

"Nope."

"Mexico?"

"I've been to Canada."

"Oh. That's something, but we're going to have to do something about your lack of travel experience." Violet was all excited again.

"We're doing something about it right now, aren't we?"

"Here we go." Roland pulled into the parking lot of what appeared to be a shack.

"What is this place?" I asked as politely as possible. I'd heard of hidden dives, but this place was going to have to have amazing food to make up for the lack of curb appeal.

"It's a restaurant." Hugh opened his door.

"What kind of restaurant?"

"You'll see." Roland got out and started heading for the door.

"Why does everything have to be such a mystery?"

Violet laughed. "Don't worry, it can't be that bad. They know I'm picky, yet they brought me here."

"So you haven't been here either?" That surprised me and once again left me wondering how long this trio had been together. Hugh had said he'd known Violet for the majority of his life, but when did Roland come into the mix?

"Nope, but I'm always up to try something new."

"Usually I am too." I slowly opened my door and got out.

By the time Violet and I pushed open the worn wooden door of the shack-restaurant, the boys were already seated and talking away with a man who I assumed was the chef.

"Welcome!" The chef rolled up the sleeves of his white coat. "So glad you all stopped in today."

"We're excited to try your food." Violet walked the few steps to the boys' table. There were only half a dozen tables crammed into the small space, so she didn't have to go far.

The chef nodded. "I've been told to stick to vegetarian."

"I can pick if necessary," Violet said politely, "And I think Daisy eats everything."

"Maybe not everything…" I wasn't picky, but I wasn't the most adventurous eater in the world.

"I know just the thing. If you'll excuse me." The chef hurried off.

"Is this place even open?" I asked, glancing around at the otherwise empty room.

"Technically not for another hour, but Reggie doesn't care."

"He doesn't care because he knows you, or because you made him not care?" I asked suspiciously.

"Would I do something like that?" Roland smiled.

"You're despicable."

"Why? Because I played on the excitement he already has? How is that despicable?"

"People are entitled to feel the way they want to. You shouldn't use their feelings to get what you want."

"Everyone manipulates people. We just do it with finesse." Hugh laughed.

"I'm actually not hungry. I'm going to wait in the car." I pushed back my chair and walked outside. I'd lost my appetite the minute I found out the chef was being manipulated. What was the fun in enjoying a meal that was made under duress?

I tried the car, but it was locked. It must have locked automatically. I refused to go back inside, so I took a seat on the curb next to it. What was I even doing? I had no idea whether their friend Cade could find Owen. I should have stayed in New Orleans, or gone home, or even stayed with Louie. At least I could be learning something about what was happening to me.

"Hey, you need some help?"

I glanced up to see a guy around my age standing a few feet away. He was holding the leash of a large chocolate lab.

The guy broke into a huge smile when I looked at him. "Whoa. You're beautiful."

I groaned. "Hi. I'm fine, but thanks."

"What are you doing out here alone? Can I give you a lift somewhere?"

"A lift in what?" I definitely hadn't seen or heard another car pull in.

"My car. It's parked by my apartment over there." He pointed down the road.

"I'm fine. I'm waiting for my friends to finish eating."

"Why aren't you eating with them?" He switched the leash into his left hand.

"I needed some fresh air."

"Same here. Well, and Snickers here. He needed it."

"Snickers? Is that the dog?"

"Yup." The dog tugged on the leash.

"I think Snickers wants to keep walking."

"He can wait." He stared at me.

"You should go."

"Can't you come with me?"

"No. I'm fine where I am."

"Can I get your number?"

"No. Sorry."

"Why not?"

"Please leave me alone." I blinked a few times. I was too stressed out to handle this guy.

"Just give me a chance."

I felt a ball of anger welling inside me, but I didn't want to feel angry. It wasn't this guy's fault he was being so pushy. I tried to relax. I started slow breathing in and out before I was suddenly hit with a thought. "You're lonely. Don't you have a girlfriend or something?"

"We broke up last week."

"Go to her and tell her you want to make up. She's the one you really want."

He nodded. "That's exactly what I'm going to do." He turned and walked away. I felt a wave of euphoria like I'd never felt. It was more of a physical sensation that reverberated through my whole body.

I was ripped from the high by clapping coming from behind me. "You're a natural."

I turned to face Roland. "What are you talking about?"

"You're a natural. You did that on the first try."

"I didn't do anything."

"Are you sure?"

"Yes." I thought over the conversation. I'd been as polite as possible.

"You mean that guy didn't go from being ready to jump all over you to trying to make up with his ex-girlfriend?"

"He realized what I was saying was rational. He was lonely."

"Does that usually work? Do men hooked on you usually just crawl back to their exes?"

"No. But this one was different."

"You manipulated him. You used the loneliness he felt and twisted it. I also think you played with his horniness a little. I bet he's going to try to get himself some make-up sex."

"No." I shook my head. "I didn't do anything."

"It's nothing to be embarrassed of. You did nothing wrong. We all wondered if you had that ability too."

"I can't manipulate people. I'm not like you. " I could feel the anger returning.

"Then explain what just happened. People don't do things like that on their own. They don't suddenly do what you want them to."

Fear, anger, and regret circled me. "I screwed with an innocent person?"

"You don't know that you screwed him. Maybe you helped him. Maybe his ex was the one, and now they'll get married and have their perfect little family." Roland sneered.

"Do you have something against that? About happy little families?"

"No." He shook his head. "I'm going to go finish eating. You coming?"

"I already told you I wasn't eating."

"Even now? Even when you did the same thing?"

"You just told me it wasn't the same thing. You told me I helped him."

"You may have. On the flip side, maybe she was abusive. Maybe you just sent him back to hell."

"Ugh, why are you doing this to me?"

He put his hands on my hips, in a gesture that might have been intimate but wasn't. "Because you're going to have to stop worrying about it. No matter which way it goes, it happened. It's over. You had your fun. Don't you feel good?"

"No." I shook my head, but I remembered the euphoria. It had felt good. But maybe that was because I was excited he'd left me alone. That was it. I'd never do something like that to someone who wasn't coming on to me. Right? And it was only one time. I'd find a way to stop the effects of the magic.

CHAPTER EIGHTEEN

DAISY

"You really should have had some lunch." Hugh said without turning around from his spot in the driver's seat. He'd taken over the wheel again.

"I'm fine." All I could focus on was how close we were to getting to LA. Even though I knew it was doubtful that Owen was with their friend, I was still hopeful he'd help lead us in the right direction.

"Your stomach is growling. You're hungry."

"I'm fine," I repeated. I didn't need anyone paying more attention to me. I just wanted to get there.

Roland leaned over closer. "It makes you hungry. Eventually you'll get so used to it that it won't affect you like that, but at first it's going to leave you famished. It's pretty much the only time you really want or need food."

"I don't know what you're talking about." Denial seemed like the best option. If I didn't think about it, it would never happen again.

"Roland told us everything. You need to accept it," Violet said carefully. "It's bound to keep happening. Just like with the attraction. It's going to get stronger."

"Accept it? She needs to embrace it." Hugh turned to look at me. He needed to keep his eyes on the road.

"She will when she does it a few more times." Roland stole a glance at me before turning away.

"Are we almost to your friend's house?" I was focusing on Owen again. I needed to keep my thoughts off the guy with the dog. What if Roland was right and I'd sent him back to a bad relationship? I couldn't take the chance of letting that happen again. I needed to be more careful.

"We're getting close." Hugh slowed down as we hit traffic. "Or we were."

"Oh, city life." I sighed.

"Have you lived in one?" Violet asked.

"I went to college right outside of Atlanta, so I understand traffic a bit."

"Yeah, I've heard the traffic is bad there." Violet seemed intent on keeping the conversation moving.

"We're flying back to Louie's after this." Hugh rolled down his window. "I'm not doing this drive again."

"That's fine," Violet said simply. "As long as we stay together."

"Do you guys always stay together?" I asked. "I mean how come Roland and Hugh had been to that restaurant but you hadn't?"

"Sometimes we need breaks." Violet popped a piece of gum in her mouth. "Want a piece?"

I shook my head. "No thanks." They weren't the only ones who needed a break. I needed a break. I needed a break from all of the insanity in my life. Not only were the things around me going crazy, but things inside me were going crazy too. How had I not even realized what I was doing?

"Let's hope Cade can help us track down Owen. We don't have much time."

"Do you guys have some place you need to be?" I thought I was the only one in a rush.

"Not exactly." Hugh tapped the wheel.

"This whole random cryptic messages thing is getting old."

"I figured you'd like some stability in your life. You know, keep something the same."

"I'd prefer to know what in the world you guys were alluding to."

"Looks like traffic is opening up. We'll be there in no time." Violet snapped back into happy mode.

"Great."

"Don't you want to find Owen?" Roland crossed his arms. "Because if you don't, we could have probably have found an easier way to track down the witch."

"Of course I want to find him!"

"Then stop complaining."

I groaned. "This Cade guy better be able to help."

"Or what? Is there a threat in those words?" Hugh chuckled.

"There would be if I thought I was capable of harming you in any way." I rolled my eyes. Hurting anyone else definitely wasn't on my to-do list.

"There are ways. I'll teach you." Violet sounded serious, but I couldn't tell. All three of them were hard to read.

Violet was right about the traffic opening up. Maybe she had a sense about it like she did about the rain. I tapped my foot impatiently as we wound our way through neighborhoods lined with beautiful mansions and palm trees. I felt like I was on a celebrity bus tour. Finally, Hugh stopped in front of a gate. Another gate. What was with these paranormal creatures and their gates?

Hugh pressed the buzzer. A booming voice spoke. "State your business with the king."

Hugh leaned his head out of the window to talk. "We like Cade and he likes us."

"Speak in normal terms please."

"Tell Cade his favorite trio is here."

"One moment."

We waited until finally the gates opened. "He calls you his favorite trio?"

"No, but I knew he'd understand."

"We're not a trio anymore though," Violet said excitedly. "We're a quartet."

"I'm glad you didn't say foursome."

"Such coarse humor, Daisy."

I shrugged. "Just being honest."

Hugh drove us up the circular brick drive toward the sprawling mansion. He parked behind a red Jeep, and even though no one moved to get out, I did. I was tired of waiting for everyone else to do things first.

"You weren't who I was expecting." A guy maybe a few years older than me walked right over to where I waited. He was wearing a button down linen shirt with a few buttons open at the top and a pair of khaki pants. He was barefoot.

"Neither are you. I guess it's time I stop expecting kings to look a certain way." Something was seriously wrong with me. I was incapable of keeping my thoughts to myself.

He laughed. "I assume you're referring to Levi then? He's had the pleasure of meeting you too?"

"I don't know if he'd call it a pleasure."

"Well, I will." He took my hand and kissed it.

I resisted the urge to roll my eyes. Speaking my mind or not, I didn't need to anger the guy who was supposed to help me.

"I take it you know I'm Cade. May I ask what your name is?"

"Daisy." I gently pulled my hand back.

"Daisy. Another flower."

Finally, the others got out of the car. I assumed they'd stayed inside to talk about me. Surprisingly it didn't bother me as much as I would have thought.

"Hello, Cade." Violet smiled, but she didn't walk over to him. Evidently she wasn't as friendly with him as she was with Louie. Maybe they preferred to keep to their own.

"Always a pleasure to see you." He didn't hold back. He walked over and hugged her.

She laughed. "And I see you met our new friend."

"I did. I didn't know you guys spent time with humans." He watched Violet carefully.

"She's got something special to her."

He turned his attention to me. "I see."

Cade shook hands with Roland and then Hugh. "To what honor do I owe this visit?"

"You're looking right at her." Violet nodded in the direction where I stood.

Cade looked me over again. I tried to hide just how uncomfortable he was making me. He needed to turn away. "Is there something I can do for you, Daisy?"

We were still standing on the circular drive. I was slightly surprised he hadn't invited us in.

"I've been told you might be able to help me find someone." I forced myself to look him in the eye.

"Have you, now? Well, that depends on who you're looking for and why." His tone was serious. His flirtatious mannerisms disappeared.

"I'm looking for a Pteron named Owen, and I'm doing it because I need to say thank you."

"And because she needs closure," Roland quickly added.

"Owen Kaye?"

"Blond hair from New Orleans Owen. I don't know his last name."

"Aren't you in the wrong place?"

"I don't know why I'm here. Violet seemed to think you could help."

"I see." He looked over them suspiciously. "You thought I could help you find Owen even though you were just with Levi?"

"Levi claims he's off the grid. She needs to find him," Violet argued on my behalf. "I'm afraid we might be running out of time."

"You're Allures. You have all the time in the world." He crossed his arms.

"But Daisy doesn't…" Violet said quietly. "Do I really need to say more?"

"Oh." Cade glanced back at his house. "Although I don't believe in coincidences, I may be able to help you. Or let me rephrase this, a visitor of mine might be able to help."

"Who? The owner of the Jeep?" Violet asked. She pointed the red vehicle. "We didn't mean to interrupt your company."

"It's not that kind of company."

"Cade?" a girl with long red hair walked down the front steps. "Who are they?"

"That one's looking for your brother." He pointed at me.

Brother? Wait. Was this Hailey? The one Andrew was obsessed with?

"My brother?" She quickly took the stairs and walked over. "What do you want with my brother?"

I took a moment to compose myself. What was going on? Why was she here? "I want to thank him."

"Thank him for…"

"Saving her life," Cade filled in.

"When and how did my brother save your life?" She crossed her arms.

"In New Orleans a few years ago. I was nearly drained by vampires."

"Oh my god." She grinned. "You're Halloween girl."

"Halloween girl?"

"Yeah. I heard Owen talking to Levi about it when it happened."

"Glad to know I was important enough to repeat." I tried to play it off, but my heart was about to beat out of my chest. Owen had talked about me!

"But why now? Why are you suddenly looking for him?" She stepped closer. "And why are you with these people? What are they?"

Cade put a hand on Hailey's arm. "They're Allures."

"Allures?" Hailey asked with confusion. "I thought they all left."

Hugh laughed. "Really? You thought we all packed our bags and left your world?"

"Yes…" Hailey's face didn't falter. If she was intimidated by Hugh she didn't show it.

"We've been here. We just don't need to check in with The Society much." Violet smiled in a way that once again let me know she was hiding something.

"And you knew about this, Cade?" Hailey turned to him.

"Yes. I met these three a few years back."

Hailey turned back to Violet. "And what are you doing with a human? You aren't planning to hurt her, are you?"

"Of course not!" Violet put a hand to her chest. "We're trying to help her."

"Help her?"

"She's desperate to find your brother. We're trying to help." Violet sighed. "Why is that so hard to believe?"

"What's in it for you?" Hailey asked suspiciously. "No one helps someone to this extent if they're not getting something out of it."

"She's going to help us track down a witch we need to speak with," Roland jumped in.

"Meaning?" Hailey put a hand on her hip.

"Meaning if something seems off with Daisy, it is. She was given a magic paste that contains our essence."

"Wait? What?" Cade stumbled back. "Is that why she has a strange aura?"

"Off?" I asked. "What do you mean?"

"I sensed it too, but she's human." Hailey moved her hair all over to one shoulder.

"None of that matters now though. We need to help her find Owen."

"Why? This still seems extreme." Cade shifted his weight from foot to foot.

"She's in love with him," Violet said softly.

"In love with him?" Cade and Hailey said at the same time.

"Why is that so hard for you to understand?" Violet asked. "Don't young people still fall in love these days?"

"I never said I loved him." Was it possible to love someone after meeting them once—kissing them once?

"You do." Violet kept her eyes on Hailey. "Don't waste your breath denying it."

"Does he know that?" Hailey asked.

"I haven't talked to him since that night."

"You're still into him, and you haven't talked to him in what, three years?" Hailey asked incredulously.

"Two years and almost seven months."

"Not that she's counting." Hugh laughed.

"Do you think we can trust them?" Hailey asked Cade. "You think they're telling the truth?"

"Do you know where he is?" I stepped toward Hailey. "Could you help me find him?"

"I don't know."

"You don't know where he is, or you don't know if you want to help?" I wasn't going to beat around the bush. Not when I was this close.

"I don't know if I should. He's my brother. I don't want to see him getting hurt."

"He's going to get hurt." Violet said it simply. "But that's beside the point."

I glared at her. I thought she was on my side.

"I'm not going to hurt him! How could I hurt him? I just want to see him again."

"Why?" Hailey turned to me. "Give me a reason other than wanting to thank him because if that's really it, I'll send him the message for you."

"I need to know if he feels the same way I do."

"Tell her about the kiss, Daisy," Violet urged me.

"The kiss? You guys kissed?" Hailey's breath hitched.

"Yes. I've never felt anything like it. It was like time paused and he seeped under my skin. It's crazy, but that one kiss changed me." I didn't care how pathetic I sounded anymore. Nothing felt more important than finding him. I needed to find him.

Hailey nodded. "I'll take you."

"You'll take me?"

"If Cade doesn't mind lending us his plane it will take no time at all."

"I won't give you my plane to borrow, but you can use it if I come with you. I don't mind tagging along to witness this reunion. Should be interesting." Cade winked.

"If Hailey wasn't here, would you have been able to find Owen?" Things were working out too easily. I almost didn't trust it.

"Probably if you gave me enough time. I can usually find people even if they don't want to be found."

"How soon can we go?" Now that I knew we were close to finding him I could hardly wait.

"Anytime, do you want to stay and eat first?"

I shook my head. "No. I want to go."

"Fine. Let's do this."

CHAPTER NINETEEN

DAISY

I shifted nervously in my seat as Cade's private jet carried us to Owen. After years of searching, I was finally going to see him again, and now I didn't know how to feel. What if he pretended not to know me? Or worse, what if he knew me but didn't care? What if the feelings were all one sided, and he just stared at me like the first time we met and asked me what I wanted? I'd been rejected plenty of times before, but could I handle Owen's rejection? Maybe it would be a good thing. As Roland liked to remind me, I was doing this for closure.

"So you really like my brother, huh?" Hailey sat in a seat across from me. She'd been watching me for a while, but I'd tried to ignore her stare. I was too nervous and overwhelmed to worry about what his sister thought of me.

I couldn't ignore her question though. "Yes." Now wasn't the time to waver. I knew what my feelings were, as strange as they were after such a long passage of time. "He made quite an impression."

"He could use a girlfriend, but preferably one that doesn't come with so much baggage."

"Yeah, well." What was I supposed to say? It wasn't my fault that I couldn't get rid of the magic.

"What are you planning to do when you see him?"

"Say hello."

"Really? That's it?" She arched an eyebrow.

"I don't know. I've been so busy figuring out how I was going to see him. I wasn't worried about what I'd do when I did." Although there were many things I wanted to do. Most involved his lips and mine.

"She's going to slap him and then kiss him." Hugh slumped down in the seat next to me. He'd been sitting on the other side of the plane, but evidently he'd been listening in to the conversation. "We've discussed this before."

"If by discuss you mean that you told me that's what I'd do, then sure."

Hailey laughed. "Owen's going to totally freak out when we get there."

"Freak out?" My stomach dropped. Was it going to be worse than I thought? "Why?"

"Because he went out to Colorado to be alone. He didn't like me visiting, but I was one person. We're a whole group, and he doesn't know your friends."

"If I could go alone, I would." I wasn't exactly thrilled about having a whole group of people with me either.

"But you can't." Hugh stretched out his legs. "You're stuck with us."

"For now," I mumbled.

"You're not getting rid of us that easily."

"Do we have to do this right now?"

"What's wrong with now?" He crossed one leg over the other. "We're stuck on this plane doing nothing."

"She's nervous." Hailey smiled. "Can't you tell?"

"What is there to be nervous about?" Hugh asked.

"Are you kidding?" Hailey sat forward in her seat. "She hasn't seen him in years. Who knows what's going to happen?"

"Thanks for reminding me."

"I'm just saying it like it is."

"Thanks then. That's always nice."

"Ok, I'll say it like it is." Hugh dug into his pocket and pulled something out. "You might need this."

"What?" I gasped at the condom in his hand. "Are you kidding me?"

"Ugh. You're talking about my brother." Hailey stood up. "Owen was right. I shouldn't worry about his sex life." She walked off.

Hugh laughed. "That bought us some alone time."

"Would you put that away?"

"Take it. You might need it."

"I'm not worried about sex." I bounced my knee. I couldn't sit still when we were getting so close to Owen.

Hugh pushed the condom into my hand. "Trust me on this."

"Fine." I stuffed it into my pocket so I wouldn't have to look at it again.

"Do I need to get Roland over here?"

"Why?"

"To relax you."

"Why does he do that, and why does it seem so weird to you?" I forced my knee to stay still by sheer will power. I needed to calm down on my own.

"I have no idea why, but it's significant if you understand how Allures are born."

"But I don't understand it. Louie was about to tell me, but he stopped."

"And I'm stopping too. No reason to worry about it right now." He hooked his arm over the back of the seat next to him. At least someone was comfortable.

"Try to relax. We'll be there soon."

"But now you've got me even more curious about how Allures are made!"

"Exactly. If you're thinking about that, you can't worry about Owen." He smiled.

"I think you might be on to something."

He laughed. "Don't act like it's the first time."

I leaned my head back and looked out the window. I had no idea what was going to happen, but at least I was getting my chance. After two and a half years, the wait was down to one hour. Who knew the last hour would feel like the longest?

CHAPTER TWENTY

OWEN

I sat up with a start. I'd been having another one of my endlessly recurring nightmares about Daisy. I wasn't going to sit and wait around much longer. I heard faint voices and jumped out of bed. Someone was outside. Had Levi come out to see me already? All annoyance disappeared when I realized he could have news about Daisy.

I walked to the front door and listened. I heard a number of voices, but none of them was Levi's. There was one voice I definitely recognized though. I'd know Hailey's voice from a mile away.

I was going to kill her. Kill her. I ask Hailey to keep my location a secret, and she shows up with a whole crowd of people? She was lucky she was my sister.

As soon as I heard her reach the front steps, I wrenched open the door and stepped out on the porch rather than inviting her in. "What are you doing here so soon, and who are those people?" Even with my night vision I couldn't make out any faces since no one was looking at me, but there was definitely a group of people standing down at the bottom of my gravel drive.

Hailey glanced down at the gathering before holding up a hand to silence me. "Before you get upset, I need you to do me a favor."

"Why would I do you a favor when you're the one who has explaining to do?" Sometimes Hailey was impossible to understand.

"Do you remember the girl you saved a few years ago? The one who was nearly drained by vamps?"

"Wait. What?" I tried to process what she was saying. "You've talked to Daisy too?"

"Uh, when you say 'too,' I assume you know she's been asking about you everywhere?"

"Yes. I talked to Levi." I smiled despite my annoyance. I liked knowing she was asking about me.

"What?" She got up in my face. "When? What about all this secretive, 'he can't know where I am' talk?"

"Thanks to you I had to talk to him." I shifted my weight. I was wearing only a pair of boxer shorts, so I hoped her friends didn't plan to stay around and chat.

"What did I do?"

"You led some bears out here. Levi had them tail you to get me to call him."

She put a hand on her hip. "How did I drive that far without noticing I was being followed? That's not like me at all."

I shrugged. "Maybe you were distracted."

"I'll worry about that later. Right now I need you to tell me what you know. What did Levi tell you about Daisy?"

"Why? Why does that matter?"

"I need to know what I'm working with here."

I peered out into the dark, trying to see the faces of the two girls in the group. "Is she here?" I didn't wait for an answer. I pushed past Hailey, not caring that it was the middle of the night and I was in only my boxers.

And that's when I saw her. She watched me approach with a mix of fear and excitement on her face I was positive matched the expression on mine. My chest tightened, and my entire body ached to touch her.

"Hi." She waved.

"Hi." I smiled. I didn't know what else to do. I didn't know how to feel.

"Uh, why don't we save the introductions for later?" A tall girl with black hair reminded me that Daisy and I weren't alone. I looked around. There were two guys I didn't know and Cade. The girl and guys had something strange about them. They obviously weren't human, but I couldn't pin point what they were.

I turned to Cade. "How you're messed up in all this I don't want to know."

"You do want to know, but Violet is right. As much as I'd love to stay and watch this awkward fest, we should probably give you two some space."

"You're leaving?" Daisy asked the girl nervously. "Where will you go?"

"We'll find some place close to hang out. Don't worry, we'll be back." She blew Daisy a kiss before turning around.

Hailey gave Daisy a stern look. "Don't hurt my brother."

"I'm not going to hurt him," she spoke softly.

"And we can all say the same to you." One of the two guys wagged a finger at me. Who was he to her? Why was he protective? I felt my own protective side rising up in response.

"He's not going to hurt me." Daisy spoke with such conviction. At least she was sure about that.

Once everyone else disappeared into the night, I could focus on Daisy. I stared at her face, glad she looked exactly like my memories. Absolutely beautiful. Two years was such a long, yet short, period of time depending on how you looked at it.

"You look good." Her eyes ran up and down my body. I didn't mind. I wanted to do exactly the same thing, but she was wearing a whole lot more clothing than I was.

"You can see me in this little light?" I hadn't questioned it at first, but the only light was coming from inside my cabin.

"Wait. Weird." She looked at her hands as though they'd provide answers. "I guess my night vision is getting better."

"Really?" I thought about what Levi said, about her seeming a little different.

"Maybe I'll get something good from all this craziness."

"Are you all right?"

She nodded. "Yes. Things have just been strange. That's all."

"Do you want to come inside?" It was the only logical thing I could come up with to say.

"Sure." She ran her teeth over her bottom lip. I couldn't pull my eyes away from them. "Did you mean now?" Her question brought me back to reality.

"Yeah. If that's okay with you." What, was I fifteen? I blamed my inability to speak normally on the strangeness of the situation.

"It's okay." She ran her hand up and down her arm. Either she was cold or extremely nervous. Maybe both. I could take care of the cold part easily by getting her inside.

"Good." I turned and headed for the house. She followed silently.

I held open the door for her to walk into the small cabin. She walked in, and I followed closing the door behind me.

She glanced around. "Nice place."

"It suits my needs."

"Yeah…" She stood just inside the doorway.

"Uh, I should probably get dressed. Feel free to take a seat or something."

"You don't have to get dressed." Her face turned red.

The blush was cute, but the words were cuter. "I think it might make you more comfortable." I hurried into my room and jumped into some jeans. I grabbed a t-shirt, and pulled it on as I walked.

She was still standing in the same place I'd left her.

"You don't have to stand there all night."

"I know… I just. This is weird, right? I shouldn't have come."

"It's weird, but you should have come. Or, well, I'm glad you did." Could I get anymore awkward? My friends would be laughing in my face if they could hear me, but luckily they couldn't.

"Are you?" She looked up at me nervously.

"Yes. I'm surprised you went through all the effort, but I'm glad you did."

"Yeah. Same here." She stuffed her hands in the pockets of her jeans.

We stood awkwardly for another moment before I had to break the silence. "It's been a while."

"Two and a half years."

"I thought about you the past few Halloweens."

"I thought about you more than that. It's actually pretty humiliating now that I'm standing in the same room with you. I don't know what I was thinking." She looked away.

"I lied."

"About?"

I walked toward her. I had to wipe that regret off her face. "I thought about you a lot more than just Halloween."

"Yeah?"

"Yeah." I stopped right in front of her. "You were very memorable."

"So were you." She licked her lips. Again with the lips.

"I probably should ask you a million questions right now, but would it be okay if we put those off and did something else?"

"I guess that depends on what else you want to do?" Her eyes widened slightly.

"I want to kiss you."

"I'm okay with that." Her eyes seemed to sparkle.

"Yeah?"

"Yeah."

I didn't wait for her to change her mind. I brushed my lips against hers gently. I was going to keep it short, but I had to know if I was glorifying the last kiss.

She moved her lips against mine, and any thoughts of keeping it short disappeared. I wrapped my arms around her as I deepened the kiss, greedily pushing for access beyond those irresistible lips of hers. She opened up, welcoming me in with the same intoxicating taste as she had the last time.

She moaned, encouraging me to continue the kiss. I didn't need the encouragement. I lifted her up and carried her over to the couch. I sat down, settling her on my lap. I needed her close, closer than standing would allow.

Her fingers tangled in my hair as she let me explore her mouth. My hands ached to explore more, but I didn't want to rush it. I'd waited over two years to taste her lips again, and I was going to enjoy every second of it.

I lost all sense of time before we eventually broke the kiss.

Neither of us said anything for a few moments. We stared into each other's eyes breathlessly.

"You can really kiss." She remained on my lap.

I rested my hands on her hips. "I could say the same thing about you."

"I guess I didn't exaggerate how good that kiss was last time."

"It might have even been better this time." I ran a hand through her long brown hair.

"You think?"

"Maybe we should try it again to make sure."

"That sounds like a very good idea."

My lips met hers again, and this time I knew I couldn't keep my hands to myself. I slipped my hand just underneath the bottom of her t-shirt, needing to feel her skin. She was warm and soft, and everything I wanted. Everything I needed. She slipped her hand under my t-shirt, spreading out her fingers as she ran them up and down my chest. Her touch felt amazing and combined with the kiss, I could hardly contain myself.

I lifted her off my lap and laid her down on the couch, doing my best to keep our lips connected, but there was a moment's separation. She moaned in protest at the brief interruption, but I quickly returned, holding most of my weight on my hands while hovering just above her.

"I want you closer." This time she broke the kiss as she pulled me down on top of her.

She ran her hands under my t-shirt and up my back, stopping when her fingers found the small slits that served as the only evidence that I had wings.

She broke the kiss. I stilled. Did she remember? Was she going to push me away?

"Can I see them again?"

"My wings?" I'd barely caught my breath, and the relief that she wasn't running had my heart beating a mile a minute.

"Yes. Can I?"

"Sure." In a mild state of shock, I pulled off my t-shirt. I carefully transformed, forcing my mind to stay human while my wings spread out behind me.

"Beautiful…." She slowly ran her fingers over the feathers. I wasn't used to someone touching them, and my body both tensed up and felt like it was on fire—in the best sort of way.

"You really think that?"

"Of course." She moved on to the other wing, carefully running her hands up and down the area she could reach.

"Why?" Maybe I was putting too much pressure on her, but I needed to understand. Why did she like something that other people ran from?

"Because they are beautiful. Each feather looks and feels so delicate, but together they make up such large, strong wings. The black color is beautiful." She continued to run her hands along them.

"Not as beautiful as you."

She smiled. "You really aren't affected by the Seduction's Kiss? Those feelings are yours?"

"What do you mean? Are you talking about the magic that Mayanne got rid of?"

"The magic she *tried* to get rid of…"

"Wait…" My hunch was right. "Is it still there? Is that why you have night vision now?"

"I don't know what's happening to me." She closed her eyes.

"Is it making you sick at all?"

"No. It's changing me somehow. First the crazy attraction stuff, and now the night vision and the manipulation."

"Wait. Manipulation?"

She opened her eyes. "It only happened once, but it happened. I think."

"What happened?"

"Supposedly there was Allure essence in the paste, and my body didn't reject it."

"Allure essence? That's impossible. They've been gone for centuries." I retracted my wings.

"Tell that to the three Allures I've been traveling with the past few days."

"Those people? They're Allures?" I sat up more.

"Yeah, and now that stupid paste seems to be having more of an effect. Do you think that witch, Mayanne, could help me again? The Allures don't seem to think it could work, but I have to try."

"We can talk to her, but first tell me. You said you manipulated someone. What did you do exactly?"

"I feel horrible about it. Horrible. How I could possibly violate someone in that way?" A stray tear slid down her beautiful face, and it nearly undid me.

"Don't cry. I'm sure it wasn't that bad." I didn't know much about the nearly mythical creatures who were said to be descendants from the gods, but I knew they were powerful and capable of crazy things, but not Daisy. There was such a sweetness to her that I knew she couldn't be corrupted by magic.

She rested her head against my chest. "I manipulated someone. I played with his feelings and made him do something he didn't want to do."

"Did you mean to?"

"No." She gripped my shirt with her hand. "I hadn't realized I'd actually done it until Roland told me."

"Roland? It that one of those guys?"

"Yeah." She closed her eyes again. She was exhausted.

"I need the whole story. I need all the details, but I'm not so sure you're up to that right now."

"Can I stay with you a little bit longer? I need that."

"Do you really think I'm going to kick you out?"

She shrugged. "I don't know what to think anymore."

"I don't know what to think either, but I know two things."

She looked up at me through tear soaked eyelashes. "What things?"

"That there's something between us, and you need help. Those two things combined mean that I'm going to try to keep you close."

"Close is good." She yawned.

"Do you want me to see if your friends are around? Or do you want to go to sleep for a few hours first?"

"That depends."

"On?"

"Whether you're going to stay with me."

"I told you that I was going to try to keep you close." I brushed some stray hair away from her face.

"That doesn't mean you weren't going to go try to find out more without me."

"You are exhausted. You can sleep here, or you can feel free to use my bed." *Say my bed.* The thought of her lying in my sheets had my whole body excited.

"Will you rest with me in your room?" She gazed up at me with puppy dog eyes.

"Do you want me to?"

She nodded.

"Okay." How could I say no to this girl who'd traveled days to find me? And who was I kidding? I wanted to be with her as much as she wanted to be with me. She filled a hole in me that no one had filled for a long time. After years of dreaming about her, she was finally here.

I took her hand and led her into the one bedroom in the small cabin.

"Is there a bathroom I could use first?"

"Of course." I pointed to the bathroom right outside my room.

"Be right out."

I waited impatiently for her. Now that the thought of having her in my bed had crossed my mind, I wanted it. I didn't want her to suddenly change her mind.

The door to the bathroom opened. "Thanks."

"You're welcome..." Was I supposed to say you're welcome? It's not like she needed to thank me for letting her use my bathroom.

She walked into my room, but paused in front of my bed. "I don't want to get your sheets dirty wearing my jeans."

"I don't care, but do you want to borrow a t-shirt to sleep in?" I eagerly anticipated a yes. The thought of her wearing only one of my shirts had me so aroused my jeans were becoming my worst enemy.

"That would be great."

I pulled out a white t-shirt from the small wooden dresser and handed it to her. "Hope this works."

"It's perfect." She glanced around the room.

"Want me to leave so you can change?" I didn't want to go anywhere. I was struggling to hold myself together as it was.

"No. That's okay." She turned her back to me. I turned away, despite my desire to get a glimpse of her bare back. I couldn't be a perv. She deserved better than that.

"You can turn around now," she said a moment later.

My eyes went immediately to her bare legs. "Wow. You look good in that."

She laughed nervously. "Thanks." She pulled back the blanket and sheets and slipped in. "Aren't you going to get changed?"

"Oh. I didn't know how you felt about that."

"I've already seen you in boxers."

"True." I quickly stripped down to my boxers and got in the bed beside her. I turned off the light before she noticed the crystal clear evidence of exactly how turned on she was making me. What was I doing? I barely knew the girl. That wasn't true, and I knew it. Years of yearning had to count for something, especially if it was reciprocated.

"I've dreamed about you a lot." She ran her fingers down my arm.

"I've dreamed about you too." I rested my hand on her hip.

"Good dreams?" There was nervousness in her voice.

"Very good dreams." I didn't need to tell her about the nightmares. I didn't want to scare her off.

"You're real." She rolled toward me. Her face was inches from mine.

"I am real."

"Everyone tried to convince me I made you up. Even Reyna. You guys really cleared her mind."

"I'm sorry. I know that must have been terrible for you. I'd hate it if people didn't believe me."

"I knew it was real. That you were real."

"I'm glad." I ran my hands through her hair. I hadn't realized how much I'd missed her until she was next to me.

"Well, I did doubt it when I got to New Orleans and discovered that everyone and everything from my last visit was gone."

"Even me."

"Even you."

"How'd you track me down?" In the end it didn't matter. She'd made it here, but the fact that I'd gone from completely off the grid to easily accessible in a few days' time was a bit surprising.

"It's a really long story, but the big part was that Violet assumed Cade would know."

"Because Cade knew Allures…"

"Evidently."

"And Hailey was there?"

"Yup. Pretty convenient."

"It is." I smiled.

"Are you completely weirded out?"

"About what?"

"About me showing up… about having an Allure essence in me?"

"I was part of that kiss, so that should give you the answer to the part about you showing up. As to the Allure stuff, I have wings. Do you think the fact that you have some paranormal traits bothers me?"

"Do you think there's a chance to make it go away?" She sat up on one elbow.

"There's always a chance."

"Do you know someone who might be able to help? Besides Mayanne?"

"Yes." I smiled, knowing exactly who I'd ask. "But she's back in New Orleans."

Daisy laid her head back down. "I'm supposed to go back and see this quasi-Allure leader in Arizona after this."

"You don't have to do anything you don't want to do."

"I want to believe that, but I also need to figure out what's happening with me."

"Can you tell me about it?"

"Could it wait?"

"Sure. Whenever you're ready."

"It's just that I've been waiting more than two years to see you again."

Hearing her say that would never get old. "I know the feeling."

"Do you?" She moved closer. "Do you know how hard it's been? How no other man could even come close? You ruined me with that kiss."

"I can do one better."

"Yeah?" she asked breathlessly.

"I lost interest in kissing anyone else once I kissed you." I hoped she took my words as a compliment not as an admission of my lameness.

"At least you still have interest in kissing me."

"Lots of interest." My eyes fixed on her lips again. I needed another taste.

"Then do it again."

I let out a deep breath. "As much as I want to, we both know that things might go a lot farther than a kiss this time."

"You mean the fact that we already want to rip each other's clothes off might be accentuated by the fact that we're half naked in your bed?" She put a hand over her mouth. "And I did it again. I just said exactly what was on my mind."

"If it helps, it's exactly what was on my mind."

"That definitely helps."

"You ready for that kiss?"

"I'm always ready for your kisses."

"You might not be saying that in a few days."

"A few days?" She ran her hand down my chest. "You think I'm staying around that long?"

"I figure that after waiting two and a half years to see me, I'd have to really be a letdown to make you leave any sooner."

"You're not going to be a letdown."

"I guess there's only one way to find out."

"And what way would that be?" She ran her teeth over her bottom lip again.

"This way." I crushed my lips against hers, not bothering to take the kiss slow this time.

I took advantage of her momentary surprise to slip into her mouth, hungrily devouring every inch I could get. She moaned softly, as her hands raked up and down my back. I slipped my hand underneath the t-shirt, exploring the soft skin of her stomach.

"Wait." She broke the kiss, and I tried to cool myself off. Before I could get close she pulled off her t-shirt and tossed it on the edge of the bed. My eyes took in the site of her in just a bra and panties.

It was her turn to surprise me as she picked up the kiss exactly where we'd left off.

CHAPTER TWENTY-ONE

DAISY

My body pulsated with a hunger so strong I could barely control myself. Lucky for me, Owen definitely didn't mind. His hands immediately took advantage of the skin I'd exposed.

I was usually self-conscious the first time I let a man touch me, but it was different with Owen. It was both exciting and natural.

His hands explored my body as the kiss grew more and more fevered until I needed to come up for a breath.

Owen only gave me a few seconds before returning to my mouth. He cupped my breast through my bra, and I needed to get the fabric out of the way. He must have had the same thought, because he had my bra unclasped and tossed aside in seconds. He broke the kiss again and gazed at me with hungry eyes.

"God, you're so beautiful." His mouth descended on my other breast, and I closed my eyes. I moaned as his teeth grazed my nipple.

I needed more of him. I needed all of him. I slipped my hand into his boxers, eagerly taking him in my hand. He groaned as I stroked him gently. "You're killing me, Daisy."

"How do you think I feel?"

"I haven't even started," He grinned wickedly before slipping his hand between my legs. I resisted at first, nervous about letting him in, but his gentle coaxing had me opening up to him. He returned his mouth to my breast as his fingers gave me a pleasure I'd never felt before.

"Owen," I moaned.

"We have one slight problem." He lifted his head.

I had a feeling I knew exactly what that problem was. "I have a condom in my jeans." I was grateful that Hugh had slipped it to me. "Don't ask."

"If it means I get to have you, I really don't care."

"You already know you can have me."

"Good." He pulled off my panties and tossed them into the pile of the rest of our clothes. His boxers followed.

I waited impatiently as he unwrapped the condom. "I guess it's time for my test."

"You've already passed."

"Well, then let's see if I can get some extra credit."

"I never imagined you'd go for the teacher innuendo."

"Neither did I." He positioned himself over me.

I closed my eyes.

"Open your eyes for this."

I listened. I opened my eyes, and they immediately locked on his. "You're incredible, Daisy." He thrust into me.

I gasped, taking a moment to adjust to the feel of him inside me. He moved slowly at first, easing in and out. "Tell me if I'm hurting you."

"I don't care. I want you." I didn't care. He was larger than the few other guys I'd been with, but I knew he'd fit perfectly. I knew every moment would be perfect.

"I never want to hurt you." He stilled.

"Please, Owen. The only way you're going to hurt me now is if you stop."

"Then I won't." He sped up his movements, and I wrapped my legs around him. He moved in deeper and deeper, until the full length of him filled me.

I moaned, and that seemed to be what he needed to hear. He continued, on and on until I was digging my nails into his back. "Can you let me see the real you again?"

"My wings?"

"Yes."

His eyes darkened and his body heated up. He moved even harder and faster as his large black wings released from his back.

The pleasure I was feeling before was nothing compared to what I started to feel after he transformed. I reached up and stroked one of his wings. I was hot, nearly on fire, and my vision was hazy.

He pushed me over the edge, and I thought that was it, but he didn't stop. My body both begged for him to continue and to stop, because I wasn't sure how much more I could take.

He pushed me over the edge again before his body shuddered, and he reached his own release.

I couldn't speak. I didn't have the capacity or the breath.

He lay next to me, watching me with a mix of adoration and shock. "Wow."

"Uh… I hope that means it was good for you?"

"Amazing. I mean, I knew it would be, but I never imagined that."

"Amazing is a good way to describe it."

"So it was good for you too?" He ran his hand down my arm. "I didn't hurt you?"

"I may be a little sore, but it was definitely worth it."

"You'll just have to get used to it."

"Again you're assuming I'm going to come back for more?"

"Are you going to deny it… after that?"

"No. I'm not denying anything when it comes to you."

"Good, because if I was determined to keep you close before, that determination is even stronger now."

"There's one slight problem though. Or ok. Two."

"What are they?" He left tiny kisses along my jaw line.

"I'm wide awake, and we don't have any more condoms."

He laughed. "We can find other ways to spend our time."

"Yeah? Care to show me?"

"How bad would it be if I used the oral exam line?"

I laughed. "You kind of already used it."

"I did, didn't I?"

***

I woke up as sun streamed through the small window in Owen's room. I snuggled deeper into his side, unwilling to face the day if it meant pulling me away from the best night of my life.

"Good morning, beautiful."

"Good morning." I turned to look up at him. "How long have you been up?"

"Most of the night."

"What?" I tried to pull away, but he wrapped me up in his arms. "You couldn't sleep?"

"I don't need much sleep, so I watched you instead."

"Watched me?"

"Uh huh. You're adorable."

"Great." I tried to pull away again, but he rolled me on top of him. "I could really get used to waking up with you next to me."

"I could get used to falling asleep next to you."

"That kind of works out then."

"More than kind of." He kissed me gently on the lips.

"Before we do any more of that, you don't happen to have an extra toothbrush, do you?"

"I actually do."

"Perfect."

"I also have plenty of soap in the shower."

"Owen."

"Yes?"

"Wanting to brush my teeth doesn't mean I'm asking to shower with you." Not that the thought of it bothered me. Owen wet. I could handle that image.

"How did you know I was implying a shower together?"

"Because of the giant smile on your face, and the bulge pressing against me."

"We're going to have to do some condom shopping later, but that's not all."

"No?"

He gently shifted me to his side. "In all seriousness, we need to slow down."

"Uh… what?" Could he say mixed signals?

"Not in here. No. I'm not doing that, but I need to take you out for a real date."

"What is a real date exactly?" Any date with Owen sounded good, but I was curious what he had in mind.

"One that involves dinner and something before the sex."

"I wouldn't mind that." I wouldn't mind anything with Owen, especially not if it meant he wanted to be with me.

"Good." He brushed his lips against mine.

Loud knocking on the front door got both of our attention.

I groaned. "Do you think that's for you or me?"

"Probably both of us." He sighed. "I guess that means we'll have to postpone the shower."

"I guess so." I reluctantly pulled myself out of bed and searched around for my clothes.

Owen handed me my panties and bra. "Hopefully I play the date well enough to get a repeat of last night."

"I say your chances are good." I hooked my bra.

"Like 80% good? 90%?" He stepped into his jeans.

"More like 99.9%." I found my t-shirt on the dresser where I left it.

He walked over and pulled my tank top the rest of the way down. He was still completely naked. "Where's the last .01%?"

"I have to give you a little bit to work for, don't I?"

He laughed. "You're too perfect."

"Perfect?" I shook my head. "Not really."

"You are whether you know it or not." He watched as I buttoned my jeans. "Ready to face the world?"

"Aren't you going to put a shirt on?"

"That possessive already? Don't want me showing off my chest?"

"I'm fine with it, as long as you keep the wings for me."

He grinned. "I might have to show them off when I'm flying once in awhile, but otherwise it's a deal."

"Good."

He pulled on a navy blue t-shirt. "But that means your body is for me too."

"I'd worry about you getting possessive, but I guess I started it."

"You did…" He wrapped his arms around my waist. "But I'm finishing it." His lips moved to my neck.

The knocking started again.

"All right, no more distractions."

"Fine. I suppose they're not going to leave until they see us." He took my hand in his and led us to the front door.

He pulled it open, and we came face to face with the three Allures, Hailey, and Cade.

Cade grinned. "Good morning."

"Same to you." I didn't bother hiding my broad smile.

Cade laughed. "Somehow I think you guys had a much better morning than us."

"And a better night." Owen grinned.

"Ok, enough of that." Roland stepped toward the door. "We gave you time. It's time to go."

"Go?" I asked with confusion. "We can't go yet."

"We can't stay long," Violet said with a slight smile. "But we don't have to leave this second, especially not if Owen helps us out."

"What do you need help with?" Owen asked immediately.

"Has Daisy filled you in? Do you understand what the witch did to her?"

"I understand she still has magic in her."

"It's more than magic," Hugh grumbled.

Violet gave Hugh a dirty look. "Daisy mentioned that you took her to another witch for help. Could you tell us where to find her?"

"That depends. Why do you need to find her?"

"Because we need to find Kalisa, the witch who used the magic."

"She might be able to help me," I added. "At least their friend seems to think so."

"I'll do anything to help Daisy. You really think the witch can reverse it?"

Violet shrugged. "Maybe. We won't know until we find her."

"I can put you in touch with someone who can help, but I'm not getting Mayanne in trouble."

"I understand." Violet nodded. "Point us in the right direction, and we'll be fine."

"Can I see your phone?" he asked.

"Yes." Violet pulled out her phone and handed it to him.

Owen typed something in. "Call that number and say you got it from Owen. He'll help you track her down."

"Thanks. That's perfect." Violet beamed.

"Great. I'm taking Daisy out tonight." Owen smiled at me. "We're not going anywhere before I do that."

"We?" Roland crossed his arms.

"Yes, I'm going anywhere Daisy goes." Owen put his arm around my waist. "In case anyone was wondering, we're together now."

"I would have had no idea." Hailey rolled her eyes.

"How about a compromise?" Violet fixed her smile on Owen. "Take her to lunch."

"Lunch isn't good enough. It has to be dinner." Owen's resistance to the appeal of an Allure definitely came in handy.

Violet sighed dramatically. "Fine. I suppose we can agree to that, but we need to leave tomorrow."

"We'll leave when Kalisa is found. There is no reason to leave—" Owen's protest was drowned out by the sound of a truck on Owen's dirt drive. It had us all turning, and thankfully seemed to calm everyone down.

"Damn it." Owen sighed.

Hailey laughed. "Don't tell me, is that Clyde?"

"Of course."

I had no idea who Clyde was, but I wasn't in the mood for any more company.

The truck stopped and a guy around my age wearing a cowboy hat stepped out. He gave us all a long look before walking over. "Hey, Owen. You didn't tell me you were expecting so many guests."

"It came as a surprise." Owen tightened his arm around me.

"And who is this?" Violet asked sweetly. Oh no. What was she going to do?

"I'm Clyde." He took off his hat. "And what's your name?"

"Violet." She held out her hand. "It isn't often I get a chance to meet a real cowboy."

Roland laughed.

Clyde grinned. "A cowboy? If that's what you want to call me." He winked before turning his attention to me. "How about you? Excited to meet a cowboy?"

"Uh, sure."

"She's with me, Clyde," Owen warned.

"With you, with you? I had no idea you had a girl, man."

"Yeah, it's new."

"Aren't you going to say hello to me?" Hailey turned to him, saving us from the awkward conversation.

"Of course, Hailey." Even as he spoke he was watching me and Violet. I had a feeling the beautiful red head wasn't used to sharing attention.

"I came over to discuss some business with you, Owen, but if it's a bad time, I can come back."

"It's a wonderful time." Violet put a hand on Clyde's arm. "Why don't you and Owen go inside and chat? We'll wait out here."

"That sounds like a great idea." Clyde grinned. "Smart and beautiful."

"Isn't she?" Hugh smirked.

"Daisy can join in on our discussion too." Owen touched my arm lightly.

"I assure you I'm not going to whisk her away, Owen, but she and I need to talk." Violet kept the smile plastered on her face, but her words were anything but light.

I tensed. Why was she being so combative with him? Wasn't she the one who insisted we rush out to find him?

"Now isn't the time to talk business, Clyde." Owen's tone was harsh, but I knew he wasn't trying to direct it at Clyde.

"I understand. What are you up to today then?"

"Owen's going to take Daisy out to lunch."

"Dinner." He glared at Violet.

If they weren't arguing about me, it might have been comical.

"But I have absolutely nothing to do today. Any chance you could show me around town?" Violet bit her lip in a ridiculously exaggerated way.

"Of course. Want to go now?"

"I'd love to!"

"Violet, could I talk to you for a second?" I asked.

"Me?" Violet put her hand to her chest. "I thought you guys were too busy."

"Violet." I glared at her.

"Fine." She smiled.

"Wait for me, Clyde." She gave him another grin before following me inside.

"Don't hurt that guy."

"Why would I hurt him?" she asked innocently.

"What else would you be doing with him? You want to manipulate him."

"No, I wanted to talk to you."

"Wait? You were only doing that because you knew I'd do this?"

"I may not have known you long, Dais, but I *know* you well."

I ignored her use of the nickname again. It was the least of my problems. "What is it then? What's so important that we need to talk?"

"We can't stay here. You knew this was only a short visit."

"No I didn't… besides things have changed."

"What's changed?"

"Owen… he feels the same way as I do."

"And that changes what exactly?"

"I want to stay out here a bit. See what happens." After all these years it was happening. I'd found Owen.

"You can't."

"Why not? Louie doesn't have Kalisa yet. What's the rush?"

"We should be there when he brings her in."

"Why? Why does that part matter?"

"I'm beginning to think you don't care about getting rid of the magic."

"I do, but I also care about spending time with Owen."

"Don't get too attached to him. I warned you about that."

I shook my head. "No you didn't. You never told me that."

"Then I'm telling you that now. Don't get too attached."

"Why?"

"Because most likely Kalisa won't fix you, and if she doesn't, then things are going to change with Owen."

"No they won't. He doesn't care."

"This isn't about him." She put her hands on my shoulders. "This is about *you*."

"My feelings for him aren't going to change." Nothing could change them. I'd been crazy about him before, but everything had intensified now. Being with him was even more amazing than I'd imagined.

"That's the thing, they are." She dropped her hands. "You can have tonight, but that's it. I refuse to stand by and watch you both get hurt."

"Then don't." I had no idea what she was talking about, but I wasn't in the mood to listen. After years of searching, I'd finally found him. I was giving us a chance.

"Don't what?"

"Stand by and watch. I'll return to Louie's when he has Kalisa and is ready for me. We can split up for a while."

"Split up? That's not possible."

"Of course it is. We'll have both upheld our side of the bargain, and I'll be magic free."

"It's not that simple."

"I'll be fine."

"You won't. You don't understand the changes happening in you. This is only the beginning. You need to be ready for it."

"It's going to be fine." I brushed her off and walked outside. I refused to let her ruin my mood.

"It's not going to be fine."

"Daisy, you ok?" Owen met me out on the porch.

"I'm fine." I took a deep breath. "Violet's getting ready to go spend some time with Clyde."

"Think about what I'm telling you, Daisy. Please." She sent me a fleeting look before walking down the driveway.

"Are you sure you're okay?"

"I'm fine." I tried to clear my head so I could focus on the important things, like my date with Owen.

CHAPTER TWENTY-TWO

OWEN

I had absolutely no clue what I was doing. It had been so long since I'd dated anyone, but I needed to do something special for Daisy. We'd spent an amazing night together, and I refused to let that be the only one we shared. If something was going to come of our crazy connection, I needed to anchor our physical attraction into something real.

As soon as Daisy slipped off to take a shower—unfortunately without me—I started planning. I headed out onto the back porch, and Hailey followed.

"You can't take her to the diner." Hailey decided to but in even though I never asked for her opinion.

"Where else am I supposed to take her? The one nice place in town is closed on Mondays."

"Be creative." She pulled her hair back into a bun and secured it with the hair tie she always seemed to have around her wrist.

"Or, you could share the idea you obviously have. You know, actually help me for a change."

"For a change? I brought the girl to you, didn't I?"

"You did. Technically. I owe you."

"Are you sure you want to owe me more?" She hopped up on the back porch railing.

"I already have one idea. I just need help to make that happen."

"I'll help if it's good. I'm not helping with anything lame." She swung her legs.

"I want to take her to the movies."

"But there's no movie theater in town. You told me that last time I was here."

"There isn't, but we could make one."

"You don't even have a TV."

"Maybe not, but we have Cade's jet. We could get anything and everything we want."

"And that fits with *my* idea. We need to figure out her all-time favorite meal, and you need to cook it for her."

"Cook it for her? You want me to cook?" Hailey was well aware of my ineptitude in the kitchen.

"I told you I'd help."

"Actually you said I'd cook it for her."

"For all intents and purposes, you're cooking it. That's the romantic part. Whether you get help or not is another story. So now all we need to do is find out her favorite movie and food."

"Easier said than done if we want to surprise her." I heard the shower shut off inside. "And we're out of time."

"Leave the snooping to me. I'll get the details. You keep her busy while I get things ready."

"I don't mind keeping her busy." I smiled thinking of the many ways I could do that.

"No. None of that. You're the one who reminded me that your sex life was none of my business."

"It isn't your business, but it's mine."

She made a disgusted face. "I'll go talk to her."

"She just got out of the shower."

"So? I'm a girl. It's not going to bother her." She hopped down off the railing.

"She doesn't even know you."

"She barely knows you, but she had no problem getting naked with you." Hailey laughed.

"I liked you better when you were sulking."

"I was never sulking."

"Yes you were."

"Whatever. Go find Cade and have him figure out your movie screen problem. I'll text you all the details." She started for the back door.

"Why are you helping me?"

"Because you're my brother, and despite all your short comings I kind of love you."

"You kind of love me?"

"That's all I'm admitting to." She walked inside.

I shook my head. Hailey was something else.

It didn't take me long to find Cade holding court with his friends. Although I could tolerate him more the longer I knew him, his showmanship tendencies were annoying.

"Well, hello there. I didn't expect to see you surface today." Cade grinned.

"Oh yeah, because I was planning to sleep with Daisy while Hailey hung out with us."

"I don't know, Pterons are known to have done worse things." Roland glared at me.

"Do you have a problem with me?" I didn't like the way he looked at me—or Daisy. Was he into her or something?

"Yes, but it doesn't matter. After tonight we won't be seeing you anymore."

"I agree. After tonight you won't have to see me or Daisy again. I, however, will be seeing her plenty."

"Why?" He stood up. "You never looked for her in years, yet now she shows up and you're suddenly meant to be?"

"I don't have to explain myself to you."

"You don't have to, but you could." Roland crossed his arms. "If you're so crazy about Daisy, explaining it shouldn't be difficult."

"I never looked for her because I didn't think it was an option." That was putting it mildly. I knew she didn't want to be found by someone like me. I generally considered myself a confident man, but not when it came to humans. My ex-girlfriend had done a number on me.

Roland scowled. "You work for the king. You could have tracked her down."

"I mean because it wasn't an option to be with her."

"Why not?" Roland asked. "She wasn't good enough for you?"

"No, the opposite. I don't have to explain myself to you. The only one I need to explain anything to is Daisy, and she gets it. There's something between us. It was there two years ago, and it's here now." How could I begin to explain my fears, or the nightmares that had plagued me since that night?

"It doesn't matter anyway. She's leaving."

Violet put her hands up between us. "Enough. Both of you. Roland, you need to settle down. Owen isn't trying to hurt Daisy. Give him the benefit of the doubt. Owen, hopefully your information will lead us to Kalisa quickly."

"The sooner we help Daisy, the better." That was something I'd agree with them on.

"Exactly. Roland, let's take a walk." She linked her arm with Roland and headed for the woods. Hugh followed.

"Aren't you supposed to be planning a date?" Cade immediately picked up the conversation as though the others hadn't just walked off.

"Yes. That's why I came out here. I need your help."

"Oh?" He smiled. "This is going to be interesting."

CHAPTER TWENTY-THREE

DAISY

I needed air. I could have stayed glued to Owen all day, but I couldn't say the same thing about the others. They all meant well in their own ways (at least I hope they did), but the tension and fighting was getting ridiculous. Violet and the guys wanted me to leave, Owen wanted me to stay, and Hailey and Cade wanted me to have more answers. Despite my euphoria at finding Owen, I found myself kind of missing my quiet life before I knew about vampires, witches, and winged superheroes.

I treated myself to a hot shower, staying in way longer than necessary. The hot water felt good, and it gave me some much needed peace and quiet. I was half convinced that if I closed my eyes without Owen around the Allures would have me tied down in the backseat of a car on my way back to Louie's. They weren't keen on waiting until he found Kalisa.

The only thing motivating me to get out of the shower was the thought of seeing Owen. Even fifteen minutes apart made me miss him.

I wrapped up in my towel and went back toward Owen's room to get dressed. Violet had come back from her outing with Clyde with some fresh clothes at least. I didn't need to ask her whether she'd actually paid for them. I was positive she hadn't.

I'd just pulled on the cotton sun dress Violet had picked out for me when Hailey barged in. "Hey!"

"Hi…" I smoothed out the navy blue dress. "Did I take too long or something?"

"No, not at all. I wanted to make sure you didn't need anything."

"Oh. Thanks. I'm good."

"You sure? There's no food you're totally craving?"

"I probably should eat something." I thought about how long it had been since I last ate. How was I even standing?

"What should we get?"

"Oh, whatever everyone else wants."

"It's your choice," she pushed.

"Is this a test or something?"

"A test?"

"Like to see if I have similar taste to your brother or something?"

"No! Of course not. I'm only trying to be polite."

"Does Owen have anything for sandwiches, or eggs or something?" I tried to come up with the simplest meal possible.

"Sandwiches? Eggs?" She threw her hands up. "You're impossible."

"Uh…"

She sat down on the end of the bed. "Sorry, I'm really bad at this."

"Bad at what?"

"Inconspicuously getting information. I prefer just getting it, but I was trying to be tricky."

"Why would you need to know what kind of food I like?"

"So Owen could surprise you."

"Surprise me?" I couldn't deny the excitement I felt at the thought of him wanting to go out of his way to surprise me. I knew what we had was more than physical attraction—but it was nice to have some proof.

"I don't want to ruin the rest of the surprise, so just tell me your favorite food and favorite movie, and we can pretend this went down much better."

I laughed. Hailey was really cool and quirky. She'd be a lot of fun to hang out with. "I love seafood and pretty much any film adaption of a Tennessee Williams play."

"Interesting."

"Why is that interesting?"

"Well, I took a seminar on Tennessee Williams last semester. I didn't know anyone actually watched those movies for fun, but to each their own. Oh, and Owen loves seafood too."

"Oh, cool."

"Yeah. It is cool." She stood up. "Ok, pretend this conversation never happened." She disappeared out the door.

I shook my head. She was definitely a character.

***

"This is incredible." I took another bite of the linguine and clams. The clams were perfectly cooked, and the sauce was to die for. I had no idea how he'd gotten fresh clams in Colorado, but he told me to thank Cade. I guess there's nothing you can't do when you have a private jet and connections.

"I'm glad you like it." Owen smiled at me across the table. He was different than I expected him to be. There was a vulnerability about him that didn't fit with the strong exterior he wore.

"Of course I do." I still couldn't believe I was sitting at a table with him.

"Are you okay?"

"Yes, of course."

"You seemed to be zoned out for a second."

"I was reflecting on things."

"Reflecting on them?" He raised an eyebrow. "In other words you were analyzing the situation."

"Just thinking about things."

"What kind of things?" He sipped his red wine.

"On why you never looked for me." I looked down, instantly regretting the words. Was I going to ruin everything?

"Daisy?" he said my name quietly.

"Yes?"

"You really don't know why?"

"No. I don't."

"Because I assumed you wouldn't want to see me. Eventually you'd have gotten over the shock of things and realized you kissed someone who wasn't human. I didn't want to deal with your rejection."

Was that really it? He was worried about me rejecting him? "That's ridiculous. How could you think that? I've searched for you for years!"

"I didn't know that." He put his hand over mine. "And now I wonder if I'm a disappointment."

"You seemed a lot more confident last night." I sipped my wine.

"It was easier."

"Easier when you were naked?"

He laughed. "Easier when I could let our physical urges rule."

"Stop worrying. It's true you're not exactly what I was expecting, but that's a good thing. You're so real and complicated, and everything I want."

"And you're everything I want. You know that, right?" He scooted his chair closer to me. "I'm not using you or anything. I want to see where this goes."

"I'm just glad you admitted you remembered me." I forced a laugh. He had no idea how terrified I'd been when we arrived at his place.

"Of course I remembered you."

"Am I what you remembered?" I'd assuaged his fears. It was my turn to ask. I braced myself in case his answer wasn't the one I was expecting.

"You are everything and anything I've ever wanted in a woman. I knew you were special back then, but now? Well, now I know you're perfect."

"I'm not perfect. I'm far from it."

"Perfect for me. You feel it too. I know you do. This isn't normal, but what is?"

"What's not normal? Our attraction to each other?"

"The chemistry between us."

"Do you think it's the magic?"

He cupped my chin in his hand. "No. It's not magic. I'm immune to it, so you never have to worry that my feelings aren't real."

"So I can feel confident that you're going to ask me on a second date?"

"Of course, but this date isn't over yet. You ready for the next part of our evening?"

I looked down at my completely cleared plate. "Yes, I believe I am."

"Great." He stood and walked around to my chair. He held out his hand. "Ready?"

I accepted his hand. "Ready once we clear the dishes."

"Hailey said she'd take care of it. I'll pay her back later."

"You sure?" I hated leaving things a mess.

"I'm sure."

We walked outside, and I broke into a grin. He'd set up a huge movie screen along the back of a large shed behind the house and spread out a blanket in front of it. "I brought the movies to you."

"Wow." Now I knew why Hailey had asked about my favorites.

"How does *Cat on a Hot Tin Roof* sound?"

I laughed. "I have no idea how you figured out I loved Tennessee Williams."

He led me over to the blanket that was laid out on the freshly cut grass. "It was a lucky guess."

"Such a random one."

He laughed. "She means well." He sat down on the blanket, and I sat right next to him. He pulled me back so I was leaning into his muscular chest.

"I can tell." I rested my head against him.

The movie started and I took advantage of my proximity to Owen by running my hands down his arms. I'd never get tired of touching him.

"I want to know everything about you." His lips trailed down my neck.

"Everything?"

"Everything."

"Most of it isn't very exciting." Almost none of it was.

"Sure it is." He returned his lips to the most sensitive spot on my neck.

"I don't even know where to start." I stopped trying to pay attention to the movie. It was no match for his lips.

"What's your favorite color?" he whispered against my skin as though he were asking a highly intimate question.

"Blue."

"Like the ocean or the sky?"

"Like your eyes."

He turned me so I was straddling him. "If anyone else had said that I might have considered it corny."

"What was it coming from me?"

"Wonderful."

"I aim to please."

"Do you?"

"Not always." I put my hands on his shoulders. "What's your favorite color?"

"Brown."

"You better not say because of my eyes."

"The color of your hair…"

I laughed. "Ok, technically different."

"Favorite season?"

"Spring. I love the weather, the flowers, even the rain. Yours?"

"Winter."

"Really?"

"Does that surprise you?" He covered my hand with his.

"I'm not used to people saying that much."

"Maybe it's because I grew up in New Orleans, and we have mild winters. Whenever I get the chance to go somewhere with snow, I jump on it."

"Do you ski?"

"I have, but it's not really a Pteron thing."

"I guess it isn't as exciting when you can fly."

"Kind of." He put a hand on my hip.

"My turn. What's your favorite number?"

"Two."

"Mine's four."

"Two and two make four."

"Really? I had no clue."

Without warning he started to tickle me. I moved off his lap, and he gently pushed me down on the blanket while I burst into a fit of giggles. "Going to play it that way, huh?"

"Maybe."

He ran his lips over my neck again. "Your skin is so soft."

"So are your lips."

He slipped his hand under the hem of my dress. "What about my hands? How do they feel?"

"Good. Very good." All thoughts of watching the movie disappeared as his hands and lips continued their journey.

"Sorry to interrupt." Violet's voice carried over the sound from the movie.

Owen moved his hand immediately, and I quickly worked to reposition my dress.

"What is it?" Owen asked impatiently. He didn't like getting interrupted any more than I did.

"We have to go." Violet stared down at us.

"Why?" I forced my eyes to stay on her even though they wanted to wander to the screen behind her. I really did love that movie.

"Louie found Kalisa."

"Already?" I sat up straighter. "How did he find her so quick?"

"Louie has his ways, and Owen's tip paid off. It doesn't matter. She's been found, and we need to get back to his place immediately."

"Does he still think she can help me?"

"If she can help, she will. Louie isn't someone anyone says no to." Violet's words sent a chill through me. I hoped I never had a run in with him. In the back of my head I heard a voice telling me that without question I eventually would.

"I will obviously be accompanying Daisy." Owen wove his fingers through mine.

"You can come on the plane, but if Louie tells you to leave, you will listen." She gave Owen a knowing look.

"We'll deal with that when the time comes." He moved to standing, helping me up in the process.

"The plane? I guess that means you're taking mine?" Cade appeared with Hailey.

"Yes. We'll need it." Violet kept her eyes on Owen.

"I'm coming too." Hailey walked over.

"Not a chance." Owen shook his head. "This isn't a game, Hailey."

"You might need me."

"What I need is for you to stay here."

"Why?"

"So I can contact you to get help if we need it." Owen had snapped into protective older brother mode, and it seemed really natural on him.

"Don't worry, Hailey." Cade put an arm around her. "I'll stay and keep you company."

Hailey huffed. "Fine, I'm only doing it once though."

"We're still taking your plane." Violet wasn't asking a question.

"It's fine, I'll have the pilot fly back. Hailey and I have our own wings if we need to leave before then." Cade grinned.

"Either way, we were taking it. Have your pilot ready the plane." Violet turned to us. "Sorry to cut your date short, but we don't have any time to waste."

"Once we do this, we're out. Do you understand?" Owen asked her.

"You may be, but she's not."

CHAPTER TWENTY-FOUR

DAISY

"Are you sure it's really Kalisa?" I asked as I found myself on a private jet for the second time in my life. I had a passing thought about how cool it would be to tell my friends and family, but then I realized they probably wouldn't believe me. It wasn't worth even bothering to share it. Besides, I already had a dozen voicemail messages from my mom checking on me. I needed to call her back before she called the cops.

"Yes." Violet nodded emphatically. She was sitting across from where I sat next to Owen. "She's been found."

"And what's going to happen to her?"

"She's going to help you if she can and answer for her crimes."

"Which means we need to call Levi. He's the only one authorized to handle a trial of this sort." Owen shifted in his seat.

"No. Allures don't answer to Pterons. We'll be doing our own trial."

"That's not allowed."

"Owen," Violet crossed her legs. "How would you handle things if a witch killed a Pteron? Would you hand that witch over to someone else?"

He nodded in understanding. "Not a chance."

"Exactly."

"But are we sure that's what she did? What if she got the essence from someone else and didn't know what it was?" I wasn't happy with what Kalisa did to me, but I also had no clue how much she knew.

"Not just anyone can make the paste she made. She knew what she was doing." Violet crossed her legs in the opposite direction.

"We have to protect Daisy in all this." Owen put an arm around me. "If this witch was powerful enough to take out an Allure, she's dangerous. We can't let our guard down."

"She'll be fine. Daisy is stronger than you give her credit for."

"I understand she's strong, but she's still human."

Violet crossed her legs yet again. "I'm not going to let anyone hurt her."

"Can I ask you something?" Owen ran his fingers up and down my arm but looked at Violet.

"You can ask me anything, but it doesn't mean I'm going to answer."

"I thought the Allure's were all gone... how many of you are there?"

"Enough of us." She pressed her lips together for a second as though she were debating whether to say more. "Any other questions?"

"None that are polite."

"Then don't ask them." She stood up. "I'll give you guys some time."

I rested my head on Owen's chest. "Hopefully our second date won't end so eventfully."

"Or at least not in this kind of event." He stroked my back. "I should have expected it. My life rarely stays calm."

"Neither does mine."

"You've had some rough years."

"I have."

He leaned in close. "We're going to see this witch and figure everything else out. Even if she can't help, that doesn't mean it's time to give up. I have some ideas of who can help."

"I hope so." I tried to hide my fear, but it wasn't going anywhere. The one benefit of hanging out with only Allures and Pterons was that I didn't have to worry about accidently manipulating someone again.

"What are your plans? We haven't talked about that yet." He continued to gently rub my back.

"I don't have any other plans now. The only thing I wanted to do was find you. I did that."

"That you did." He ran his lips up and down my jaw line.

I closed my eyes, focusing on his touch rather than the craziness that was likely to ensue. I was beginning to understand that quality time was fleeting. I needed to enjoy every second I could. Still, I had questions to ask. "What about you? What are your plans?"

"Right now my plan is to make sure you're okay."

"I mean beyond that. Before me."

"Before you isn't as simple as it sounds, but if you mean before last night, I planned to go back to New Orleans eventually."

"Are you still going to?"

"That depends."

"On?" I opened my eyes.

"Whether you're going with me."

"Once again expecting me to stay around for more?"

He smiled. "Not expecting. Just hoping."

"If I ever go back to that city it's going to be with you."

"I'll take that." He snuggled me against his side.

***

I must have dozed off because before I knew it I was lurched awake as the plane started its descent.

Owen put his arm around me. "You okay?"

"Yeah. I just don't like flying."

He smiled. "I hope you mean on planes. If so, I agree with you there."

"Yeah, I wouldn't mind flying with you again."

"Good." He kissed my forehead. "I wouldn't mind taking you with me again."

The plane lurched again as the landing gear made contact with the tarmac. I glanced out the window at the desert landscape. I squeezed Owen's hand. Part of me was ready to get this confrontation over with, but the rest of me wanted to stay on board. What if Kalisa struck against the one person she could—me?

"You ready?" Owen asked as we unbuckled.

"I don't really have a choice, do I?"

"You always have a choice."

"Not always."

"Always." He led me up the aisle toward where the Allures had already disembarked.

"He really has a landing strip at his house?" I glanced around at the field. The plane was on the one strip of pavement.

"We told you his house was opulent." Hugh put and arm around Violet. "Let's find Louie."

"A landing strip goes beyond opulent," I mumbled. Focusing on a detail like that helped me forget I was about to come face to face with the woman who had changed my life so completely.

Owen seemed to sense my discomfort and grabbed my hand. "I can get us out of here in seconds if I have to."

"That's very convenient." I hadn't adequately considered the benefits of dating a guy with wings.

"I know."

"Welcome!" Louie met us before we'd made it halfway to his house.

I stopped. "Where is she?" I wasn't going to play around and act like we were there for any other reason.

"That excited to see the witch?" he asked.

"I'm ready to get rid of this magic." I'd been ready for years.

"I already warned you it wasn't likely she could help." He looked me square in the eye. "I told you not to get your hopes up."

"You didn't say that exactly, but either way I still need to find out. Have you asked her yet?"

"She says she can't."

"And you believe her?"

"Yes, but not because I'm taking her word for it."

"Where is she? Can I see her myself?"

"If you want to see her, I'd be happy to let you see her before she's transported."

"Transported? Where? Where are you taking her?"

"It's nowhere that needs to concern you now."

"What about the trial?" I looked at Violet. "You promised a trial."

She looked away, avoiding my gaze.

"If she can't help me, then why am I here? Owen and I might as well go."

"Go? Why would you go anywhere when this is where you belong?" Louie gestured to his property.

"Where I belong?" I asked. "I don't belong anywhere but where I want to be." I was filled with a sudden burst of confidence.

"So she hasn't figured it out yet?" Louie asked. "And no one's told her? And what about her Pteron over there? Is he blissfully unaware too?"

"Violet wanted to give them time." Roland walked over. "She had a good point about letting Daisy build some good memories now so she wouldn't hate us later."

"Hate you?" Louie appeared taken aback. "What could she possibly hate you for?"

"It's been a long time since you were human." Violet finally looked at me. "It's been a long time for me too, but I'll never forget."

Louie turned to Owen. "Pteron, you need to leave. We appreciate you escorting Daisy here, but that's where your role ends."

Owen tightened his hold on me. "Fine. Daisy and I will be on our way."

"Daisy is not leaving with you." Louie turned his head to the side slightly. "Haven't you figured it out? They told me you were the king's advisor."

"I am."

"Then surely you have a base level of intelligence." Louie sneered.

"Get to the point." Owen held my hand firmly in his own.

"I believe it's time we give Daisy and Owen a little bit of an education on Allures."

"I've been asking for one for days." I didn't keep the annoyance out of my voice.

"Let's move to the patio. We'll be more comfortable there."

"I'm fine right here." I stood my ground. I was done being toyed with.

"Allures are only born from other Allures."

"Born in what way?" I knew we weren't talking about human conception here.

"An Allure has only one gift to give. She can give half her essence only once to a deserving human she wishes to have as a companion."

"Why would she have to give half her essence to spend time with him?" It's not like Allures had trouble making friends.

"Let me continue. When I'm done, I'm sure you'll understand."

I nodded. "Continue then."

"Once given the essence, that human becomes an Allure with all that comes with it." Louie smiled. "It's truly the greatest gift, and you've gotten it double."

"What do you mean?" Owen asked. "She was only given some in a magic paste."

"She was given the entire essence of one of our kind. Not just half."

"What does that mean?" My body started to shake from a mixture of anger and fear.

"I don't know yet, but I can't wait to find out." Louie reached out a hand to me and then dropped it. "We'll get to find out together. Roland will be with us too."

"Together? Roland? What are you even talking about?" My head was spinning as I tried to process what he was saying.

"Roland, would you like to explain, or should I?"

"Might I explain?" Violet said softly. "Daisy might prefer to hear it from me."

"Go ahead."

"As Louie explained, when we give half our essence to a human they become an Allure and stay as our companion."

"You keep saying companion. What does that mean exactly?"

"It can mean anything. Usually what it sounds like: companionship, company, someone to pass the time with."

"Pass the time with? That doesn't sound like an exciting way to spend your life." I thought back to the cab driver from New Orleans. He'd reminded me of the importance of living your life instead of standing back and watching.

"We have a lot of time, Daisy." She pursed her lips.

"Meaning?"

"They're immortal…" Owen squeezed my hand. "I'd always heard that, but I've never met an immortal creature before."

"Immortal? As in you live forever?"

"Yes." Violet smiled. "We stop aging when we become an Allure."

"Oh wow…" They'd dropped hints, and now it was all coming together. But that wasn't what we'd been discussing. "But what does Roland have to do with figuring things out?"

"Hugh is my companion. I made him. My maker has moved on to a new role that pulled him away, so it's just us."

"Then why's Roland with you?"

"My maker disappeared years ago." Roland moved toward me. "I'd searched for her across the globe, with no sign."

"Oh. I'm sorry."

"You get it, right?" Hugh asked. "The pieces are falling into place?"

"Huh?"

Roland smiled at me. "We share a special bond with those who make us and those we make. We are most comfortable when we're together."

"You're losing me."

"How do I make you feel, Daisy?" Roland asked.

"You relax me…" Then everything dawned on me. "The essence I have, it's from your maker?"

"Yes." Louie was the one to answer. "And from the Allure I made."

"Wait. What?"

"That's why I said the three of us would figure this out together. You've joined our family, so to speak."

"No. I'm not joining any family. I'm not an Allure. This change can be stopped. Even without Kalisa's help we can figure this out." I wasn't becoming one of them. I refused to let it happen. I was human, and I wasn't going to let that change.

"There's has to be a way to separate the essence from her." Owen pulled me close to his side. "She doesn't want to be an Allure."

"It's a gift. Of course she wants it. Who wouldn't want immortality and immeasurable power?" Louie stepped toward me. "It's going to be wonderful, Daisy."

I shook my head. "I'm not an Allure. We can stop this. Give it to someone who wants it."

"Why? You deserve it. It only works on someone worthy."

I shook my head again. "No. I'm human. I want to be human."

"Let's go, Daisy. We can leave." Owen tightened his hold on me.

Louie glared at Owen. "Daisy is becoming an Allure. She needs to be with her own."

"Since when do creatures have to stick to their own? That's never been mandated or recommended by The Society."

"The Society? Again with that? We don't care about The Society." Hugh crossed his arms.

"Either way we're going."

"She needs to know the rest. She has to know everything," Violet said sadly.

"What else is there? What else do I have to know?"

Violet pursed her lips. "With all the gifts, come loss."

"What kind of loss?" Owen asked when I couldn't.

"Loss of real feelings."

"What?" I choked out. "What do you mean?"

"Why do you think I've been telling you to hold on to your memories of Owen? Those are the only feelings of love you're ever going to have. Once you fully change you'll be incapable of it."

"That's impossible. Someone can't be incapable of love." What was the point of anything if you couldn't feel love? Isn't that what our lives are all about?

"They can if they're an Allure." Violet watched me. "We can touch everyone else's emotions, and we understand them still, but we don't really feel them. Like me right now. I'm sad for you, but I don't really feel it. It doesn't hurt me. We still have sensations, like the high you get after touching someone else's emotions, but that's it."

"No! I'm not losing my ability to feel. That's all I have. What am I without it? That's what being human means."

"And you won't be human." Hugh sighed. "Once you fully turn it won't matter anyway. You won't feel the loss."

"But you'll remember from time to time." Violet fixed her eyes on me.

"There has to be a way to stop this. Owen's right. We can separate the essence from me and give it back. You can find someone else." I was in panic mode mixed with shock. If it weren't for Owen's strong hold on me I wouldn't have been standing.

"Good luck with that." Louie laughed dryly. "You think it's that easy?"

"We'll figure it out. If there's a way, we'll find it." Owen went stone still.

"This is all so entertaining: a Pteron so desperate to hold on to his human love that he'll promise the impossible." Louie clasped his hands in front of him. "Perfect really."

"Violet, help me. Please," I begged. "How do I do this? What do I do?"

"Violet will not help you." Louie stepped in front of Violet, blocking her from view. "There's no help she can provide. Separating the essence from you would kill both you and the essence unless it was done the right way."

"Then do it the right way!" Owen jumped into Louie's face. "Do it." His eyes darkened and his wings spanned out, ripping through his t-shirt.

Louie stepped back. "Simmer down, bird."

"Fix her *now*." Owen's eyes were now completely black. Combined with enormous wings and an incredibly muscular body, Owen was a formidable sight.

"There's only a few beings capable of fixing her, and even if you found them they wouldn't do it. They'd see her potential and refuse."

"We'll find them. We'll convince them." We had to.

"Like I said, good luck with that. When you're fully changed come find me, Daisy. I look forward to welcoming you." Louie took my free hand and kissed it.

I shook Louie off. "Violet, please. Where can I find help?"

"She can't help you, Daisy. You're on your own." Louie's eyes locked with mine.

"Please. Something."

"Don't make this harder than it has to be." Louie looked mildly sympathetic, but I didn't trust it. I didn't trust anything. It's then that I realized something.

"You knew she couldn't help me. You knew it before you called Violet, yet you still had them bring me here."

"Of course. I knew from the moment I met you that the change couldn't be undone. The others knew it too. Violet knew before she even brought you here."

Violet scowled. "It's not like that. I didn't know for sure. Everything I did was for your own good. You need to believe that."

"Wait. This whole time you knew Kalisa couldn't help?"

Roland nodded. "We knew it wasn't likely in the beginning, and once you manipulated that guy we knew you were fully changing. I'm sorry, but we had to get you back here. You belong with us. We're the only ones who can make your change better for you."

"No! I'm not changing!"

I heard a door slam, and I turned toward the house in time to watch two men dragging Kalisa down the stairs. I watched in a state of shock as she struggled against them.

"I'm not changing," I repeated, much quieter this time.

"Bring her over here," Louie ordered his men.

Owen's arm tightened around me, and without looking I knew his eyes were probably black again. I swallowed hard, trying to prepare myself.

"It's you. How are you, child?" Kalisa's eyes twinkled.

"How am I? How can you even ask that?" I searched her face for some sort of explanation. Surely she'd had a reason for cursing me that way. "Why did you do this to me? Why?"

"I was only doing what my master willed me to do." She grinned, revealing her rows of capped teeth. "I do as I am told."

"What? You aren't making sense. No one else was there that day."

"He spoke to me here." She touched her temple.

"You put a spell on Daisy because of voices in your head?" Owen stepped toward her. "Are you crazy?"

She laughed again. "I've been called worse."

"Please. Reverse the spell. I'm begging you." I yanked myself free from Owen's hand and fell to my knees.

"I can't, but I can tell you who can."

"Who?"

"No one can. Don't listen to her. Can't you tell she's crazy?" Louie stepped between us.

I looked around him. "Tell me, please. Make this up to me."

"Find the Creators in Energo. That is the only way." She started laughing again, and the men started to pull her away.

"Energo? Where's that?" Owen called after her.

She glanced back over her shoulder. "Somewhere you'll never find on your maps."

Owen looked at her and then back at me, as if debating whether to follow after her. He stayed at my side.

"I'm sorry, Daisy." Violet turned her back to me.

"You're sorry? For what exactly? For lying to me? For forgetting to tell me I'm turning into one of you? Let's go, Owen. Get us out of here." I squeezed his hand.

"Absolutely." Owen wrapped his arms around my waist.

"Come and find me when you're ready." Roland watched me sadly. "I'll make myself easy to find."

Before I could respond, Owen took off, and my stomach lurched. It had been years since I'd flown with him, and this time I was too numb by the recent news to enjoy it.

He flew for a few minutes before he landed behind a formation of rocks. He set me down carefully. "You okay?"

"What am I going to do?" I fell to my knees. "What the hell am I going to do?"

Owen held out his hand to me. "You're going to stop saying I."

I accepted his hand and moved to standing. "Why?"

"Because we're in this together."

"Why? Why are you willing to help me?"

"Because I'm not losing the best thing to ever happen to me."

"You don't owe me anything. You can go on with your life."

"Daisy," He took my face in his hands. "Look into my eyes. Does it look like I can just walk away and go on with my life?"

"I don't know. You pretty much just met me."

"You and I both know that isn't true."

"We do?"

"Do I need to remind you of how long I've known you?"

I nodded.

His lips crashed into mine, and I eagerly welcomed him. I needed to taste him, to feel the way his body felt wrapped around mine. I needed to feel, to remember why finding a way to stay human was so important. Becoming an Allure meant losing this—losing my love for Owen, and after years of searching, I wasn't losing him again.

Daisy and Owen's story continues in *Lust (The Allure Chronicles #2)* releasing in 2015! Please keep reading for a preview of *Dire (The Dire Wolves Chronicles #1)* an NA Paranormal Romance by Alyssa Rose Ivy.

www.AlyssaRoseIvy.com
www.facebook.com/AlyssaRoseIvy
twitter.com/AlyssaRoseIvy
AlyssaRoseIvy@gmail.com

To stay up to date on Alyssa's new releases, join her mailing list: http://eepurl.com/ktlSj

DIRE

The Dire Wolves Chronicles

ALYSSA ROSE IVY

PREFACE

A single howl made me stop short. "The wolves!"

"Let's hope they are farther away than they sound." Gage tightened his hold on my hand and pulled me forward.

Three more howls filled the night. "They sound closer."

We picked up the pace, and I chanced a glance behind me. That was a mistake. Several large grey wolves came into view. "Run!"

Gage didn't need to be told twice. He broke into a run without letting go of my hand.

I ran as fast as possible over the frozen snow, but we didn't get far before the wolves started circling around us. "Oh my god." Could things get any worse?

"You have to make a run for it." Gage's voice quivered. "They're going to kill us."

"I'm not leaving you." I tried to stay strong, and I kept my eyes locked on the wolves. There were five of them. All of them were massive, much larger than any wolf I'd seen before, but one of them was even bigger and had a large silver streak running down its back. That wolf seemed to be staring right at me.

"I'll distract them. You run. I'll catch up."

I spotted an opening next to one of the smaller of the wolves and went for it. I didn't make it far before one of the wolves stepped in front of me. I froze, paralyzed with fear, before my legs were knocked from under me. Suddenly, I was lying in the snow with a giant wolf hovering over me.

"We're fucked." Gage voiced exactly what I was thinking.

The silver streaked wolf stared down at me. It's almost glowing eyes bored into mine. Was I really going to die as half-frozen food for a giant wild animal?

Then things got hazy and the air seemed to buzz. Moments later it wasn't a wolf on top of me—it was a man. A completely naked man with a faint scar across his face.

"What the heck?" I tried to scurry back, but Hunter didn't move. His very exposed parts nearly touched me. I didn't want to notice his size, but I did. He was huge. He also didn't look remotely concerned with the cold.

His lips brushed against my ear. "Were you going somewhere?"

CHAPTER ONE

MARY ANNE

He wore black athletic shorts that sat low on his hips and gave me a fantastic view of his perfectly sculpted abs. I had a strong desire to touch those abs with my hands and quite possibly my tongue. His bare chest was equally as alluring, all muscle with just a little bit of sweat sliding down.

"Thanks for waiting up for me." He walked into his room and closed the door. "I was worried you'd have fallen asleep already." He slipped off those black shorts and walked toward his bed that amazingly enough I was already tucked into. He pulled back the blanket. "And you're wearing the lingerie I like best." He grinned wickedly as he slipped in beside me.

"Isn't the best part taking it off me?" I bit my lip, knowing that it would only turn him on more.

"You remembered." He slipped the strap down off my right shoulder.

"I remember everything about you. I always have."

"How'd I get so lucky?" He slipped off the other strap as he left tiny kisses from my shoulder up toward my neck.

"You know you're the only one I've ever wanted."

"I know." He pushed my top down and out of the way. "I feel exactly the same way." His mouth closed around my breast.

"Mary Anne!"

My eyes flew open as someone pounded on the door to my dorm room. I blinked a few times, trying to hold on to the remnants of my dream.

"Mary Anne!" The voice yelled louder.

I grudgingly dragged myself across the room and opened the door. I wasn't surprised to see Genevieve standing there.

"Finally!" She pushed into the room. I closed the door and cut her off before she could sit on my bed. I needed to make it first. I pulled back my jersey knit lime green sheets and navy blue comforter. As soon as I smoothed out the comforter, she took a seat.

I sat in my desk chair and watched her. "As lovely as it is to see you, I'm guessing there's a reason you're here?"

"Aren't you a little grouchy this morning?" Suddenly her glossy lips twisted up into a smile. "Wait….you were dreaming about him again."

"Why do you have to say it like it's a bad thing? Most women have some sort of sexual dreams. It isn't at all abnormal." I ran my fingers through my long red hair to get out the tangles.

"Mary Anne, I'm only saying this because I'm a friend and I care about you, but you're obsessed." She crossed her legs. "Most women may have sex dreams, but they're about celebrities, not a guy they actually know. Plus, the frequency is the crazy part."

"There's nothing wrong with dreaming about Gage."

"There is. If you want him so bad, just get with him. It's not like he'd say no. He's gotten with half the girls on this campus already."

I groaned. "That's not entirely true. I admit he has a reputation, but he doesn't actually sleep with everyone. Plus, I can't just sleep with him. We have a history. We're from the same town." Maybe claiming we had a history was a bit of an overstatement, but I had known him practically my entire life.

"Is he still driving you home for break?" She leaned back on her hands.

"Of course. Why would that change?"

"I thought you might have considered taking Roy up on his offer to drop you off on his way home." She raised an eyebrow.

"Gage and I are going to the same place. It makes sense to have him drive me. Plus, my parents know him."

"Mary Anne." Genevieve was in the habit of saying my name far more often than necessary. She was the best friend I had at Eastern U, so I didn't remind her of how annoying the practice was. "You know what you're doing, right?"

"Are we still discussing my plans to get a ride home with Gage?"

"More specifically we're discussing your decision to say no to Roy's offer. You're chicken. You're afraid of accepting an overture from a guy who you actually have a chance with. A guy who is really interested in you."

"I wonder why you want me to give Roy another shot?" I bit back the smile that was ready to come out. "This would have nothing to do with his best friend, would it?" I'd gone out on one date with Roy, and although there was nothing particularly wrong with it, I had no intention of seeing him again.

"What?" She put a hand on her chest. "Of course not."

"Oh? It wouldn't be convenient for you if I were dating Roy?"

"Sure, it would be convenient to have an excuse to spend time with Tony, but that's not why I want you to give Roy another chance. He's a nice guy."

"He is nice. He's also intelligent and cute, but that doesn't mean I want to spend four hours in a car with him."

"Not when you can spend the same amount of time in a car with Gage."

"Gage drives a truck."

Genevieve sighed. "Same thing. My point is that you have no excuse to be sitting around pining over a guy when you have real, good options knocking down your door."

I didn't take the bait. I was too stressed out to get into a fight about my love life. "I'm taking a shower." I walked over to my closet and pulled down my favorite pair of worn in jeans. I took a purple thermal shirt from my dresser. December in Boston was cold.

"I'm sure it's going to be a cold shower." Genevieve made no move to leave my room.

"I hadn't even gotten to the good part in my dream, so a hot shower will be perfectly fine."

"I'll wait here." She lay back on my bed. "We can walk over to the exam together."

I hesitated with my hand on the door knob. "That sounds great, but please no more overanalyzing my choice of men. I need to keep my mind focused on the test."

"You're going to ace it. You know this stuff inside and out."

"Let's hope. I refuse to become the first member of my family not to get the Youngston Fellowship, and I need to ace calculus to get it."

"You'll ace it, but so what if you don't get the fellowship? You'll still get into grad school, and you'll be able to do exactly what you want anyway."

"You don't know my parents."

She sat up. "I've met them."

"Meeting them is different than knowing them."

"Yeah, but you said they wouldn't mind you getting a ride home with Gage. That makes me question their sanity." She laughed. "Ok, take that shower. We don't have much time."

"I wonder why not."

"Don't start. Your alarm would just be going off."

As if to prove her point, the dinging of my alarm started. Genevieve turned it off, and I headed down the hall to the bathroom. Four hours in the car with Gage. I could hardly wait.

Dire is available now!

Want to stay up to date on Alyssa Rose Ivy's releases? Join her mailing list: http://eepurl.com/ktlSj

ACKNOWLEDGEMENTS

As always, this book would not have been possible without the support of my family. Grant, I can't imagine taking this journey without you.

Thanks to Nicole Stephenson for the fantastic editing. Thanks also to Kelly Simmon of Inkslinger PR for your continued support.

Thanks to all the bloggers who have continued to help me spread the word about my books, and to my readers for giving me the opportunity to share another story with you.

Printed in Great Britain
by Amazon.co.uk, Ltd.,
Marston Gate.